THE
GOOD
DETECTIVE

Center Point
Large Print

**This Large Print Book carries the
Seal of Approval of N.A.V.H.**

THE
GOOD
DETECTIVE

JOHN McMAHON

CENTER POINT LARGE PRINT
THORNDIKE, MAINE

This Center Point Large Print edition
is published in the year 2019 by arrangement with
G.P. Putnam's Sons, an imprint of Penguin Publishing
Group, a division of Penguin Random House LLC.

The text of this Large Print edition is unabridged.
In other aspects, this book may vary
from the original edition.
Printed in the United States of America
on permanent paper.
Set in 16-point Times New Roman type.

ISBN: 978-1-64358-221-4

Library of Congress Cataloging-in-Publication Data

Names: McMahon, John, 1970- author.
Title: The good detective / John McMahon.
Description: Center Point Large Print edition. | Thorndike, Maine :
    Center Point Large Print, 2019.
Identifiers: LCCN 2019012162 | ISBN 9781643582214 (hardcover :
    alk. paper)
Subjects: LCSH: Large type books. | GSAFD: Mystery fiction.
Classification: LCC PS3613.C5843 G66 2019b | DDC 813/.6—dc23
LC record available at https://lccn.loc.gov/2019012162

For Maggie,
because faith and patience
are not small things

THE
GOOD
DETECTIVE

1

A fist banged on my driver's-side window, and my eyes flew open. I lunged for my Glock 42. Nearly shot my foot off.

Two white eyeballs glared at me through the darkness.

Horace Ordell.

"You okay, P.T.?" he hollered.

The first thing you gotta know about Horace is that his ass is the size of a small nation. So to get him moving takes an act of war.

I looked at the clock in my Ford F-150: 2:47 a.m.

"You were screaming in your sleep," Horace said. The big man's body was parked a foot outside my door. "Could hear you way the hell yonder."

My eyes drifted to the bouncer's stool where Horace resided most nights. A neon sign above it read *The Landing Patch*, and two curved strips of light displayed what very unsubtly looked like a woman's legs, opening and closing. And opening and closing again.

I took in the smell of tobacco plants after the rain. The scent of old Georgia dirt.

"Everything all right inside the club?" I asked, opening my truck door.

Horace bobbed his bald head, his skin dark as

night. He'd played O-line for Alabama until he blew out his knee.

Behind him, the strip club was housed in an old log mill, set along protected county land beside the Tullumy River. What were once windows for ventilation had been covered with rusted metal signs to block out the light. *Drink Coca-Cola*, one read. *Eat Utz Chips*, another.

I glanced at myself in the rearview mirror before getting out. Wavy brown hair. Bloodshot blue eyes.

I also saw into the back of the cab, where Purvis lay. Sweet Purvis, my seven-year-old bulldog. The look he gave me lately was always the same: *You're spiraling since she's gone, P.T. Grab ahold of something.*

But I'm not the type to reach out and grab. Hugs, for instance. I was never a big hugger. Even before my wife's accident.

I stepped out of the truck, and Horace kept yammering.

"I don't mean you were screaming a little, P.T.," he said. "It was more like History Channel, Army flashback type shit."

"You can go back to your post, Horace," I said. "I'm fine."

Of course I wasn't fine. I was five counties from fine.

Horace stared at the ground, his mind hatching something. "Or I could call someone?"

10

The look on his face was odd. A nervous smirk maybe. "Like who?" I said.

"I dunno." He shrugged. "Another cop? I know you had a couple drinks. Maybe he comes out here and has you walk the line. Throws some cuffs on you?" He hesitated. "Or you could tip me? A lotta folks tip me."

I almost smiled. A shit-heel like Horace threatening a detective who'd experienced what I'd been through. If brains were leather, this guy didn't have enough to saddle a june bug.

I reached into my truck, and Horace took a cautious step back. Then he saw the highball glass in my hand. I'd brought it out earlier from the Landing Patch, and it was still full.

I handed him the glass and got back in the truck. The night sky was a shade of violet, with purplish-gray cumulus clouds that looked like overstuffed pillows.

"Here's a tip," I said to Horace, "don't go mistaking grief for weakness."

I fired up the engine, and a paper crinkled in my flannel shirt pocket under my seat belt. Unfolding it, I stared at a single word as Horace walked away.

Crimson.

The penmanship was as neat as could be expected, considering it had been written in eyeliner and penned in the dark.

I flipped the paper over. The other side had an address on it: *426 E. 31st. 'B.'*

"Damn it," I said, remembering the stripper and her story from the previous night. She was a redhead with bruises that ran the length of both legs. I had promised her I'd come by and flash my badge. Scare the shit out of her abusive boyfriend.

My eyeballs were floating, and I needed to find a bathroom. I pulled onto I-32.

My name is P. T. Marsh, and Mason Falls, Georgia, is my town. It's not a huge place, but it's grown to a decent size in the last decade. Lately we top out around 130,000 souls. A lot of that growth has come from two airlines setting up shop here as a place where they refurbish commercial airplanes. The bulk of those planes get repainted and sold to overseas airlines you've never heard of. But some of them end up right back in the friendly skies above. It's kind of like plastic surgery in the better neighborhoods of Buckhead. Slap on a fresh coat of paint and some new carpet, and no one notices how worn-out the bodies are underneath.

I made it through the cute areas of town. The parts where, during the day, tourists window-shop for Civil War–era vases. Where college kids eat chicken-fried steak and get drunk on buckets of Terrapin Rye.

The numbered streets came then, and along with them, the parts of town where folks lived who worked on those airplanes. The scrubbers, recarpeters, and painters.

I passed 15th Street, 20th, 25th. It had rained while I was asleep at the Landing Patch, and small lakes formed in poorly paved side streets.

I parked my truck behind an abandoned Big Lots off 30th and got out, cutting through the dark neighborhood on foot.

After a few minutes, I found the address on the paper, a worn-down bungalow home. The letter *B* and an arrow had been spray-painted on the driveway, pointing at a detached back unit.

Crimson's place.

Small white Christmas lights were on in one window, the only sign of the coming holiday. I walked closer. The bedroom had an entrance that led in from the driveway. Through the screen door, I could see Crimson, faceup on the bed.

The redhead lay there in cutoff jeans and a V-neck with no bra. Her cheeks showed fresh bruises, and her T-shirt bore the face of a Georgia bulldog in pink. I had told her that I'd come by official, with a squad car, a day earlier.

Don't make promises you can't keep, P.T.

It was Purvis's voice that I heard. Of course, he's a brown and white bulldog with a bad underbite, and I'd left him back in the truck by the Big Lots. So maybe it was my voice and his face. The subconscious works in strange ways. Or is that God?

I made my way inside, hurrying to see if Crimson was alive. I leaned over and checked

13

her pulse. She'd been knocked to hell and back, but her breathing was fine.

I shook her awake, and it took a moment for her to recognize me.

"Your boyfriend here?" I asked.

In the dim light, she pointed to the living room. "He's sleeping."

"You got a friend you can stay with for a couple hours? Let me talk some sense into him?"

Crimson nodded, grabbing her sweatshirt and purse.

I moved to the living room, and my eyes adjusted to the dark. Crimson's boyfriend was passed out in a sitting pose on the couch in a dirty tank top and jeans.

A brick of weed sat on a wooden table by the couch, and one of the boyfriend's hands was wrapped in gauze. A strip of dried blood was smeared across the fabric.

So here's the thing.

You spend the first thirty-six years of your life learning a value system. What's right. What's wrong. And when to say "To hell with it" and toss the rules aside.

But you accumulate things too. A house. A mortgage. A wife and kid. And somewhere along the way, those responsibilities matter more than right and wrong. Because there's consequences. Doing absolute right can create problems for you and your family. For your career.

For me, that was the road I'd been on. A beautiful wife. Young son. And I'd been as happy as a pig in shit going down that path.

But someone came along and took my responsibilities away. Took away my family. And all they left me with was absolute justice.

I ran my flashlight over the boyfriend's chest. He looked to be in his early thirties. A muscle-bound five foot nine. Shaved head and a blond goatee. A tattoo on his biceps read *88*. The eighth letter of the alphabet, *H*. Two *H*'s, for Heil Hitler.

So you're a neo-Nazi who beats up strippers.

The man's mouth was open, and a bead of drool hung down from the corner of it. A half-empty bottle of Jack was curled under his right arm.

I sat down on an armchair a foot from him. Grabbed a dish towel nearby and wrapped the soft cloth around my fist.

"Hey, dipshit," I said.

His eyes fluttered open, and he sat up. A look to the bedroom. Maybe he had a gun there. Or maybe he was wondering if I'd seen the condition he'd left Crimson in.

"Who the hell are you?" he mumbled, disoriented. He smelled like pomade and tobacco.

"Don't worry," I said. "The cops are here."

2

I punched him hard, square in the face.

"Jesus," he said, holding his hand to his nose. Blood surged through his fingers and onto his shirt.

He glared at me, waking up now. "Y'all just can't break into people's houses—"

I hit him again. The first time was for Crimson, the second for emphasis. His head popped backward and hit the couch.

"What do you want?" He sniffed. A stripe of blood across his teeth.

I looked around the place, taking in every detail.

There was a time when the *Mason Falls Register* called me "a detective who missed nothing." And then a more recent time when a case didn't go so well and they used the word "sloppy." I guess you can't stay on top forever.

"Your full attention," I said.

The boyfriend was still playing defense. He glanced at a frog gig leaning against the far wall. Maybe he was fixin' to stick me with the two-pronged pole.

I picked up a lighter from off the table. Lit the corner of the brick of pot on fire.

"The people that belongs to," he said, "they won't care who the hell you are—"

16

"Shhh." I bent forward and laid the head of my Glock against his jeans, right at the kneecap. "Do I have your undivided attention?"

"Yeah," he said, and I tapped the gun on his knee.

"You touch her one more time." I pointed at the bedroom. "One more tiny bruise on her, and I will take that bloody fist of yours and blow each finger off. One at a time. Like target practice. Y'understand?"

He nodded slowly, and I got up. Walked out.

3

I got the call at eight a.m. while I was still sleeping.

"We got a hot one," Remy Morgan said.

Remy is my partner, and I often tell her that she smells like milk. This is my joke that she's young. Like twenty-five years young. She's also African American, so sometimes she warns me, "Don't say chocolate milk, P.T., or I'll beat your ass."

I pulled the covers off my head. "What's the case?" I asked hoarsely into my cell phone. I was still wearing my jeans, but no T-shirt or flannel.

"We got a dead guy," Remy said.

I looked around for my shirt, but didn't see it. Shook Purvis from atop my legs. This would be Remy's third murder case, and I could hear that rookie detective excitement in her voice. "Dead good guy or dead bad guy?"

"Dead bad guy," she said. "And probably beaten to death by other bad guys. I'll come get you."

I was out of the shower in five minutes. Pulled on gray slacks and tucked in a white button-down.

Cracking open the fridge, I looked for something to eat. I was developing a new diet that involved stale food, mold, and a lot of instant hot cereal. I could feel a bestseller coming. Or maybe it was a stomach flu.

A car beeped outside, and I glanced through the blue curtains that my wife, Lena, had put up before Thanksgiving of last year. That was four weeks before the accident.

Remy's '77 Alfa Romeo Spider was at the curb. I hurried out and squeezed into the passenger seat.

"Where's the scene?" I asked.

"Numbered streets," she said.

It sprinkled as we drove, and the trees in the median along Baker Street drooped under the weight of the water. Remy told me about an extreme mud run that she'd won second place in during the weekend.

"You don't get enough excitement being a cop during the week?" I asked. "You gotta pay someone to get you dirty and let off fake explosions?"

Remy scrunched her brow. She had the sculpted cheekbones of a fashion model. "Don't be an old man, P.T."

I knew how competitive Remy was. "Well, if *you* came in second, who won the thing?"

"Some fireman from Marietta."

Remy shrugged before letting out a smile. "He won twice actually. I gave him my number."

I grinned at this, cranking down my window.

19

The wet weather had begun Sunday, and the humidity in between thunderstorms had bleached the blue out of the Georgia sky and made everything a dull military gray.

As we approached 30th Street, I saw the Big Lots where I'd parked the night before, and a lump started to form in my throat. Partly because I don't believe in coincidences. But mostly because there are no coincidences.

We pulled in front of Crimson's house on 31st, and I gulped at the humid air coming in the window. The house looked even worse in daylight. More paint had peeled off the facade than was on it.

Remy got out of the car. She had on a pin-striped blouse and black slacks. She tries to dress down how good she looks with these bookish glasses and business suits. But between the two of us, we're the best-looking pair of detectives in town. Of course, in the area of homicide, there's only one other set, but hey.

Remy handed me blue latex gloves, and we walked up the driveway. I passed the letter *B* and the arrow.

"The victim's male or female?" I asked.

"Male," Remy said. "Twenty-nine years old."

When you left here, P.T., he was alive.

Quiet, Purvis. I need to concentrate.

"We got any witnesses who saw the murder?" I asked.

"Not so far," Remy said. "But the day's young. We haven't canvassed yet."

I looked around. The next-door neighbor's house had plywood covering the side windows. There were thick dark knots soaked with rain that caused the wood to bow.

I nodded to Darren Gattling, who stood by the front door. Darren's a blue-suiter who I'd mentored five years earlier.

"M.E. here?" I asked, looking around for the medical examiner.

"Inside," Gattling said.

I stepped through the front door and saw the room from a different angle than the night before.

The body of Crimson's dead boyfriend was propped up in a sitting pose, same as when I'd left. Around both eyes were black-and-blue rings. Dried blood clogged his nostrils.

I scanned the room, seeing details I hadn't noticed in the dark. Hefty bags full of trash overflowed in the corners. An Everlast punching bag hung by the window.

Hovering over the man was Sarah Raines, the county medical examiner, dressed in a blue crime scene coverall.

"Detective Marsh," the M.E. said without looking up.

Sarah was mid-thirties and blond. She'd bumped into me in the hallway two weeks ago and asked me to dinner. Since I'd politely declined, I hadn't seen much of her in my side of the building.

"Doc," I said.

Remy pulled up beside me. She had an iPad Mini she took notes in and was using a gloved finger to page down through them.

"His name's Virgil Rowe." Remy motioned at the body. "He did seven years at Telfair for aggravated assault. Been out eleven months with no job."

I reached out a gloved hand and picked up the brick of pot. It weighed around three pounds. "Looks like he was self-employed," I said. "What do you put the street value of this at, Rem? Two g's?"

Remy gripped it. "More like thirty-five hundred." She raised an eyebrow. "But whoever killed him—*they* didn't take it."

I turned to Sarah. "You got a range on time of death?"

The M.E.'s blond hair was tied back in a purple scrunchy, but a few strands hung down over her face. "I'd put T.O.D. at four to six hours ago."

"So between two and four a.m." Remy typed into her iPad.

I took a moment, thinking about what time I'd left here last night. Must've been half past three.

"Who called it in?" I asked.

"Corinne Stables," Remy said, bringing up a picture. "She's Virgil's girlfriend."

I stared at the iPad. Corinne was Crimson's legal name. Which made Crimson her stage name.

"She's here?" I asked.

"And beaten up pretty good," Remy said. "Looks like Virgil gave her the business. Then someone gave it to him."

My reflection warped through the gold veins of a weathered mirror on the far wall. Had Corinne come back after I'd left and finished off her boyfriend? Or had I stayed longer than I remembered?

Patrolman Gattling was standing inside the door. "We got her in a black and white at the curb, P.T., but she's already asked for a lawyer."

My God. Corinne was outside?

"And Rowe?" I looked to the M.E. "What do we know about his injuries?"

"He's got a broken nose. Some cracked ribs." Sarah moved around to the back side of the couch. "And there's this." She motioned at his neck. "His C5 and C6 are fractured. I'll know more when I get him on the table, but I would guess that someone choked him."

"So two guys?" I said. "One beating him up out here. The other holding him from behind?"

Sarah shrugged. "Could've just as easily been one guy. Broke his nose and some ribs. Then once Rowe was knocked out, he came around here and finished him off."

The tip of a yellow plastic lighter peeked out

below the coffee table. It was the same one I'd used to light the brick five hours ago.

Your prints are on that lighter.

"Did patrol search the bedroom?" I asked.

"They did a once-over," Remy said. As she turned toward the bedroom, I used the tip of my loafer to push the lighter under the table.

I walked into the bedroom with Remy, noticing Corinne had cleaned up a bit.

"Ms. Stables was at a girlfriend's house all night," Remy read from patrol's notes. "Came home around seven and found her boyfriend like this. Called 911 at 7:03 a.m."

From the bedroom, I saw Alvin Gerbin, our crime scene tech, coming in the front door. Gerbin's a big man, red-faced and from Texas. You can usually hear his voice a full minute before he gets anywhere.

Gerbin plopped down in the chair where I'd sat five hours ago. He wore khakis and a cheap Hawaiian shirt. "If you're done," he said to the M.E., "I'ma start printin' the shit out of this place. Starting right here at the epicenter."

I stepped out the side door and onto the driveway.

"What's wrong?" Remy asked.

I glanced back at the house. The bottle of Jack from last night was gone. Someone had come after I'd left. Killed Virgil. Then taken his liquor with them, but not the weed.

"There are a lot of things wrong," I said. I took a few steps down the driveway toward the street. Stood there a full minute. Corinne was hunched in the back of a cruiser, her body small in the black and white.

"Boss," Remy hollered, and I turned.

My partner had walked the other way up the driveway. She had the garage door flung open and was crouched over, putting on new gloves.

I needed to tell Remy about the stripper. Before I got in too deep.

"We need to talk," I said, heading toward her.

But as I got closer, the smell of gasoline burned at my nostrils. Nine five-gallon gas containers were lined up just inside the threshold.

"Five of these are full," Remy said. "The others don't have a lick in 'em." She looked around. "No lawn mower. No gas generator. Nothing that requires gasoline here."

Behind the gas jugs were three pints of turpentine. Some kerosene. And six cans of butane, the same size as spray paint canisters.

Remy picked up one of the butane cans, shaking it so I could tell it was empty. "You see the news this weekend?"

"My TV's broken," I said. Which was technically true. I'd put my foot through it in response to a police reenactment show that had reminded me of my wife's death.

I pointed down the driveway. "I know her."

"There was an arson off State 903 yesterday," Remy continued. "A gas fire with a butane accelerant. Ten acres burned."

I'd read about this fire. The *Mason Falls Register* had been in the bathroom at the Landing Patch, and I'd scanned it for top stories. Fire at a farm nearby. Missing kid. Stolen shipment of electronics from Walmart.

But Remy was stuck back on what I'd said.

"Her who?" Remy said. "You know the stripper?"

I was buying time. Thinking.

I remembered hitting Virgil Rowe twice. But then nothing else 'til Remy called an hour ago. When I woke up, my T-shirt and flannel were gone. So was Virgil Rowe's bottle of Jack Daniel's.

Who does that sound like? Purvis said inside my head.

I knew what my bulldog was implying. Someone who liked booze but wouldn't touch marijuana. And that maybe I'd stayed longer than I remembered. Choked Virgil to death while I sipped his Tennessee whisky.

"P.T.," Remy said, "do you know Corinne Stables?"

"No, the M.E.," I said, pointing toward the house. "Sarah asked me out two weeks ago. I didn't want it to be awkward . . . if you didn't know."

26

Remy cocked her head at me. Almost a smile. "Are you and the medical examiner dating?"

I felt light-headed and needed to eat something. "I wasn't ready," I said.

My partner nodded, her brow wrinkling. Confused as to why the hell I'd brought it up in the first place.

"This dead guy could be our arsonist, P.T."

Remy tapped at one of the empty containers. "Maybe there's others involved . . . one of them wanted to shut him up after the fire? They came here. Choked him out."

My head was a mess. "I dunno," I said.

"I'm just spitballing." Remy stood up, her voice unsure all of a sudden. "You told me to always come up with a theory of the crime. But be open to changing it."

"No, that's good," I said. I saw a trash can by the garage and wandered over to it. Thinking about the bottle of Jack and my missing T-shirt.

Keep it together, P.T. Your shirt isn't in that trash. You didn't kill this jerk.

I flipped the trash open, and Purvis was right. There was no T-shirt or flannel inside. Or bottle of J.D.

"What are you thinking?" Remy asked.

"I'm trying to marry all these details," I said. "You saw his tattoo, right?"

I took off my gloves and dropped them in the trash can, heading back inside.

"Neo-Nazi," she said. "Yeah."

"And the brick of pot," I said. "Whoever killed him—they didn't take that?"

I headed into the living room with Remy on my heels. "Yeah," she said. "Haven't figured out how that makes sense yet."

I eased down onto the chair beside Gerbin, the crime tech.

"You okay?" he said. "You don't look well."

"I don't feel well," I said. I leaned my elbows on my knees, and put my head down, counting to three. Then I reached down and grabbed the lighter. Put it on the table. I braced my hands against the edge of the coffee table, right near Gerbin, and waited.

"Boss," Remy said, "your gloves!"

Gerbin stared at me.

"Shit," I said. "I took 'em off outside. I felt light-headed and needed to sit down."

Gerbin was cataloguing everything. "You touched the lighter, the tabletop, the chair arms. Probably the knob to the side door."

I thought of all the areas I'd made contact with last night.

"I'm sorry," I said to Gerbin.

"Alvin can exclude your prints, Detective." This from Sarah, the M.E.

Remy handed me new gloves, and I put them on.

"Why don't you get some cool air on your face,

Detective," Sarah said. "Sit in a squad car. Blast the AC."

I looked at the brick of pot. Thought about Corinne.

"I'll be outside," I said.

I moved out the door and down the driveway to where patrol was. Remy was confused. Not sure whether to follow me or not.

"Go through every drawer, Rem," I said to my partner. "Find us something on this girl."

Remy nodded, and I turned to the patrolman by the squad car. "Take a powder, will ya, buddy." I got in the front passenger seat of the cruiser.

Corinne Stables sat in the back, her hands cuffed in front of her. This was protocol in domestic violence situations.

In daylight, her bruises were worse than at night. Under light makeup, I could see a purple mark above her right eye. She smelled like a mix of Chanel No. 5 and Vaseline.

"I hope you're not expecting me to say thank you." Corinne glared.

There were different ways to take this, but none of them were good.

"I didn't do that to your man," I said. "We just talked."

"Well, neither did I," Corinne said. "So unless you're fixin' to join me back here, you better get me out of these cuffs."

I shifted to looking straight ahead. Communicating with Corinne through the rearview mirror.

"How long have you lived here, Corinne?" I asked.

"Two years."

"Your name on the lease or his?"

"Both ours," Corinne said. Unsure of where I was going with this.

I paused a moment. Bit at my lip.

What a dud, I thought. And I was talking about myself here, not her. I oughta have my head examined for thinking I was gonna help this girl. She told me a sad story while I was having a smoke outside a strip bar. Meanwhile she loved her bigot peckerwood boyfriend and signed a lease with him?

"Do you understand the rules around possession of marijuana versus sale in the state of Georgia? When a brick that size is found in your home?"

"It's not mine," Corinne said.

"It doesn't matter," I said. "That much pot is intent to distribute for anyone who's on that lease. Felony conviction. One year minimum. Ten max. Five thousand dollar fine."

"Fuck," she said.

"Exactly. Fuck." I motioned at the house. "Who owns this place?"

"Some guy two blocks over," she said. "Randall Moon. Red house on the corner."

"I'm gonna be the one to talk to him," I said. "To ask him for the lease on the property."

Corinne took this in.

"Is he a smart guy, Corinne? Street-smart?"

"Yeah."

"'Cause I'm gonna tell him if he gives me a lease with your name on it, his place will be deemed a drug house. His property locked down for a year during the trial. Which means no rent money for him."

"But if only Virgil's name is on the lease?" Corinne asked.

"Well, Virgil ain't here to dispute it, so that means you were an overnight guest. And you're no longer a dealer headed to prison. You know what they'd do to a pretty girl like you in Swainsboro women's prison?"

"What do you want?" Corinne asked.

"You never met me."

"My pleasure," she said.

"And get out of town," I said. "If you're from somewhere, go back there. If you're from here— it's time to leave."

Her brown eyes never left mine. Wondering still. *Did I do it? Did I kill him?*

"You got a question?" I asked.

She hesitated. "For you? Why would I ask you anything? You're just some random pig. I don't know you."

"Good," I said, and got out of the car.

31

4

Remy pulled her sports car to the side of State Route 903 in an area known as Harmony, about twenty miles from downtown Mason Falls.

It was an hour later, and we'd bagged all the evidence and left the house where Virgil Rowe had been killed.

A day ago this country had been gorgeous. Patches of wild cotton and greenery growing right by the roadside. And honeysuckle. You've never lived until you've been a kid in the South and dripped honeysuckle nectar in your mouth.

We stared out Remy's open window. The ten or fifteen acres between the highway and the nearby farm were a scourge of black from the weekend fire.

Remy'd insisted we drive out here while we waited for the M.E. to process our dead neo-Nazi. She had a hunch that Virgil Rowe's death and those gas containers might be connected to this fire. I wanted to support her, but at the same time I was her mentor. I got paid to pick at the decisions she made.

"You grew up out here, right?" I asked.

"Two miles that way." Remy motioned.

The field had an odd burn pattern. Parts of the land were scorched to the dirt. Other areas still had green weeds three feet high, the tops of them barely dusted with black.

"So tell me what you're thinking," I said.

Remy bit at her lip, the two of us still in the car. "Well, Rowe's obviously a white supremacist, and most of the folks in Harmony are black," she said. "This farm is white-owned and employs locals. Maybe Rowe decided he didn't like that."

A strip of yellow crime scene tape ran from a pine fence to our west, about a hundred yards along the highway. The tape blew limp in areas.

"Okay," I said. It was a start.

Remy got out of her Alfa and walked a few feet closer to the field. "What if we found the same brand of butane can out here?" she asked.

"Wouldn't hurt," I said, getting out of the car. "But mashed potatoes don't necessarily mean gravy."

Remy pointed. "Because something metal is shining over there."

I hesitated, explaining to Remy that the crime scene belonged to the other two detectives in town. Kaplan and Berry. I wouldn't want them traipsing over our scene.

"It's a thirty-second walk, P.T.," Remy said, handing me a pair of gloves.

I nodded, and Remy moved under the tape. I sniffed at the air. "Smells funny."

"Funny how?" she said, moving ahead of me.

"Like foot."

"Five hours of rain yesterday, meet cow shit," she said. "Cow shit, meet five hours of rain."

I turned in the direction of the smell and walked to my right.

The ground became less burnt dirt and more weedy. Thick kudzu came up to my knees.

"Just an old can of pop over here," Remy hollered.

We had moved a good eighty feet apart, and I slowed near a tall loblolly pine.

About ten feet out, I saw what I'd smelled.

A body was half-buried in a pile of burnt tree branches, about six feet from the base of the pine tree.

I could tell that it was a child, but the body was black with soot from the fire. As I moved closer, I saw that the chest and hands were burned to a dark color and the head deformed.

My eyes moved along the victim's frame, stopping on an area of unburnt skin along the right leg, buried amid branches.

A black boy.

I squinted, moving closer.

A combine harvester made a noise in the distance, but other than that, it was dead quiet.

"Damn it," I said.

"What is it?" Remy yelled.

My eyes focused on a thick piece of nylon rope that had been singed to a dark brown color. It was wound around the boy's neck.

34

A black boy.

Lynched.

I ran a hand through my hair. Swallowed.

I scanned up the loblolly's trunk to a high branch, which was clearly broken off. The leaves and twigs that fell must have covered the boy from being noticed before.

"Jesus," Remy said. She was standing beside me now, a hand over her mouth. "My granny told me about this sort of thing, but . . ."

My eyes studied the boy's face. The fire had blackened his left cheek, but on the right side, the flesh around his mouth was gone. It exposed the metal wires of braces.

"Gotta be thirteen or fourteen," I said.

Behind me, Remy began retching.

I thought of my own son. My sweet Jonas. He'd never done a thing to anyone and was taken from me.

Through the burnt branches that covered the victim's legs, I saw that the boy's shorts had survived the fire. I stared at a patch of unburnt skin below his right knee. "His shin and knee." I pointed. "They're unscathed."

Remy spit something from her mouth. "That's weird, right?"

More like impossible, Purvis said.

I glanced around. Up the hill, rows of pecan trees curved over the horizon, but the area we were standing in was unplanted. Why hadn't more land burned? Had fire crews made it out here that fast?

"What is it?" Remy asked.

"A blue-suiter shot an old man out this way when I was a rook," I said. "The city covered it up. Got sued."

"I remember that," Remy said. "I was in high school."

Electric lines buzzed in the distance, whispering some foreign language into the wind. It had stopped raining, and I glanced down. My hands were shaking.

What if Virgil Rowe had done this?

Had murdered some innocent kid?

What if Rowe was the only one who had information on this boy and the motive for hanging him in the fire?

And what if I'd choked Rowe to death?

5

When the boy awoke, a cloth was jammed in his mouth, and he spit it out, his eyes darting left and right.

He was lying on his stomach in the dark, and the ground all around him was covered in muddy water.

He could smell mint from chewing tobacco.

"Who's there?" the boy yelled.

The pain surged then. His right arm was on fire.

Then he felt pressure on his left arm, as both were being pulled backward by some rope behind him.

His hands were yanked even farther, and he felt his back arch and the pain increase.

A popping noise echoed against the walls around him, and the torn muscles in his elbows caused his arms to flail unnaturally, like they were made of jelly.

Hot white colors smeared across the insides of his eyes, and the boy howled in pain.

He screamed, but couldn't hear his own words.

And somewhere in the dark, a man chuckled.

6

As I stood in the field, a thought came to mind.

A boy had gone missing yesterday, and an Amber Alert had been issued. I'd seen it in the paper at the Landing Patch, but also in a police bulletin I'd scanned on my phone as Remy drove in that morning.

"Kendrick Webster," Remy said, staring at her cell.

I looked at the missing persons picture. Kendrick was handsome, with caramel-colored skin and a short Afro.

"You think it's him?" Remy asked.

I shrugged. With the condition of the body, it was impossible to say.

My first call was to my boss, Chief of Police Miles Dooger. I told him how we'd stumbled onto the body.

"How old is he?"

"If it's the missing kid," I said, "fifteen."

"Je-sus," Miles said, the cadence of his voice familiar from years of working together. The chief had been my mentor coming up in the department, and we were close. "Media's gonna have us for lunch, dinner, and dessert, P.T."

Miles asked me to take over the arson

investigation, which would now be an arson-murder. He'd break the news to Detectives Kaplan and Berry, who would come out and give us any background they had so far on the fire.

Remy and I walked up a gravel driveway to the main house at Harmony Farms and introduced ourselves to Tripp Unger, who owned the place.

Unger was white and in his sixties, with reddish-brown hair the color of dried pampas grass. He had the body of a distance runner and wore old jeans and a green T-shirt with a John Deere logo on it.

We explained what we'd found, leaving out the rope around the boy's neck. The farmer's head dropped.

"I don't understand," he said. "There were cops and firemen out here yesterday going whole hog. They didn't see this kid?"

"We're still sorting through the details," I said, pulling out the Amber Alert photo of Kendrick. "Does this boy look familiar?"

Unger shook his head. "Is that him?"

"We don't know yet," Remy said.

I turned for a second to examine the vantage point that the farmhouse had on where the victim's body lay. Elevation-wise, Unger's home was higher than most of the land around it. I could see Remy's sports car down on the road—from up here, a toy car.

"Were you the one who reported the fire?" I asked.

"No," Unger said. "My wife and I were gone at a sunrise service at Sediment Rock. Someone called 911."

Sediment Rock was thirty minutes out east, on the edge of a protected forest. It had stunning quartz monzonite peaks that church groups used.

"Is that something you do every Sunday?" Remy asked. "You're gone each week at that time?"

As the farmer nodded, I glanced down the hill. We needed to be at the crime scene when patrolmen arrived to cordon off the scene. Before it got crazy.

"And what church is that?" Remy asked.

"First Son of God."

"I couldn't help noticing, Mr. Unger." I pointed down the hill. "The burned land is kind of at a dead end down there—and unplanted. Will the fire affect your business?"

"Probably not," Unger said. "We can hardly afford to farm half this place."

We thanked him and asked him not to talk to any media.

As we walked back down the hill, a flicker of lightning illuminated the field, framing a towering live oak nearby. The tree had a dozen light patches of Spanish moss that swayed in the morning light like a family of ghosts. It was an unusual sight, a tree like that so far inland. Far from places like Savannah, where it was common.

A moment later, the lightning came again, but this time it hit the ground in six or seven places, all at once. A surge of electricity moved across the land and spread through my body. The tingling moved into my fingers, and my body buzzed with a strange sensation.

"Did you feel that?" I asked Remy.

But she didn't answer. She was looking the other way. At a patrol car that was hauling ass along 903, about a mile off. Another two cars trailed behind the first.

We got back near the road, and I crouched by the boy's body.

"Take some pictures of this, will ya, Rem?" I motioned at the rope around the victim's neck. "Good ones for evidence."

Remy took her phone out and started shooting. I did the same with mine.

"In five minutes there's gonna be thirty cops out here," I said.

Remy cocked her head at me, unsure of where I was going.

"I'm taking off the rope," I said. "This many people. Snapchat? Twitter? We'll have a riot across half this city by sundown."

"I think I know which half," she said.

I pulled the rope from around the boy's

41

deformed head, and Remy bagged it, carrying the evidence to her car.

"This is gonna be bad, isn't it?" she said when she returned. "This case?"

"No," I lied.

7

By noon Harmony Farms was swarming with cops. A regular convention of blue-suiters and bad-tie-wearers. This didn't include me or Remy, who always looked ready for the cover of *Southern Cop Weekly*. I could imagine next month's issue, Remy with her pockets overflowing with blue crime scene gloves, and me, a confused look on my mug, wondering if I'd killed the killer.

"So you didn't think to call us first?" Detective Abe Kaplan glared at Remy. "Before y'all went strolling through our crime scene?"

Abe is an odd-looking guy. He's six foot one with curly hair that doesn't grow properly in places. He's half black and half Russian Jew. The combination is a warning to less-than-average-looking folks in both groups to no longer meet in dark bars.

I stepped in between him and Remy. I was Abe's partner two years ago, and he could start an argument in an empty house. "Dooger already went over this with you, Abe, so let's leave out the theatrics."

"Well, what the hell we doin' here?" Merle Berry asked. Merle is Abe's partner. He's heavy-set with a giant paunch and gray hair that

43

becomes nuclear white above his ears. Merle's accent is backwoods Georgia. A twang I'd heard more as a kid than I did nowadays.

"We need the particulars on the fire," I said. "Who called it in? When? And who have you guys talked to so far?"

Berry hiked his pants up using one hand on his belt. "A crop duster called it in," he said. "The old fella saw it blazin' Sunday morn about half past five. The farmer here was gone at services."

"You bring in the crop duster yet?" Remy asked.

"Nope," Berry said.

Berry was old-school, and Remy might be accidentally poking the bear. I stepped in.

"What's your take on the farmer, Merle?" I asked. "Remy and I talked to him briefly, but what did you guys get?"

"Times are tough, and he wasn't farming that piece of land anyway," Merle said.

"He didn't seem too broken up about it," Abe added.

Across the burnt field, I saw Sarah Raines, the M.E., her hands on her hips. She wore a fresh blue coverall; because of the drizzling, she'd tucked it into black rubber boots.

"How 'bout this?" Berry said. "Abe and I'll write up any open items, put 'em in our case file, and leave it on your desk by three."

"Great," I said.

A crowd was starting to gather. Some folks were probably employees of the farm, reporting in late. Others, I'd guess, were citizens of Harmony. This many cops in their neighborhood rarely was good, and too often it meant we'd done something wrong.

My eyes moved back to Sarah. I was giving her space to inspect the victim. I had told Chief Dooger and her about the rope, but no one else.

I moved toward her. As I got close, I noticed the dirt near the loblolly had tiny green crystals dried into it. They shined like gold specks in beach sand, and I shot a picture with my phone.

"Doc," I said, "you got any idea on C.O.D.?"

Sarah looked around to see if anyone was within earshot. "When I get him on the table, I can look at his neck and check the content of his lungs. See if the hanging killed him before the fire did. If he was alive when they strung him up."

Sarah had moved the tree branches off the boy's lower body, and I got a closer look at the rest of him.

"Is he the missing kid?" I asked.

"I think so." She pointed at a mark on his right leg where the boy's skin was only slightly singed. "The missing persons report mentioned a scar on his shin from skateboarding."

Sarah crouched by the boy. "I also noticed this," she said.

45

There was a section of his shorts that hadn't burned, and using tweezers, she reached under the bottom cuff of the leg. Teased out a white tag.

"S.E.G. Uni," I read the logo off the tag. "So the shorts are part of a uniform?"

I grabbed my phone and pulled up the website of Paragon Baptist, a Harmony high school that I visited each year for the D.A.R.E. program.

As the page loaded, I stared at shots of boys in the same blue shorts. Remy came up beside me. "Have you flipped the tag over?" she asked. "At uniformed schools, everything starts to look the same unless you put your name in it."

Sarah twisted the tweezers so we could see the back of the label. On it was a set of initials written in ink.

K.W.

As in Kendrick Webster.

"My momma did that when I was a kid," Remy said. "Otherwise my girlfriends would go home with my sweatshirts, and me with theirs."

I looked down at the Amber Alert information on Kendrick. Saw the words listed under "father's occupation."

"Well, shit," I said.

Because in Georgia, certain issues lit powder kegs. Race was the first, and it was already at play here. But right behind race was religion. And according to Missing Persons, Kendrick's dad was a Baptist preacher.

8

Two hours had passed, and I was in the precinct's main conference room, staring at a flyer for an event at Reverend Webster's church called "Remembering Our History."

I'd drafted Abe Kaplan onto our team. Then I'd sent Remy and Abe to do the notification at the Websters' home. We'd decided as a group not to inform the parents about the rope around their son's neck.

Remy stood in front of me, her voice betraying a tremor as she tried to sound professional.

"After we told them," she said, "the parents broke down, P.T. Real shock. Real tears."

"And this was on their fridge?" I asked, keeping Remy focused on the flyer she'd handed me.

"Yeah." She nodded.

The picture in the center of the paper was from 1946. It showed a black man hanging from a tree. The date for the lecture was two days ago. The same night Kendrick had gone missing.

I thought about the impossibility of coincidence. Of this horror happening to Kendrick the same night his parents hosted this lecture.

Abe came in. He wore a linen suit over a black shirt. A porkpie hat covered his head.

While Remy and Abe had done the notification,

I'd taped sheets of brown craft paper on the conference room windows that faced into the precinct.

Abe motioned at the paper. "You expecting leaks from our own people?"

Out the opposite window, raindrops slapped off a line of red dogwoods. The door was a few inches ajar, and I pushed it closed.

"I'm expecting a shit storm," I said. "So lock this door when one of us isn't here, and plan on late nights."

Abe was a veteran. He nodded. Remy sat up straighter.

"Tell me about the boy's momma and daddy," I said.

"Dad's thirty-eight. A preacher," Remy said. "Reggie's his name. Mom is Grace and works at the church. Volunteer programs mostly."

I grabbed a chair and turned it backward. In any other situation, I would've done the notification myself, to read the parents' faces as they received the worst news of their lives. But the gravity of race and this crime motivated a different course. Plus, I was fortunate we had two great black detectives on the squad.

"Mom is young," Abe said. "Must've been nineteen when she had Kendrick."

"They were devastated, P.T.," Remy said.

"What do we know about Kendrick?"

"Only child." Remy consulted her iPad. "Fifteen. His best friend, Jayme, had a sleepover

Saturday night. Apparently Kendrick biked there and texted his mom when he arrived."

I grabbed a pen and turned, facing the craft paper. I had a second use for it, in addition to privacy. I wrote *TIMELINE* across the top and marked a series of dots along a horizontal line. Above the far left dot, I wrote *Kendrick texts mom. At sleepover.*

"When was that?" I asked.

"Quarter to six Saturday night," Abe said, looking at his reporter's notebook. "Apparently the kid hosting became a little shit."

"The best buddy?" I asked.

"Jayme McClure." Remy said. "The kid's mom stepped in, canceled the sleepover, and sent her son's two friends packing. That was around seven p.m."

Remy waited until I was done putting this on the timeline.

"The following morning," Remy continued, "Grace Webster's texts to Kendrick go unanswered."

"This is Sunday morning?" I confirmed.

Remy nodded. "The mom called over to the McClure house. Found out about the thing being canceled—"

"Kendrick never came home, and his BMX bike is missing," Abe said.

I took this all in. "You said *two* kids were at the sleepover."

Remy scrolled through her iPad. "Eric Sumpter's the other one. Lives in Falls West and made it home Saturday night by seven forty-five. Safe and sound."

"Eric's a black kid or a white kid?" I asked.

"Eric's black like Kendrick," Abe said. "The McClure kid hosting is white. Kendrick's mom started driving the streets then. It's Sunday morning around church time, and she's looking for him. Calling his phone. We've requested Kendrick's cell records."

"An Amber Alert went out at ten-twenty a.m.," Remy said.

Outside, a gust of wind blew the dogwoods southward.

"But in Kendrick's case, it was all for nothing," I said. "If he was burned in a fire Sunday morning at five-thirty a.m., Kendrick was dead hours before his mom even met with patrol."

Everyone nodded. Which brought us back to our timeline. Sometime between seven p.m. Saturday night and five-thirty a.m. Sunday morning, fifteen-year-old Kendrick Webster had been abducted and lynched.

"Let's start with where he went missing." I stood up. "Who saw him last?"

"The McClures," Remy said.

"And the other murder?" Abe asked. "You think our dead Nazi Virgil Rowe is connected to Kendrick's death?"

I stared at a picture of Kendrick on the wall, and my son's face flashed in my head. Jonas and me, playing with toy cars on his bed.

"What?" I said.

Abe stared at me. "The Rowe case, P.T. You think it's related to this kid?"

"I don't know," I said. "Do we know if Mr. Rowe was affiliated with any local hate group?" I motioned at the flyer with the lynching photo. "The shortest distance between two points."

Remy tapped at a picture of the *88* ink on Virgil Rowe's biceps. "Well, we saw this."

"Sure, but that's a statement about the master brand," Abe said. "That's not a local membership badge."

Abe and I were thinking the same way: the tattoo just meant that he was a neo-Nazi. "So maybe there's other ink on his body we haven't seen yet but the M.E. has," I said.

"I'll check with Sarah," Abe said. "So how do you want to handle these two cases?"

"For now, let's assume the crimes are related, but separate. Tape everything for Virgil Rowe on the east wall and everything for Kendrick Webster on the west."

I handed Abe a photo of a bike print in mud. "This was found after you guys left for the notification. About thirty yards from the body."

"A motorcycle?" Remy asked.

"Judging by the tread of the tire, it's a crotch

51

rocket," I said. "A speed bike. But the mud was too wet to cast. Unger said that kids come onto the farm all the time. Ride through the unplanted fields. For all we know, it's nothing."

I grabbed my satchel. "Remy and I will head to the McClures' while you set up here," I said to Abe.

It was at that point in the investigation when anything was possible, and hope was at its apex. But Remy still sat there, her iPad on her lap.

"What's wrong?" I asked.

"Kendrick went missing at seven on Saturday night," she said. "But he wasn't abducted on Unger's property."

I turned and stared at the timeline.

"He was brought there to die," Remy said. "But grabbed somewhere else. And there's ten hours in between. We're still short one crime scene."

I nodded. Remy was right.

"Let's find it then," I said. "Even more reason to start at the McClures', where he was last seen."

9

As Remy drove to the McClures', she told me about the state lotto results from the weekend, which were spreading through social media. Two people had won a share of $200 million.

"They split it then?" I asked.

Remy nodded. "And one of them was from Harmony," she said. "Can you believe that? There's probably only a thousand people living there."

We moved out of Mason Falls to an area east of town, unincorporated with no name.

"They both had the same numbers?" I asked.

Remy shook her head at me. "Yes, old man, the same numbers. That's how it works. You never played your badge number?"

I shook my head back. "I'm not much for superstition."

Remy slowed at an intersection out in the country, just beside an inlet from the Tullumy River.

Twenty or so people, most of whom were black, were dressed in spectral white for a baptism.

The man getting dipped came up from the water. His outstretched hand pointed at me, and his mouth made the shape of a single word.

Paul, he said. My birth name.

I stared at Remy. "You see that?"

She shrugged, nonplussed. "His baptized Christian name, I imagine," she said. "After Saint Paul."

I nodded, and Remy accelerated past the group.

The land on both sides became farmland. Peaches mostly, with some tobacco and pecans mixed in.

"So what do we know about the McClures?" Remy asked.

"Not much," I said. "No one in the family's got a sheet."

After a minute, Remy slowed the car. Kendrick's best friend's house sat on a small square of land, set amid a half-dozen large farms.

There was a brick path that led from the gravel road to the front porch. All around it, where a lawn might be, was crushed white rock. The rains had lifted the rocks up and moved them about, forming white islands here and there. Tiny oceans stood between them.

Remy rang the bell, but no one answered. A giant inflatable Santa lay on its side on the porch, deflated and wet.

"Why don't we hang out for a minute," she said. "See if they come home."

"Sure." I moved back toward the Alfa.

Confederate jasmine grew wild at the front of the property, the blooms encircling the McClures' wooden mailbox. The fragrance was thick in the muggy afternoon air. A tow truck was parked about twenty yards down the long driveway.

I stared across the nearby field. "How long you figure it is from here to First Baptist, Rem? Twenty-five minutes?"

Kendrick's house was on a plot of land next to his dad's church. I was trying to guess at the time it would take for him to bike home.

"By bike—probably more," Remy said. "You gotta head all the way down Falls Road. Then cut up along the interstate—"

Remy was interrupted by the sound of a small engine. Two pre-teens on a red ATV were coming down the road toward the McClure house. They turned before the property. Cut behind a line of pine trees at the back.

I watched them pop out a second later behind the McClures' land. They rode atop a concrete levee in between the fields. An irrigation channel that carried water.

"How about if you go that way?" I pointed.

I took out my phone and punched in the Websters' home address. On my cell, a grid of farms formed. Green squares were bisected by easements and irrigation channels colored in gray.

"Let's take a walk," I said.

We began where the ATV had gone, walking down a concrete strip that ran between two fields. The path ended, and another one headed in a southern direction toward Harmony. This new one had two concrete strips, one on each side of an open V-shaped irrigation ditch.

"You're thinking he went home this way?" Remy asked, walking with me along the concrete path.

"Kendrick had a scar from a skateboard accident on his leg," I said. "He rode a BMX bike. He was young and athletic. We should think like a kid."

Remy pointed to the concrete. "When the gulch is dry, you could ride up and down the sides. Do jumps off the top."

I nodded. "When it's full of water like this week, you ride up here."

We kept moving, walking along the concrete path. The rain had filled the bottom of the channel beside us with muddy water, six inches deep.

After about ten minutes, Remy stopped. We were approaching a break between two fields. A small road ran perpendicular to us. The V-shaped channel ran underground, and a grate blocked access, letting just water move through.

"There's something down there." Remy pointed.

I walked down the incline and stepped into the muddy water at the bottom. I could feel my socks squish around inside my dress shoes.

Remy took off her flats and left them on the concrete path. The cuffs of her slacks floated in the mud at the bottom of the trench. "My dry-cleaning bill just got picked up by the department."

"Consider it another mud run," I said.

I walked closer to the dark area, where the water moved into a sluice below the road. A black BMX bike was lying down against the grate, half covered in weeds.

Remy gloved up and grabbed the handlebar, standing it up.

"So someone stops him out here," Remy said. "And does what? Grabs him and tosses his bike? They still gotta get him out of here against his will. He's fifteen. It's not like you can get a car into the middle of this field."

I looked around. "Why would you stop in the first place, if you're Kendrick?" I asked. "You're a kid, hauling ass home on your bike. It's late. Dark out."

I climbed up the incline and stared around. The countryside was flatter than a gander's arch. A mile across the field you could see the edge of Falls West, where the other boy who'd been at the sleepover had made it home safe.

"You think it's possible he fell?" Remy hollered from down inside the trench. "Or someone called him out for being here? He's *on* private property."

57

"We need to find out who owns this land," I said.

I walked toward a line of tobacco plants. The leaves were a yellow color, which meant they were near harvest. About every five or six rows, a line of mature pecan trees stood tall.

I walked to the closest row.

Molded pecan husks covered the base of the tree, but the dirt beneath the nearest one looked tamped down, as if it had been walked on recently.

Around the base of a big tree, someone had carved a symbol in the trunk—the "all-seeing eye" from the dollar bill, complete with rays pointing outward. I ran my fingers along it, and I could tell it was a fresh carving. The sap of the tree was wet at the deepest areas of the cut.

An industrial cable was wrapped around the same tree trunk. The cord was the smooth, galvanized-steel kind that you'd build a zip line out of. I picked up what must've been forty feet of cable, half-buried in the dirt. "What time is sundown, Rem?" I hollered, glancing up at the darkening sky above us.

"Maybe five-thirty or six," she yelled back. Still standing down in the water.

I carried the galvanized-steel cable out of the field and onto the concrete path next to the channel. Then down into the water where Remy was and back up the other side onto the other concrete path.

I pulled the cable taut, and it was three feet off the ground. Running from the tree on one side of the little ditch all the way to the path on the other side.

I saw circular cut marks around the trunk of a nearby pecan, where the cable might've been tied.

"If the sleepover ends at seven, it's dark," I said. "Someone holds this cord tight while Kendrick comes riding down the path."

"They'd clothesline him," Remy said. "His bike would shoot out from under him. He'd fly off the back."

I pictured Kendrick. Cruising along on his bike.

Had someone been lying in wait for *any* kid, not caring who it was? Or was the abduction intended for Kendrick?

I grabbed my cell and dialed up Sarah Raines. She told me she was in her lab, the body of Kendrick in front of her.

"Do you have any evidence of a head injury?" I asked.

"I've got a subdural hematoma," she said. "Anterior of his head."

I described what we'd found, and it matched with what Sarah was seeing. "Would it have killed him?" I asked.

"Not what I'm looking at," she said. "But it could've knocked him out."

I thought I heard someone behind me and

turned toward the field. Four-o'clocks grew wild in the ditch between the tobacco plants, but no one was there.

"P.T.," Sarah said, "I've found some other things we should go over."

"Give me the highlights," I mumbled.

"In person," Sarah came back with. "This one's too ugly to do over the phone."

My phone vibrated, and I held it up, staring at a text from Abe.

I'd sent him a picture to confirm it was Kendrick's bike, and he already had an answer.

We were standing at the abduction site.

10

The boy's eyes scanned the darkness. It was a cave of some sort. But how had he gotten here?

The last thing he remembered was Eric.

Eric—trying to convince him to play video games. But he went home instead.

The smell of rotten meat pushed the bile up his throat and into his mouth.

He'd been riding through the fields, the cool evening air against his hair. He'd wondered if there was any dinner left over at home.

And suddenly he was flying. Not on his bike, but through the air.

His father once described the hand of God like a lightning bolt, grabbing at you. Waking you up to life.

This bolt had hit him hard. Knocking the breath out of his chest and tossing him through the air.

He'd looked around when he landed. Saw blood covering his kneecap. Concrete. Concrete and the shadow of a man.

That was the last memory before being here, in the cave.

Now someone was lighting small candles in the darkness. The boy lifted his head and saw the bony skulls of animals, each atop a wooden stick.

And then there were fresh kills. The bloody decapitated head of a goat. The fluffy white head of a lamb, smeared with red.

"What is this?" the boy yelled. "Who are you people?"

11

By seven-thirty p.m., our crime scene tech, Alvin Gerbin, had arrived in the field.

The sun had gone down, and heavy shadows fell on the unlit irrigation ditch where we'd found the bike. In the distance, lights from cars up on SR-902 flickered in the spaces between pecan trees.

We'd found nothing else since discovering the metal cord, but Gerbin would print the hell out of it, and the bike too.

Remy hung back with our crime scene tech, and I walked up to the highway.

As I got a ride in with patrol, I thought about the first twelve hours of the case and the horror the Websters were going through.

Somebody had ambushed Kendrick out in this field, but then killed him miles away at Unger's farm. What had happened in between?

The black and white pulled to the curb outside the station and let me out. As it drove away, a high-intensity light nearly blinded me.

"Detective Marsh." The voice of Deb Newberry broke through. "Can you confirm the dead child found in Harmony is Kendrick Webster?"

Newberry was a brash field reporter for the local Fox channel, and the brightness of the camera caught me off guard. I could hardly see where I was walking.

"Jesus, Deb," I said. "I'm gonna break my ankle out here if I can't get around you."

I moved past the reporter and her cameraman, but they followed me to the front door of the precinct.

"Is it true the department is heavily concerned about leaks in this investigation?"

"We're concerned about leaks in *every* investigation."

"But you don't always block off a room, do you?" Newberry asked. "Away from your fellow officers—for your evidence and timeline? Cover the windows with craft paper?"

My face gave away my answer. Her question also made me second-guess everyone around me. I opened the door to the precinct.

"Do you see the case as an opportunity to address the racial insensitivity in the police department?"

"There is no racial insensitivity on my squad," I said. "Every homicide is our top homicide, regardless of race."

I let the door swing shut on her face and moved inside the precinct, but my mind was conflicted about the decision to remove the rope from Kendrick's neck. Sooner or later the details of the lynching would come out. If we didn't have our killer in custody, folks like Deb Newberry would skewer me. And I'd deserve it.

I made my way to the conference room and plopped down in a chair next to Abe. "Tell me you found something new on Kendrick."

Abe picked up his notebook. "Well, I know how much you love coincidences, P.T. So here's one for you. Our vic, Virgil Rowe, out in the numbered streets? He's got some ink on his back."

Abe pulled out a photo, a tattoo on pale skin. An eagle, riding on a black cloud. "It's a local neo-Nazi group called StormCloud."

"What do we know about them?" I asked.

"They started as an online bulletin board in the '90s," Abe said. "Flew under the radar until 2005, when they made a website denying the Holocaust. Recent tax returns say they run a two-million-dollar budget."

"They must have legitimate businesses then."

"Now you're thinking, podna," he said, slipping into the diction of his youth. Abe was originally from New Orleans, the son of a riverboat waitress and an oil-derrick driller. "They own a towing company," he said. "Stormin' Norman Tow."

I looked up from the tattoo.

"*Vaughn McClure* has a towing company," I said. "We saw one of his trucks in the driveway."

"Exactly," Abe said. "McClure's an independent with five trucks. So far I haven't found anything to connect him to Stormin' Norman. But there's the optics of it."

"Which don't look good," I said.

I sat back. Putting things together in my head. I'd been trying to figure out how someone would know Kendrick was coming down the irrigation ditch at that exact time.

I hadn't considered a different option. That Kendrick was sent away from the sleepover on purpose. That the McClures might have deliberately driven him into the arms of an ambusher.

"No one was home at the McClure house when we tried them," I said. "Have you been able to reach Vaughn McClure at his business?"

Abe shook his head. "Put wishes in one hand and shit in the other. See which fills up first."

"What else?" I asked.

"Well," Abe said, "we got a big lead on Virgil Rowe's killer."

"The neo-Nazi?"

Abe nodded. "This lady Martha Velasquez called into the tip line. She lives on 30th Street in the numbereds. A block over from Virgil."

"Who is she?" I asked.

"Retired school counselor. Sixty-three. Hispanic," Abe said. "Her Pekingese woke her up Sunday morning around three a.m. She took the pooch out for a piss. Saw some white guy walking down from the boulevard."

"At three a.m.?" I asked. "She could see then?"

"Per Velasquez, this guy entered the property

where Virgil was killed. Two minutes later—out comes Corinne, the stripper."

I swallowed hard.

That's you, Purvis said. *I thought you were careful.*

"Now, if you remember, P.T.," Abe said. "Corinne told patrol that she was gone at her girlfriend's house from midnight to seven a.m. This means she lied."

I attempted a nod but my head just kind of bobbed.

"I'm thinking that whoever came over," Abe said, "they told Corinne to make herself scarce while they killed Virgil. Which means Corinne knows the killer."

We're dead, Purvis huffed.

"So I sent patrol to pick the stripper up," Abe continued. "But apparently she split town."

I hadn't inhaled in about a minute.

"So we lost her?" I said.

"Don't worry," Abe said. "She uses plastic and she's ours. Plus, I put in a request to pull traffic cams up on the boulevard. How many cars you think are driving around the numbered streets at three a.m.?"

I swallowed again. Sick to my stomach.

Breathe, Purvis said.

"I'm tired as all get out." Abe stood up. "There's a box of Banquet microwave chicken with my name on it. And a soft pillow."

I nodded as Abe grabbed his old leather bag. Put his notebook inside. "Kendrick's pop came up here, by the way. Talked to Chief Dooger."

"Does the dad have some information for us?" I asked.

"He doesn't want you leading the investigation," Abe said. "That's his information."

"He offer a reason?"

"Nothing in particular," Abe said. "He'd done some minor recon on you. Pointed out some cases he didn't love the outcome on. But mostly, you didn't come for the notification."

There was a reason I'd sent two black cops out on day one. I was trying to keep this city under control.

"What'd the boss say?" I asked. "He want you leading this?"

Abe shook his head and patted me on the shoulder. "Miles said to keep doing what we're doing."

Abe headed out then, and I moved to my office.

Sliding open the top drawer in my desk, I pulled out a bottle of Thirteenth Colony. Threw a quick capful back and let the rye whisky coat my throat.

Under the liquor was a framed photo of my son sitting on the front porch.

Jonas.

I ran my hands over the glass frame.

My son had honey-colored skin and a short

reddish Afro that was a mix of my wavy chestnut locks and his mother's beautiful black curls.

I thought of the reverend assuming I was unfit to find his son's killer. Hell, maybe I was.

But I'd experienced more than Webster thought.

I'd walked into stores. Into restaurants. I'd come to school events holding Jonas's hand and get that look. That "What's he doing with that black kid" look.

I'd also put Jonas in the ground. In a casket that was so small it broke my heart into a thousand pieces. Littered them from the mountains of northern Georgia to the wire grass of the coastal plains.

I shot back another cap of whisky and popped some gum in my mouth, put the liquor and the frame away. I threaded my way to the first floor of the building, to the medical examiner's office.

Sarah Raines sat on a stool in the lab, her flats up on the edge of a washing basin. She held a digital voice recorder in one hand. A sheet covered the body beside her.

"There you are," she said, hitting stop on the recorder and putting her feet down. "How are things out at that ditch?"

"Slow," I said. "We gotta break one more detail before I feel good about going to bed."

Sarah motioned at the body. "Well, maybe I have that for you."

I grabbed a chair from a desk nearby and slid

it over. Under her lab coat, Sarah was dressed in a sleeveless red top and black yoga pants that showed off her thin figure. Her shoulder-length blond hair had streaks of brown in it.

"Kendrick had third-degree burns covering seventy percent of his body," she said, moving to the top section of her report.

I grabbed my phone and jotted this down. It was good information, but no *Aha*.

"The initial cause of death was carbon monoxide poisoning." Sarah pointed. "But in the last hour, I've pulled enough soot from his lungs to change that to chemical edema."

"Asphyxiation," I said.

So there it was. Soot was in Kendrick's lungs.

I'd been gripping the edge of the tray Kendrick's body lay in; my knuckles were white.

"So he was alive when they burned him?"

Sarah nodded, her lips quivering. I've always been told I'm a hard person to read. Sarah was the opposite: every emotion on her face.

"Anything else?" I asked. "Gunshots? Knife wounds?"

"Yeah," Sarah said. "Something else, but not a knife or gun wound. That's why I wanted to talk in person." She got up, but didn't say anything. Reached over like she was gonna pull back the sheet, but didn't do that either.

Then I realized she was tearing up, her cheeks

glistening. I don't know why this surprised me—that coroners cried.

"Hey," I said, a hand on her shoulder. "It'll be okay."

"No," she said. "It's worse than you think. He was tortured, P.T."

I hesitated, not following her.

"Both of Kendrick's elbows were broken," Sarah said.

I blinked. "I don't understand. I thought he was hung by his neck, not his arms. The rope I took off—"

"He was," she said. "This other thing—with his elbows—it happened earlier. Before the lynching."

My brain was sore.

Sarah was talking about two separate injuries. The final hanging that I'd seen evidence of—and then something else, where Kendrick's hands had been pulled back, his elbows breaking in the process.

"Wait a sec," I said. "Elbows breaking—that doesn't happen naturally in fires? Bones break, from pressure?"

"They can," she said. "High temperature can cause muscles to contract. It can flex joints and break bones. Fires can put the body in what we call a pugilistic posture. Like someone's fighting."

"But not here?" I asked.

"No way," Sarah said, paging forward to show me an X-ray. "You see how the olecranon process is cracked?"

I nodded. "Is that post- or antemortem?"

"Ante," she said. "This is before he was dead."

I needed to put together what this meant. The sequence of things.

Someone had set up a trap to capture Kendrick, knocking him off his bike. Then they'd grabbed him. Brought him somewhere and broke both of his elbows. And then while he was still alive, they strung him up by his neck, hoisted him into a tree, and lit him on fire.

I didn't see Kendrick's body anymore. I saw my son, his age accelerated to fifteen. His eyes like mine. His hair more like his mom's. And the people who did this—they did it to my son.

I steadied my breathing.

Was this McClure? Was he some racist fuck who sent Kendrick away—into the arms of his Nazi buddies?

We had nowhere near the evidence needed to get a warrant to search the McClures' house, and another possibility flashed in my head. That maybe I could find the tow truck owner myself—do what I had to to make the world a better place without him. The only thing keeping me from doing this was the gnawing memory of Virgil Rowe. What I might've done to him. What it might cost me.

A flicker of lightning whitened the sky out the window. More rain was coming, and I hoped Remy was done out at the irrigation ditch.

Sarah used the back of her hand to wipe tears from her face. "You gotta find this son of a bitch, P.T. So he doesn't do this to any more kids."

I'd never heard Sarah curse before.

"I'll find him," I said. "And when I do, I'll watch as they stick a needle in his arm."

12

On my way out to the parking lot, I saw a light on in the corner office on the third floor and turned back. I took the stairwell up and found Chief Dooger working late.

Miles Dooger was fifty. A stocky build and a red face. He had a bushy white mustache that curved into a wide, upside-down U.

"There's my number one guy," he said as I appeared in the doorway.

Miles had had a knee surgery go bad in his forties, and he walked with a slight limp. He moved slowly around his oak desk and gave me a hug.

"I saw your light on," I said. "You busy?"

"Just more of this damn grant paperwork."

Two years ago Miles had stopped being one of us and became management. And it was a godsend. The chief before him had been a good cop but a lousy manager of men and machinery.

For me, it also didn't hurt to have a boss I'd come up in the ranks with. A friend at the top.

Miles was constantly trying to bring a variety of police-related business to Mason Falls. His latest push was for a state crime lab, to be located off I-32.

"You heading home?" he asked.

I nodded. "Just finished up with the M.E."

"Ah," Miles said. "The lovely Sarah."

I ignored where Miles was trying to take me. Instead I ran down the details of where we stood on Kendrick Webster's case. The discoveries about him being burned alive. The indications of torture.

Miles listened from the edge of his desk. As my mentor, he'd always been a "think first" detective. I could describe something horrific, and he'd react slowly. Thoughtfully.

"Well? What do you imagine Mom and Dad want?" he said, a contemplative look on his face.

"Dad wants justice," I said. "Mom, revenge."

Miles stood up.

"Well, there's what the family wants. And what the community needs. You don't plan on telling the parents their boy was burned alive, do ya?"

"Not yet." I shook my head. There was the rope too. The lynching. We were building up an arsenal of details we hadn't been forthcoming about.

Miles packed his things into a leather saddle-bag. "I'll walk out with you," he said, and we headed toward the elevator.

When we got inside, he turned to me. "I guess what I'm saying is—imagine the best outcome, and maybe, God willing, we'll get there."

Miles was an inscrutable politician. "Meaning what?" I said.

"You find the son of a bitch who did this." He shrugged. "Maybe you corner him. He makes a move and goes for his gun. And you take him down. Both parents get what they want."

The elevator door opened, and we headed out to the parking lot.

Could it be as simple as Miles had described?

I suddenly remembered what Abe had told me about Reverend Webster going to see the boss. The goal was to pull me off the case, but the chief hadn't brought it up.

"Miles," I said. "I heard the father came to you—"

Miles waved me off before I could finish the sentence. "Don't worry about him."

We got to Miles's Audi.

"Jules," the boss said, referring to his wife. "She says she's texted you three or four times to come for dinner, but you never respond."

"It's too hard to be around the kids," I said. "I'm sorry."

Miles threw his bag inside the sedan. "You staying focused?" he asked.

Which I took to mean "You staying dry?"

"Of course," I lied.

"Good." He patted me on the shoulder and opened his car door. "Work is a good distraction. But so is sleep. Don't forget to sleep, P.T."

13

Banging noises. And water. The banging of small fists against glass. But today it was louder than usual.

Then I heard my name. Not the word "Dad," which I usually imagine Jonas screaming as the car gets pulled down the Tullumy River, but my real name.

"P.T.," I heard. "Paul Thomas Marsh."

I rolled over and stared at the wood floor in my son's room. Heard the sound of Remy hollering. Banging at the front door.

A bottle of Dewar's was capped closed and half-full beside me. I rolled it under Jonas's bed and stood up. I was still in yesterday's clothes. I focused on the positive: less laundering of pajamas.

I walked to the front door and swung it open.

Remy's eyes moved over me. "Jesus," she said. Scanning my place like I'd trained her to. "I thought you were dead or something."

She was dressed in a white blouse and tan slacks that showed off her long legs. Walked a few feet in and sniffed.

"What's wrong?" I said. My head was pounding from getting up too fast.

"You tell me, partner," she responded. "I called

your cell ten times. And your place smells like ass."

I moved into the kitchen for ice water. Looked at the clock: 8:03 a.m.

"Kendrick's elbows were broken," I said.

"Yeah, you called me at four a.m. and told me," Remy said. "Then again at four-thirty."

I didn't remember doing this. I rubbed my face to wake up.

"What's on the docket today?" I said.

Remy glanced under the dining room table at a bottle of cheap Russian vodka. "Aircraft cable," she said.

The sun through the kitchen windows was unbearable.

"That's what was wrapped around the tree where Kendrick was abducted?" I asked.

Remy nodded. "Three vendors in town sell it. One's off SR-902. About two miles from Harmony."

I sat down at the dining room table. Our house was small. "Cozy" was the word people used. Lena and I had bought the place from an old couple who retired to Florida.

The kitchen, living room, and dining room were one big space, and Lena had filled them with antique furniture she'd bought secondhand on trips into the country with her twin sister, Exie.

Remy picked up a dirty plate from the kitchen counter with her thumb and pinky.

My partner had this way about her. She was a

tomboy—tough, didn't take shit from any guy—but was also probably more woman than a man like me could handle.

"Geez, boss," she said, "you ever heard of a cleaning lady?"

I grabbed the plate from Remy and put it in the sink.

Most of the antiques Lena had bought were currently functioning as wardrobe racks. When I wasn't working, I'd wear the same five or six T-shirts, hanging them over old glass sewing tables or cherry wardrobes filled with antique silver platters.

"These vendors," I said. "They work with the airport?"

"No, the name 'aircraft cable' is misleading," Remy said. "The stuff's mostly used in factories. For lifting equipment. I called a guy already. He's waiting on us."

Purvis stumbled out of Jonas's room, and Remy crouched to massage the wrinkled fur that crowded his face.

Bulldogs rest constantly. But Purvis hadn't been sleeping in there to be close to me. A year had passed, and he was still grabbing at the corners of Jonas's comforter in the morning. Waiting for his best friend to come home.

"Ten minutes," I said, and Remy told me she'd wait outside. I turned on a hot shower and let it warm my skin.

Water. Pounding fists. Screaming.

I have too much information on *how* everything happened last December to my wife and son. And not enough on why. The battery in the old Jeep had failed. The roads were slick. There was my father-in-law. Called to help. He arrived, but made things worse.

Before anyone knew it, my wife's car had slid off the road into the Tullumy River and was pulled under in seconds. The car was carried downriver with my wife and son trapped inside.

I got dressed quickly, putting on a tan sport coat over black slacks and a white collared shirt. Crouching down, I rubbed the whitish-pink fur on Purvis's face, right near his jawline. He huffed, and I moved outside, putting the mess of the past out of my head.

As I drove, Remy told me about a piece of news that was trending in Harmony. Two dozen kids had been sent home from Paragon Baptist with bloody noses, and no one knew why.

"That's Kendrick Webster's school, right?" I asked.

Remy nodded. "It's weird, huh?"

"Schools are like petri dishes," I said. "We saw it with Jonas at preschool. One kid would get sick. Then suddenly they were all sick."

I pulled off SR-902 at Stanislaw Avenue. We veered off the main road and down a one-way street, parking in front of a place called A-1

Industrial. It had a big metal awning with four trucks under it. Each was wrapped in neon green vinyl.

Inside, we introduced ourselves to Terrance Clap, who Remy had spoken to by phone. He was north of seventy, carried an extra fifty pounds in his gut, and wore a green railroad-conductor-style hat.

"We don't get many visits from the po-lice." Clap smiled, standing behind a counter that ran the length of the place. His voice was deep, and it dipped down at the ends of sentences.

Remy showed Clap a lead of cable that we'd cut from the forty-foot piece found at Kendrick's abduction site.

"What can you tell us about this, Mr. Clap?" she asked.

Clap pulled a stool under him. His gut rested atop the counter, and he used a magnifying glass to inspect the cord.

"Well, it's aircraft cable, just like I guessed by telephone." He looked more to me than Remy. "Five-sixteenths of an inch."

"And what's that traditionally used for?" I asked.

"Well, that could vary," he said. "Could be for marine or construction. What are y'all fixin' to build or lift?"

I squinted at Clap. Remy had told him by phone that this was a criminal investigation.

"We're not trying to build anything," I said. "This cable was used in a crime. We're trying to find out the type of person who'd have it handy."

Clap scrunched up his brow. Behind him were rows of shelves stocked with supplies. "Someone done choke a body with this?" he asked.

"We can't discuss the details," Remy said. "Do you sell this cord here?"

"Oh, sure," Clap said. He waddled between two aisles and came back with a wooden spool about two feet in diameter. Heaved it onto the counter.

Remy tapped at it. There was probably two hundred feet of identical cable wound around the core. "Do you keep receipts of who buys this?"

Clap hesitated, grabbing a Red Man pouch from under the counter. He threw some chew under his lip.

"We're cash-and-carry or account, hon," he said, still facing my way. "If it's cash, it's a paper receipt like this."

Clap pulled a chunk of two-by-four from under the counter. It had a nail sticking up through the board with receipts stuck on the nail.

I took the top receipt off and read what was listed under "Name" and "Address." Someone had written *Joe*. Nothing else. Just Joe. On the next one down, the name read *N/A*.

"You guys are pretty detail-oriented, aren't you?" I said.

Clap held my gaze, a stupid grin on his mug.

There are times I wake up in the morning and find myself in 1896 Georgia. It's not a bad place for me. But for my partner, it's a foreign country. A hostile land.

We were one day into the investigation, and already the media was buzzing with threats of a federal takeover of the case. There were people on both sides of the racial divide who wanted that. Some just for the pure chaos of it.

I tightened up my face. "We got a serious investigation here, Mr. Clap, and you're smiling like a dog with two peters. I gotta tell ya, I don't appreciate it. Makes me think there's all sorts of ways those trucks outside might start gettin' tickets."

Clap's face became solemn.

"Couple parking tickets," I said. "Some speeding tickets. Hell, I could see myself taking a personal interest in y'all's business. Sales tax records. Income tax." I held up the receipt that said "Joe" on it. "Like, you might think Joe here bought ten dollars' worth of parts, but the state insists it's a hundred because there's more tax on a hundred bucks. Turns out the state likes money."

"Why don't we start over," he said flatly.

"Yeah, let's do that." I held up the lead of cable. "How do you describe this stuff?"

"Well—"

"Oh, and look at my partner when she asks you a question."

He looked at me a minute, and then let it go. "We call that a seven-by-nineteen," he said. "You got one cluster of nineteen strands of cable and 'round it are six other clusters."

"And the folks who buy it," Remy asked. "What are they buying it for?"

Clap turned to face Remy.

"It holds weight," he said. "Gots what we call a low fatigue rate. The main use is pulleys. Sheaves."

"What's a sheave?" Remy asked.

The old guy walked over to a box on a shelf and pulled out one of those wheels that have a groove set into them. I'd seen them before, but never knew the name.

"A guy who buys seven-by-nineteen," Clap said to Remy. "He repairs industrial machinery. Owns a crane. Works a well. You gotta move something heavy, then you need your cable, your pulley, your sheave."

"What about a tow truck?" I asked. "It's got a winch, right? Sort of the same idea?"

Clap's fingers drummed a beat near his belly button. "Now, tow trucks, they got a specific-size cable. That's not my line of business, but yeah, I guess it's the same principle."

I bit at my lip, thinking over the connection that Abe had already found. Vaughn McClure, whose house Kendrick had left from, had a tow business. And Stormin' Norman Towing was owned by StormCloud, the neo-Nazi group.

"So if I'm a pulley guy," I asked, "or a tow guy. Would it be normal for me to have forty feet of this in my truck? For emergencies?"

Clap shrugged. "Reckon that stands to reason. Although the tow guys—I think they use a three-eighths inch, 'stead of a five-sixteenths."

Even better, I thought. The size wound around the tree wasn't normal for tow trucks. So if we found it in the back of Vaughn McClure's truck, it'd be more damning.

Then I thought of something I hadn't considered.

I thought of Kendrick, strung up in that tree. And the "how" of it. That maybe having this type of cord in your trunk had a different intention, outside of knocking Kendrick out at that ditch.

"This system you just mentioned," I said to Clap. "The pulley, the sheave. That would be perfect if I needed to pull something of weight up into, say, a tree, right? I could wrap a cable around a branch, run it through that sheave—"

"Now you're thinking," Clap said. "That way a job that would normally take two people working hard—with a pulley system, you do it real easy like, with one guy."

14

Both of the boy's arms were tied behind his back, and his face was pushed down into the water.

"You don't have to do this," the boy mumbled through the pain. He was lying on his stomach. "You could let me go. I never saw your face."

"Well, why don't I show you my face then, Kendrick," the man said.

The man knew his name.

"No," Kendrick pleaded.

But the man came around in front of him. Lifted his head up.

Pain shot along Kendrick's shoulder and down his arm.

Kendrick saw the man's eyes. A touch of stringy white drool hung from the corner of his lip.

Kendrick's face was pushed into the water again, and the man laid on top of him.

They were both clothed, but the man began sniffing along his neck. Murmuring strange words, mixed in with English. Petting and scratching at the boy's head.

"Rise," the man said in between words that sounded like something from another world.

Kendrick's head was pulled up from the water, and he gulped at air.

Sputtering. Yelling. "Get off me!"

"Burn," the man repeated next, pushing Kendrick's head back down.

Kendrick gulped at muddy water, thrashing against the man. Which sent spears of pain from his wrist to his elbow.

Kendrick was nearly out of energy when the man pulled his head up for the last time.

"Take him," the man said to someone else waiting in the darkness.

Kendrick exhaled. Was it over?

But he felt himself being yanked backward.

Dragged along a rough-hewn floor.

Then lifted up by the rope that bound his hands behind his back—his two jelly-like arms supporting all his weight. And he screamed like he'd never screamed before.

But wherever he was . . . nobody seemed to hear.

15

By noon, Remy and I had made our way to the other two supply houses that sold aircraft cable. At each, we were fortunate to find a computer on the counter. And without a subpoena, each business handed us a list of folks who'd bought our specific gauge of cable in the last month. Call it Southern hospitality.

As we drove away from the last place, I couldn't help imagining that the main use of the cable was to get Kendrick up in that loblolly.

We got onto State 902, and Remy talked about some details that had been bothering her. The lottery winnings in Harmony the same day as the murder. The strange lightning storms on the land where Kendrick had been killed.

I pulled off the highway and headed toward my house. I didn't think the storm or lotto mattered much, but the carving in the tree where someone had waited for Kendrick didn't sit well with me.

Then again, I also knew that my partner was young and impressionable. And evidence was what mattered most, not your gut.

"Every time I think there's something bigger at play on a case," I said, "I discover there's just some regular guy—some evil man doing evil things."

I turned onto my street, where Remy had left her car that morning.

"The only conspiracy," I said, "is when you and I stand idle. Let the assholes get away."

I dropped Remy outside my house, and she hung by the car window for a moment.

"I'll be in in an hour," I said. "Just gonna let Purvis out."

"It might do you well to get something solid in your system," Remy said.

It was the first time my partner had referenced my drinking out loud, and I wasn't sure how to respond.

"Okay," I said. "Thanks."

I moved inside, raiding the pantry. I found some cornmeal and self-rising flour and made batter for some hoecakes.

I let Purvis out back, and he sniffed around an old swing set that I'd built in the backyard when Jonas was five. His brown and white tail unconsciously moved left and right as he smelled the earth.

The links in the swing chains were rusty from mist from the morning sprinklers, and I noticed something I hadn't before. There had always been an area of dirt under each swing where my son's feet had dragged along the ground. Grass could never grow there, but now the two areas were overgrown with green marathon.

I made my way back to the kitchen and fried the hoecakes in Lena's old wrought-iron skillet.

I stared out the kitchen window as I cooked. The east side of the house gave way to a forested area with slash pines so dense you could hardly walk through them. But weedy cogon grass with white flowers had grown up all around them, seeding themselves into the trunks and slowly strangling the trees.

Have Remy and I gotten ourselves into something twisted? Rotten?

I ate at the stove until I was full as a tick, the grease and flour pouring into my system and soaking up any liquor left over from last night. The sun threw shadows through the blinds onto the floor, and it looked like stairs heading to nowhere. I thought about how many cases hit dead ends and how many dirtbags never got caught.

My cell rang, and it was Abe.

"I found a financial transfer between McClure Towing and Stormin' Norman Tow."

"Bullshit," I said.

"Nope, seventy-five hundred bucks. Paid from Stormin' Norman to McClure."

Money from neo-Nazis to McClure.

"We got him," I said.

"Could be everyday business," Abe warned. "But between that and the StormCloud tat on Virgil Rowe . . . plus the cord three hundred yards from the McClure house. It should be enough for a friendly judge to give us a search warrant."

An hour later, I met Abe outside of McClure Towing near downtown. The judge had denied us a warrant for the McClure residence, but gave us paper on the towing business.

Vaughn McClure met us at the door, and Abe badged him, handing him the warrant.

"The hell is this?" McClure asked. He was in his early forties. Chiseled face and thick black hair. He looked like a model for men's hair dye.

Abe motioned McClure outside to talk while I did a quick once-over of the place.

The small lobby up front was spare. Water jug for customers. Those pointy paper cups in a stack atop it. A couple worn-out chairs.

I began by rummaging through the desk drawers. Nothing. Then the file cabinet. In a folder in the last drawer, I found a stamped invoice from Stormin' Norman for the same dollar amount that Abe had located. The invoice read "Three Trucks—Supplemental Support."

Abe, meanwhile, had moved to the garage while a patrolman sat with McClure out by the curb. Abe's job was to find the aircraft cable—not the three-eighths inch used in tow trucks, but the five-sixteenths that matched the cord used in Kendrick's abduction.

I walked outside and showed Abe the file. The garage smelled of motor oil and coffee grinds. "I got jack diddly out here, P.T.," Abe said.

I placed the invoice in a sealed evidence bag,

and McClure walked over. He had white sweat stains on his black polo shirt.

"What'd you take?" McClure nodded at the evidence bag. I had a couple inches on him, but his arms were like granite.

"Why don't you come with us downtown, Mr. McClure. You can have your attorney meet you there."

McClure made a call to his wife and got in the black and white. I followed the patrol car in my truck so I could talk to Abe. It was three p.m., and I'd hoped we'd be heading back with more than the paper evidence of what Abe had already found digitally.

"There was nothing incriminating in that office," I said to Abe once we were by ourselves. "And the problem with this"—I held up the invoice—"is Stormin' Norman's a legit towing business. Per this invoice, McClure just provided some extra trucks to someone in his industry."

"Sure," Abe said. "But there's, you know—"

"The optics of it?" I finished the sentence with Abe's go-to phrase.

"If McClure is innocent and he's really just protecting his business," Abe said, "he's gonna want to talk to us now, podna."

"Says who?"

"Well, if he doesn't," Abe said, "we just give the Deb Newberrys of the world a little morsel about Stormin' Norman and the Nazi connection to Kendrick. Let the market take care of the rest."

The word "market" was Abe's expression for the press. Meaning that if the media had this information, they would make the same connection we did between the neo-Nazi tow truck company and Vaughn McClure. And then they'd eat McClure alive. Protesters outside his business. Media trucks outside his home. If he was only trying to protect his family and business, we'd use that instinct against him.

But if he was a Nazi bastard in hiding, like we suspected, he'd lawyer up hard and we'd know to start digging holes in his life 'til we found something else.

We got back to the station, and Alana McClure was already there, along with an attorney. The wife was a heavyset redhead, the lawyer a skinny white guy in his seventies who I'd seen in court. His name was Kergan.

We put the lawyer and the McClures in a room and let Kergan go for a minute. The usual attorney speech about his client being harassed.

Then I laid it down on the desk. The invoice. The article about StormCloud and their holdings. The lead of metal cord.

"I'm not gonna beg you to tell me a thing, Mr. McClure," I said. "You know what this is?" I put my hand across the table. "It's me, putting a hand out to you, while your boat goes down in a storm."

"We don't need to be here," Kergan said, pushing his chair back.

"When the press hears that you might be connected to a black boy getting burned alive," I said. "And you won't help his parents . . . ?"

"You're gonna blackmail my clients now?" Kergan interrupted.

"And our chief suspect," Abe added, "is a Nazi white supremacist who you do business with."

Abe let that hang in the air, and I dealt the final blow. "Kendrick was grabbed in the field a hundred yards from your house," I said. "To a lot of folks that might look like you purposely sent him packing Saturday night—into the arms of a neo-Nazi you get money from."

"We're leaving." Kergan stood up.

"Siddown," Vaughn McClure said to his attorney.

The lawyer took his chair.

Vaughn McClure exhaled. He seemed nervous. But just as much, he was pissed.

"This thing." He picked up the invoice. "Stormin' Norman needed a second company to help them clear some old cars off a property. So they hired us. We worked three days alongside their drivers. We never talked politics, and we didn't know shit about 'em, except they paid net ten."

"You got any eagle tats, Mr. McClure?" Abe asked. "When we book you, are we gonna find hate ink on your shoulders?"

Vaughn McClure looked to his wife and then back to me.

"We didn't want to feel like we were piling on," Vaughn McClure said. "And talk bad about Kendrick."

The energy in the room shifted.

"Meaning what?" I said.

"Listen, we love Kendrick," Alana McClure said. "He's had supper at our house twenty times. But in the last year, it's been tough to have him over. And it happened again Saturday."

"What happened?" Abe asked.

"Kendrick's behavior," Vaughn McClure said. "Pushing the other boys around. Specifically my boy. I'm no helicopter parent, but eventually I step in."

"*Kendrick's* was the bad behavior that ended the sleepover?" Abe asked.

"Go ahead and ask Eric," Vaughn McClure said. "He was there too."

"I blame some bad influences," Alana McClure spoke up. "People at the church."

This sounded like bullshit to me. Then again, we'd been looking at this from the Websters' point of view.

"Influences like who?" I asked.

"There's a guy at the church," Vaughn McClure said. "Tattoos down to here." He pointed at his wrists. "A lot of the boys think he's cool. He's been to prison. Talks to them about girls."

I looked to Abe.

"I checked every employee at First Baptist," he said.

"I think he's a volunteer," Alana McClure said. "Lives in a shed on the property. Rides a speed bike."

The motorcycle detail popped. We'd seen a single set of tracks near the crime scene.

We talked to the McClures a bit more, and then I heard three quick knocks on the observation window. This was Remy's signal, and I excused myself. Left Abe in there with them.

Inside observation, Remy had her laptop flipped open.

"Tell me this is bullshit." I pointed at the two-way window. "That we didn't just lose our best suspect."

"There's a new handyman at the church," Remy said. "Cory Burkette."

In the picture Remy had open, Burkette was a pasty shade of white. Stocky. He wore an orange prison jumpsuit.

"He got out of Rutledge a month ago," Remy said. "Served eight years for attempted robbery."

"And he rides a bike?"

"A 2011 Suzuki GSX." Remy pulled up a picture.

"How does Burkette know the Websters?"

"Some church outreach program with Rutledge prison," Remy said. "The reverend counseled

Burkette while he was locked up. After he got paroled, Webster invited him to stay at First Baptist."

Remy stepped outside to call Eric Sumpter, the other boy at the sleepover. As she did, I found the photos of the motorcycle tracks out at Unger's farm. I thought about the irrigation channel where Kendrick's BMX bike had been found. A motorcycle would be an easy way to get Kendrick's body out of there fast.

Remy opened the door, and I knew right away from her face. Eric Sumpter had verified the reason the sleepover ended. The McClures were in the clear.

"Shit," I said.

Remy shrugged, grabbing her keys. "One door closes, 'nother one opens. Right? Let's pick up Burkette."

I nodded, and twenty minutes later, we pulled onto the church grounds. The place was desolate at four p.m. on a Tuesday.

Remy knew the area from growing up around here. "There's an access road that loops around the back." She pointed.

I pulled down a curving driveway that moved behind the church and past a set of dumpsters.

"There." She pointed.

A shed, maybe ten by fifteen, was located in between the back of the church and the side of the Websters' house. It was a tan prefab fiberglass number, with a dark brown plastic roof, molded to look like shingles on top.

My eyes traced a power line running from the church, looping over a wafer ash tree and dropping down atop the shed. Burkette was probably using it to power the tiny outbuilding.

I steered to the curb and got out. As Remy crossed in front of the truck, she pulled her sidearm from under her blazer.

I shook my head at her, patting my side. She got the message about not pulling her gun on church grounds and reholstered her weapon.

The front of the shed was opposite our approach, and we crossed the lawn slowly. About halfway there, I noticed a set of tire tracks in the grass.

The marks were shallow and smooth, like the ones photographed at the crime scene.

I motioned Remy around the west side of the shed, while I moved east.

Getting around to the front, we threw the door open.

No one was there.

Inside, a mattress was set up on the floor. Beside it sat an old thirteen-inch television. The TV had rabbit ears made out of a metal hanger.

I walked into the small space. An old wooden dresser sat near the mattress, and each drawer was flung open. The place smelled of Aqua Velva aftershave and dirt.

"Someone left in a rush," Remy said.

She ran her flashlight over a single pair of white boxer briefs in the top drawer, her light ending on the tag.

A size 26 waist.

Burkette was five foot ten, two hundred pounds.

"Burkette stopped wearing a size 26 years ago, Rem."

"But Kendrick didn't," she said. "So what the hell is his underwear doing in Burkette's dresser?"

16

We put out an APB on Cory Burkette's 2011 Suzuki GSX and regrouped at the precinct.

It was Tuesday at five p.m. Less than thirty-six hours since Kendrick's body had been found.

Inside the conference room, Abe waded through a thick pile of paper. "Cory Burkette was the last person Kendrick texted."

Abe held up a printed page, reading the text aloud.

2nite is ending early. U said you'd show me when rents r asleep.

"When was that?" Remy asked.

"Seven-ten p.m.," Abe said.

I marked this on our timeline. Kendrick had left the sleepover around seven-ten. He'd texted Burkette, telling him it was over.

We stared at the words of the text.

"Well, 'rents' are parents," Remy said. "Kids said that years ago."

"And 'show me'?" I thought of the boxers we'd found. "Who thinks that sounds creepy?"

Remy raised her hand, and I walked over to the wall where we had put up our evidence. Stared at the picture of the size 26 boxers.

"So the underwear," I said. "Do we think Burkette was a pedophile? He and the boy were lovers? What?"

"What if Burkette was a creepy collector with the underwear?" Abe said. "Maybe he made his first real move on Kendrick Saturday night. The kid rejected him and threatened to out the ex-con."

"So Burkette killed Kendrick to shut him up?" I asked. "Then Burkette tells his Nazi friend he did it for the cause. They get together and burn Kendrick?"

"It's a possibility," Abe said.

"We're still assuming Burkette and Rowe knew each other?" I said. "Through what? StormCloud?"

"It's our theory," Remy said.

"Was Burkette affiliated in prison? Like Rowe was?"

"Member of the White Sons of Georgia," Remy said, staring at the handyman's prison records.

Abe looked up from his notes. "But Reverend Webster said that was all in his past. Webster met Burkette through a church program with Rutledge."

I looked at who else Abe had put under "Suspects" on the north and south walls of the room.

In the Rowe case, there was a white piece of paper with a smiley face drawn on it. Clipped to it was a copy of Martha Velasquez's DMV photo.

This was the Hispanic woman who'd seen Corinne leave at three a.m. The smiley face represented whoever a sketch artist would draw once they sat with Velasquez. If things went as I was guessing, that sketch would be of me.

Abe saw where I was staring.

"Sorry, P.T.," he said. "Ms. Velasquez left town to help her daughter with a new baby. She's up by Tray Mountain in White County. Unreachable."

"So she's not coming in?"

"She's driving back the day after tomorrow with her daughter," Abe said. "I got an artist scheduled on Christmas Eve."

I nodded, but inside I felt nauseous.

My eyes shifted to the other wall. To our suspects in Kendrick's murder. There was a booking shot of a white man I didn't recognize.

"Who's this guy?" I asked.

"His name's Bernard Kane. Came into the precinct loaded, saying he killed Kendrick."

"A drunk looking for attention?" Remy asked.

"Most likely." Abe shrugged. "It didn't take long to confirm he was in Macon at the time of the murder. Only problem is—in his intake interview—he asked patrol if Kendrick had two broken elbows."

I turned to Abe. "That didn't leak out to the press, did it?"

Abe shook his head. "I asked the blue-suiters to put him in a cell and dry him out."

"I'll talk to him on my way out," I said.

We agreed to split up then. Remy was gonna comb through the list of people who'd bought the type of cable used to stop Kendrick's bike, while I went back to Virgil and Corinne's place. We still needed evidence that Rowe and Burkette were working together. I was hoping to find it at Rowe's house.

"I got a question, Rem," I said before my partner walked out. "Did Virgil Rowe's place look tossed? When we first got there?"

"It didn't look clean," she said. "Why?"

I held up our case file with the pictures that our crime scene tech, Alvin Gerbin, had taken. The kitchen cabinet doors were open, the cups and plates inside them overturned.

"I didn't notice," she said. "But there was a lot going on."

"All right, I'll take a look," I said. I popped out of the conference room and swung by my police locker.

I'd been looking everywhere for my spare set of house keys and remembered they were in my cubby. But when I searched my locker, I found it empty except for an old workout towel.

I walked down to the first floor and scanned the paperwork on this guy Bernard, who knew about Kendrick's elbows. There were two DUIs and two disorderly conducts on his sheet.

Bernard Kane was in a cell by himself, lying on a cot, his face toward the wall.

"Bernie?" I said.

The man rolled over. He was listed as thirty-nine, but looked younger. Wore a blue sport coat and designer jeans.

"Bernard," he corrected me, standing up. The smell of urine floated through the air.

"Detective Marsh," I introduced myself. "I understand you've turned yourself in for our arson-murder."

"I have," he said.

"Can you tell me how you did it?"

His eyes lit up. "I burned the boy. Clean and simple."

"You kill him first?" I asked. "Then let his body burn? Or you burn him while he was still alive?"

Bernard bit at his lip, thinking about his options. "What do *you* think I did?" he said.

I ignored his question. "Where'd you get the blue masking tape from?" I asked.

"I bought it online," Bernard said. "Untraceable."

"There was no blue masking tape."

Bernard's face fell.

"Where'd you get the information on the elbows, Bernard?"

He walked closer to the bars, his eyes searching the corners of the hallway.

"Lean in closer and I'll tell you."

I didn't know what his game was, but I leaned in.

"I know about the details because it's not the first time, Detective. It's happened before. And they break the elbows every time."

I pulled away and saw that Bernard's eyes were glazed over. As if hypnotized. I waved my hand in front of them.

"And who are *they?*" I asked.

Focusing his eyes on me again, he moved his face into the bars. "Come closer and I'll tell you."

I leaned in again, and his hands flew through the bars and onto my shoulders.

"Jesus," I said, shoving him back into his cell.

Bernard landed on his side on the ground.

"I was trying to tell you a secret," he said. "About the luck. The luck is everything."

A guard hustled down the hall, hearing the commotion. "You okay?" he said.

"Yeah." I nodded.

Bernard crawled back to his cot and pulled the mattress close to his body. "I was just trying to warn him," he said to the guard. "I've seen things."

"The guy's nuts, P.T.," the patrolman said. "Ignore him."

I turned and headed out.

"Beware the giant," Bernard yelled as I walked away. "He's doing the dirty work."

I headed out to my truck, thinking about the sheer quantity of crazies in this city.

As I got to the parking lot, a group of men in their twenties were getting dropped off with picket signs on wooden poles.

I made eye contact with one of them, and he looked to his buddies. "That's him." He pointed. "The guy from Reddit."

I glanced over my shoulder. Was he talking about me? And what the hell was Reddit?

I fired up my engine and pulled away from the curb, just as the guy yelled after me, "Come back here, you racist."

A mile away, I took out my phone. Typed in "Reddit" and "P. T. Marsh."

The link I clicked had a picture of me at the top, from day one out at Unger's farm. The headline below asked a simple question: *Do white cops really work hard to solve black murders?*

I called Remy. "You remember that conversation we had about googling yourself?" I said. "Looking up stuff with your name?"

"You saw the article on Reddit?"

"Just now," I said. "How bad is this in the black community, Rem?"

"I think everyone's shifted to this other thing with the kids getting bloody noses."

The issue at Paragon Baptist had spiked in the last hour. One of the kids had fallen into a coma.

"Someone at the station said it's typhoid?" I said.

"Weird, right?" Remy said. "Good thing is, the kids are getting antibiotics now. So it'll die down in the news."

I finished her thought. "And our case will flare back up?"

"By Sunday service, P.T., if nothing's solved with Kendrick, famous people are gonna start showin' up here."

Meaning folks from outside the state like Al Sharpton. Also well-known televangelists and ministers inside Georgia like Creflo Dollar. All that despite the fact that we hadn't said it was a lynching yet.

"I know you care about our community," Remy said. "You married into it. But to someone who's pissed off, you're just another white cop who doesn't give a shit."

"I get it," I said. "So let's keep digging."

I hung up and pulled onto my street. Purvis hadn't been out sinch lunchtime, and I needed to give him ten minutes to pee.

But as I got out of my truck, something wasn't right.

The front door to my house was swung wide open, and Purvis was lying on the porch. His brown-and-white-striped stomach was faceup, his eyes closed.

I pulled out my Glock and moved past him

through the open door. As I did, I smelled Pine-Sol and Clorox.

A woman appeared in the doorway to the kitchen. She wore a loose-fitting tie-dyed dress.

I let out a deep breath and holstered my weapon.

My late wife's twin sister, Exie, stood there with a scrubber in one hand and a cereal bowl in the other.

"Some of these dishes, Paul," she said. "They might need to be thrown out."

"Jesus, you could've been shot," I said.

"I am quite confident you wouldn't shoot me, Paul."

I looked at my dining table. Six or seven large crystals were placed in an oval shape on top of Lena's table runner. A piece of incense was burning in a tray in the center.

"Where's Thomas?" I said, asking about her son. Exie was a single mom. Lived two hours from here.

"He's with his dad," she said.

My eyes moved over the same face and figure that my wife had. The smooth skin I missed touching.

"You can't be here," I said. "The doctor said it's not healthy. You look like her. You sound like her."

Exie offered a placating face. "And I told you I'd respect that unless there were extenuating circumstances."

"How much do you need?"

"Money?" she said. "None." Her eyes hit the floor. "I mean, I'd never turn down a loan. But that's not why I came."

I grabbed the crystals and blew out the burning stick. I had a mind to toss the whole bunch in the trash, but I carried the rocks to her purse.

I pulled out a hundred and forty bucks in twenties from my wallet. All the cash I had on me. Placed it atop the rocks. "You gotta go, Exie."

"Relax," she said. "I drove two hours up here to tell you something."

The smell of burnt sage from the incense filled the air. "What is it?" I asked.

"My twin spoke to me," Exie said. "I was doing a reading for a couple, and Lena's spirit entered it."

I handed Exie her purse.

The love of my life had been the sensible sister.

Exie, on the other hand, worked part-time as a psychic and didn't own a bra. She was also a serial shoplifter. Arrested four times. I guess she never saw the law coming in one of her readings.

"Her spirit told me, 'Someone's about to whoop Paul.'"

"Whoop?" I said. "Like beat me?"

Exie nodded.

"Lena never used the word 'whoop' in her life," I said.

"'Someone Paul knows and trusts,'" Exie continued.

"Lena never called me Paul," I said.

The truth was that only a few people did. Most of them were in my wife's family, but Lena had not been among them. Even when she was pissed, my wife screamed a single letter at me, *P*.

"Let's go," I said. "I'm going too."

"My advice is a real thing," Exie said.

"I know," I said as I hurried her out the front door. "And I thank you."

I moved outside and grabbed Purvis, watching as my sister-in-law drove away.

When the car was gone, I turned to my bulldog.

"What'd you let her in for?" I said. "We're supposed to be in this together."

Purvis just stared at me with those wide brown eyes.

I'd often wondered if he could tell the difference between Lena and Exie. Whether my wife and son's disappearance was confusing to Purvis. Or whether it was a hundred percent clear what had happened. And I was just a crappy consolation prize to be left with.

I put Purvis in my truck and locked the house, firing up the engine.

17

Back in the numbered streets, I took a right at 33rd and slowed outside the bungalow home of Randall Moon, landlord for Corinne and Virgil.

I banged on the door. I still needed to get a lease from Moon without Corinne's name on it.

A skinny Asian guy in his thirties opened the door. He wore a *Roll Tide* tank top and reeked of marijuana. I flashed him some tin, explaining why I was there.

"Yeah, I was expecting you, man. But it's all cool," he said, his hand running over a black peach-fuzz mustache and goatee. "Corinne called me. She explained it all."

Explained what all?

I looked around, scanning the streets behind me. The last thing I needed was some dopehead talking about me being inside Virgil Rowe's place the night he died.

"What exactly did she explain?" I squinted. "Because I'm doing you a favor, bud. I could have your place on 31st demoed. A tractor come in and knock it down."

Moon coughed nervously and stood up straighter. "Yeah. No. I mean she didn't say anything bad. Just that you two knew each

111

other, and like you said—you're doing us a favor."

Us? Jesus. Was Corinne with *this* clown now? I stared at the guy's pupils. He was as high as a Georgia pine.

"Is Corinne around still?" I asked.

"Yeah," he said. Trying to look me in the eye, but unable to.

"I thought she split town?"

"That's what I meant," Moon said. A line of perspiration formed on his forehead. "She's out—but somewhere else, you know? Not here in Mason Falls."

Jesus, he knows, Purvis said. *And he's lying.*

I glanced over my shoulder again, at the cars parked nearby. Looking for anyone sitting in one of them. An undercover maybe.

"Virgil Rowe is the only name on the lease, bro," Moon finally said, grabbing an envelope off the coffee table. A pile of papers was shoved inside.

Christ, what a mess. For all I knew, this guy sold Virgil the brick of weed.

Grabbing the envelope, I walked out to my truck rather than say another word to Moon.

I'd screwed up coming by to help Corinne that first night. Now this shithead junkie knew it, and maybe so did the lady who Abe was putting in front of a sketch artist.

The best I could do was to plow ahead—try

and prove that Burkette and Rowe knew each other. If they did, I'd have connected the two cases.

Minutes later, I was inside Virgil's house two blocks over and had every light in the place on.

I glanced into Rowe's master bath. Same as the kitchen: things knocked over, cabinet doors left wide open.

I decided to search the house again, going room by room, seeing if there was anything that someone might've been looking for but didn't find. This was why I'd asked Remy if the place looked tossed.

After twenty minutes, I had nothing.

I dropped into the same armchair where I'd sat when I confronted Virgil. I opened my satchel and paged through the case file.

When I got to the note about my print on the lighter, I looked up. In the last hour, I'd seen six other lighters around the place, the cheap colored type you get free at the liquor store when you buy smokes.

I stared at a box of matches on a shelf in the living room. They were the tall fireplace type—housed in an oversized "strike anywhere" box. Shoved in between two James Lee Burke paperbacks.

Was this odd in a home with no fireplace? Or to an arsonist was it some keepsake?

I grabbed the box, shaking it. It didn't rattle. As

I slid it open, I saw it was stuffed with currency. Hundreds. New bills.

I laid them out. There was ten thousand dollars. On the bottom bill, someone had written a single word across it, in black Sharpie.

Rise.

A tiny yellow Post-it was stuck to the back of the same bill. On it was scrawled the letters *P.B.* and a time, two p.m.

Who or what was P.B.?

I thought about Kendrick's initials, K.W., and others in our investigation.

The other boy at the sleepover was Eric Sumpter. E.S.

And the McClure kid. J.M.

My phone rang, and it was Abe. "You got a TV in that place?" he asked.

I found a clicker.

"Channel four," Abe said.

I punched it in and saw that since I'd left the precinct, the small group of protesters outside had grown. About a hundred folks marched with signs about equality, police brutality, and lack of diversity.

A breaking news graphic kept flashing along the bottom of the screen.

"They've been teasing a new lead for ten minutes," Abe said.

I opened a cupboard where I'd seen a bottle of no-name vodka. Took a drag on it without even thinking.

"Here we go," Abe said. I waited for the word "lynching" to come onto some graphic at the bottom of the screen. For everything to go to hell.

Instead, the footage showed me and Remy, parking at First Baptist.

"What the hell is this?" Abe said.

Someone had caught video on their cell phone of Remy pulling her weapon as she exited my truck. It cut off quickly and replayed in a loop, conveniently not showing the part where she'd put her gun away.

The graphic at the bottom of the screen read *Police pull guns on church campus.*

"Jesus," I said.

On TV, Kendrick's mom, Grace Webster, was interviewed. She was asked if she knew police had entered church property, and she shook her head.

A picture of Cory Burkette flashed on the screen, followed by a graphic that read *Arson-Murder Suspect*. The news channel must've put this together from our approach of the shed.

"P.T.," Abe said. "Sorry. Channel four wasn't the one I was waiting on. I'm in the break room and someone must've moved the dial. Switch over to eleven."

I changed channels and saw Deb Newberry from Fox standing along a rural road.

"I'm standing off SR-909 outside of Bergamot," Newberry said. "Behind me is the cabin of

Clarence Burkette, the uncle of police suspect Cory Burkette, who is wanted in connection with the death of Kendrick Webster."

"What the hell?" I said.

The camera panned to a small rustic cabin in the distance behind Newberry. "An hour ago, this reporter saw Burkette enter this small rustic cabin. He hasn't left since."

"We're getting an address," Abe said. "You want me to grab Remy? We'll meet you there?"

"On my way," I said, my keys already in hand. Then I bit at my lip, remembering something.

Remy would probably be suspended by Chief Dooger for getting caught on camera at the church.

"Just you, Abe," I said. "Tell Remy I'm sorry, but she's gotta wait for the chief."

I grabbed the money and ran out, the wooden door slamming behind me.

18

The liquid on Kendrick's clothes stung his pores and made him shiver in the night air.

It also rose up and burned the skin around the small hairs inside his nose.

It took him a minute to place the smell.

Kerosene.

Kendrick saw sky then. He was outside on his back on wet ground.

His fingers reached at strands of scrub brush, but pain came from everywhere, so he stopped moving. "God, please God," he mumbled.

He saw the moon. He'd just learned about waxing and waning moons in science, and this was a waxing gibbous. A few days before a full moon.

"Dad," he said aloud, looking around. Purple was filling the sky. The sun coming up soon.

"He's awake," a voice said. Thick and nasal-like. A man stood there, and Kendrick felt so small next to him.

Kendrick tried to lift his head, but something thick was around his neck.

"No," he yelled.

Spears of orange sunlight came alive at the corners of his eyes.

"Why?" he said to the man.

"You're chosen. And today you go free."

Free?

Hope sprang in Kendrick's chest, but it lasted only a few seconds.

He felt his body getting pulled—not by the rope that was tied behind his back earlier, but by something around his neck.

A quick tug and his body flew up into the air. A tightening as the rope gripped his throat.

And then he could feel the heat. He recognized what the spears of orange were.

Fire was burning the ground below him.

19

Cory Burkette's uncle's cabin was a one-room place, set in a valley off State Route 909.

As I drove out there, I passed two hotels built around a turnpike heading into Mason Falls. Both had *No Vacancy* signs in the windows, and I wondered if the big media had already shown up.

As I turned off the main road, I saw six patrol cars parked around the edge of the property. The evening air was buzzing. Half of the protesters from the police station had heard the news from Fox and relocated here. Signs held up read *Corrupt Cops Don't Care* and *Diversity Now!*

Law enforcement had come in force too. Around the property I saw a half-dozen SWAT guys and twenty patrolmen. I slowed my truck and moved through the gawkers.

As soon as I put the truck in park, Abe was outside my door. The air smelled like night-blooming jasmine and primrose, and a yellow moon was rising in the distance.

"Burkette's inside," Abe said.

Way up ahead of us was the uncle's log cabin, set on a square of gravel. It wasn't one of those modern cabins that looked rustic but in reality had satellite and a deep freeze. It was a tiny house built a hundred years ago. The area to the left and right of it were planted with large southern magnolias. The tips of the green branches had white saucer-sized blooms that were spread open and smelled like lemon.

"Is he by himself?" I asked.

Abe nodded. "And armed."

I stopped walking. "Are you sure?"

Abe motioned to Burkette's Suzuki, leaning against the right side of the cabin. "The patrolman who first cleared the folks from Fox outta here— he got a peek in the side window." Abe pointed. "The drapes were originally open, and he saw a .45 on a table."

"Shit," I said.

Beyond the cabin, a forest of Georgia pine went on for miles, eventually becoming state land, a protected forest.

"How about a back door?" I asked. "Or another window?"

Abe shook his head. "One way in. One way out. And now he's blocked that window with something wooden. We think it's a cutting board."

We'd gotten to within twenty yards of the place and stopped walking.

About eight cops were crouched behind two police Suburbans positioned in front of the cabin. SWAT members leaned against each SUV, their Remington pump-actions trained on the front door. Big spotlights had been set up and turned night into day.

"Is there a landline in there?" I asked.

"No," Abe said. "We have Burkette's cell, but the phone's either off or dead. And we don't know much about this guy, P.T."

"Get Reverend Webster," I said. "If he and the ex-con have some connection, let's leverage it."

Abe nodded and left. I grabbed the bullhorn and introduced myself to Burkette. Behind me I could hear the crowd way back on the highway, chanting something.

"Cory, if you got a cell phone, I'm gonna give you my number." I waited a minute and then recited it to him.

"We're in no rush," I said. Establishing rapport. "At nine p.m. a lot of us get double time. We like double time, Cory."

"I didn't do nothing to Kendrick," a voice hollered.

All right, you got him talking.

"Well, maybe you know something that can help," I said into the bullhorn. I grabbed my notebook and flipped back to Kendrick's mom's name. "Cory, it's important to Grace to know why this happened. *How* it happened."

No response from Burkette. Grace wasn't a trigger for him to talk.

I pointed a finger at each of the SWAT guys behind the cars and tapped at my chest, asking them if they were wearing Kevlar. Each nodded back.

I motioned at myself then, signaling for some-one to grab me a vest.

Getting one on, I stood up. Hustled around the perimeter and met with each cop, telling them that if at all possible, I needed Burkette alive. Wounded was acceptable, but I needed him able to talk.

Abe hustled over and crouched beside me. "Preacher's here."

Patrol had placed an E-Z Up farther back, where I'd parked. I walked back there.

Reverend Webster paced under the tent, dressed in a purple V-neck and black slacks. He was late thirties, slight of build, and maybe five foot nine, with a short fade haircut. Another hundred feet up toward the highway, two CNN news vans had cameras on us.

"Reverend," I said, turning my face away from the filming. "Mr. Burkette is armed, and honestly, I don't know how long he's gonna stay inside. With all that's gone on with your son, are you willing to speak with him?"

"Well, I don't believe Cory touched my son," Webster said.

I'd seen the reverend's wife on the news a couple times. In each instance, she seemed to blame everybody.

"You don't?" I said.

"I know my wife's been critical of Cory," he continued. "And of the police. But I watched

Cory around Kendrick. He's got a good soul. I think it was someone else."

"Did you know Cory was affiliated with neo-Nazi groups in prison?" I asked.

"Of course," Webster said. "That's how we met. He reached out to me because of my ministry in that area."

Did you know the creep had a pair of your kid's underwear in his shed? Purvis asked.

"So you gave him absolution?" I said.

"My faith doesn't work that way, Detective. Only God can do that."

I grabbed a Kevlar vest and slipped it around Webster's sweater. "Let me get this on you, sir," I said, helping his arm through each side.

"I'm sure you're aware that I didn't want you leading this case," Webster said as I tightened the vest.

"I am."

"Still, I'd like to know—are you a Christian?"

I didn't answer, velcroing the straps in place.

"I'm not trying to convert you," he said. "It's my wife that asked."

I stared at him. "Does she want to know if I can take someone's life in exchange for her son's?"

Webster's eyes were on the dirt. The reverend and his wife were not on the same page. Not just about Burkette, but about justice. Or maybe it was about vengeance.

I led Webster over to one of the Suburbans and

handed him the bullhorn. "If in your heart you believe Burkette isn't guilty—then help me get him out of here alive."

The reverend steeled himself. Said nothing for a moment. Then he held the bullhorn to his face. "Cory," Webster said. "I've just told Detective Marsh that I don't think you're capable of hurting anyone, especially Kendrick."

"Reverend?" Burkette's voice rang out.

"It's me, Cory," Webster said.

A single tear streamed down the preacher's cheek, and I thought about how impossible the situation was. Speaking with a man who most likely killed your son.

"Cory, it's okay," Webster said.

I reached over and flicked off the reverend's bullhorn. "Ask him to come out so we can talk about it. Tell him we'll hold our fire."

Webster nodded, and I flicked the bullhorn back on. "The police are gonna hold their fire, Cory. Why don't you take a step outside so we can talk."

A minute later we heard an unlocking noise. "I'm just gonna stand at the door," Burkette yelled. "We can talk from here. You come too close, and I'm back inside."

I grabbed the bullhorn. "Cory, this is Detective Marsh again. We're all going to lower our weapons except for me. This is our procedure. So you can focus on me. But you gotta come out real slow with your hands up."

I saw a single hand come out from an ajar door. Then another. I moved in between the two Suburbans, my Glock trained on Burkette's chest.

This was the first time I'd seen him in person, and he was a big guy. Pale skin and freckles. He had the body of a four-down running back. Compact and muscular. I imagined him lighting the match that killed Kendrick, and I wanted to rush him.

"I'm not coming out any farther, Marsh," he said, standing at the open door. "You can come to me."

Burkette was a foot outside, and his eyes scanned from side to side, taking in all the lights and vehicles.

I was thirty feet out. Then twenty-five.

A pile of freshly split firewood was parked by the door, and the smell of bark chips was strong in the air.

Twenty feet. Fifteen.

"There's a lot of cops out here, Marsh," Burkette said, his face ashen. He had an accent that elongated words. It reminded me of an old partner of mine, six or eight years ago. He could use three syllables to say the word "ours."

"Just look at me," I said. I lowered my gun so it was on the ground below him, ready to move up if needed.

"Okay, let's talk," he said.

I stopped moving any closer.

"I didn't do this," he said. "I know everyone says that, but I wouldn't touch Kendrick."

"Do you know a man named Virgil Rowe?"

Burkette squinted at me. He was covered in sweat. "Is he a member of the church?"

I shook my head.

"Do you like young boys, Cory?" I asked.

I wasn't trying to rile him up. I just wanted to see his facial response. Would it be confusion? Denial?

But I never got it. Something else happened instead.

And it happened like it was in slow motion.

I heard a noise. Something overhead that I suspect was a drone.

The zipping sound spooked Burkette, and he turned back toward the door, which was ajar.

His .45 was tucked into the rear waistband of his Lee jeans. As he turned back toward the cabin, he stopped, almost as if realizing at the last minute that his gun was facing us.

"I see it," I yelled, just as Burkette grabbed at the gun. He held it backward by the handle—trying to toss it into the cabin.

A single shot rang out. Then a second shot. Both from the same place behind me.

Burkette went down, and I raced over.

"Jesus," I said. Blood was pouring from his neck. "Cory, talk to me."

"Gigg. Kenttrack. Noss." Cory Burkette blubbered nonsense.

With my fingers, I tried to block a hole in his neck that was impossible to cover. His voice was unintelligible for three seconds, and then nothing. He was gone.

I stood up, staring at the gun that was thrown into the cabin as Burkette fell.

There was one cop who could hit those two points in succession, and I turned to Abe.

"C'mon, man," I said, a pleading look on my face. "I yelled that I saw it."

"You *saw* it?" Abe scrunched up his face.

"Yeah," I said. "Burkette must've realized we saw his piece, and he was trying to toss it into the cabin."

Abe shook his head at me. "Are you kidding me, P.T.? He was an ex-con who killed a kid. He reached for a gun in his waistband. It was us or him."

I kicked at the front wall of the cabin, frustrated. "I was talking to the guy, Abe. He'd just told me he didn't know Rowe."

"And every guy on death row is innocent," Abe said.

He stormed off, and I turned to Reverend Webster. He was bent over vomiting, and he lifted his head to make eye contact with me. "You knew this would happen, didn't you?"

Burkette was his friend, and we'd used the preacher to lure him to his death. Then gave the reverend a front row seat to the justice his wife wanted for their son.

"No," I said to him. "I'm sorry."

He pulled off the vest I'd strapped to him and turned, looking out at the crowd back near the highway. There were cheers as the news of Burkette's death moved among them.

"You people just killed an innocent man," Webster said. "A lamb to slaughter."

A blue-suiter took Webster away, and the crowd slowly dissipated.

The truth was that Abe was right. Burkette was a killer and had left the place armed to confront two dozen cops. A boy had been murdered. Webster might've been unused to seeing this kind of violence, but we weren't doing social work here.

I exhaled for the first time in a few days, a sense of relief coming over me. An act of horror had happened in Mason Falls. Now the two men linked to it were dead.

Abe sat on the back lip of an ambulance. A guy named Cornell Fuller talked to him. Fuller was the lead cop in Internal Affairs in Mason Falls, and he took Abe's gun.

Patrolman Gattling walked up to me.

"Burkette inherited the cabin four weeks ago from his uncle," the patrolman said. "The reporter from Fox must've found that out."

I thought about this. Did it make sense— Burkette living in a dirt-floor shed at the church after he inherited this place? Or was it the same as here? No electricity or phone at either.

And then it hit me.

How this had ended was good for me.

No Burkette aboveground meant no conversations with him about Virgil Rowe. The case would die down. Burkette would be assumed to be Kendrick's killer. Why else confront cops with a .45? And Virgil Rowe would be a known accomplice and neo-Nazi that nobody wanted to spend police time looking further into.

Which meant little chance for a conversation about me helping Corinne out by killing Virgil.

I thought about that first night at Rowe's, and then waking up the next day.

I'd still not found the flannel I'd worn. Was it covered in blood in some trash can somewhere? Had I tossed it in the river?

My instinct for justice told me there could be more here, but my instinct for self-preservation told me to finish the paperwork fast. I grabbed my keys and headed back to the precinct.

20

By the time I returned to the station house, it was a ghost town. I switched on the TV in the break room and raided the fridge for old pizza.

A so-called crime expert from Atlanta was being interviewed on CNN about Burkette's shooting.

"Police could've used Tasers or nonlethal force," the expert said.

A bottle of Jack was in a cabinet above the fridge. I filled the cap and shot it back.

A second man on the show took the counterpoint. "Why are you defending this guy? He killed a kid. Then he pulled a gun on a cop."

Someone was walking toward the kitchen, and I turned. It was Sarah Raines. Her blond hair was down, and she was dressed in a blouse and tight black pants that showed off her body.

"I thought all you guys were out celebrating," she said.

I flicked off the TV and turned back toward my office.

"I had a couple things to clean up," I said. "Trying to close out the case tonight. Maybe take a couple days off."

"How's Remy?" Sarah asked.

"Suspended for a week," I said.

"That sucks."

"Well, we got some good press today." I shrugged. "Maybe the boss'll let her out of the penalty box a couple days early."

Sarah put down her purse. "How about a drink with *me* then?"

Sarah was sweet. But I drank alone for the most part.

And you're already one drink ahead of her, Purvis said.

Rain check, I thought.

Except I didn't say those words.

"Sure," I said. "One drink and then I gotta get back. I came in to connect some dots on Burkette. I need to stay sharp."

"C'mon then," she said.

Ten minutes later we were down the street at a place called Fulman's Acre. One of those bars where the owner took the tips and staple-gunned them to the walls. Fives and ones covered every inch behind the bar; even the ceiling was dotted with money.

Sarah and I sat at the bar, bathed in a red and orange glow from a string of colored bulbs above our heads. The light and dark parts of her hair flickered in color as she talked.

Sarah had worked in Mason Falls for about ten months, but I didn't know about her life before then, other than some reference she'd made to growing up in a small town in Indiana.

"Where I was born . . ." She smiled. "Let's just say it makes Mason Falls look like the big city."

"Let me guess," I said. "Little midwestern place. A thousand people. Biggest building in town is two floors."

"Six hundred people," she said. "And a hundred of them went to my high school."

"And you ran as fast and far away as a girl could run." I smiled, joking at the stereotype of it.

Sarah hit me on the arm. "I'll tell ya," she said. "University of Michigan seemed like a different universe when I got there. Freshman year, I had an *English class* with six hundred people in it."

We talked about college and after while she nursed a Chivas and soda water.

"And that's where you went to medical school too?"

"Yup." She nodded. "Eight years in Ann Arbor. Go Blue."

"And why be a coroner?" I asked. "Why the dead?"

"That's a longer story," she said. "I guess the short version is that I took a leave during my second year in med school. My brother had stage-four cancer, and I ended up spending most of that year in Bloomington at a clinic."

"Jesus," I said.

"Yeah, it was tough," Sarah said. "I went back to medical school, but a year into it, I wasn't sure what to do. I didn't think I could handle telling patients the kind of news my family got."

"Of course not."

"One of my professors suggested pathology, and I fell in love. After residency, I got a gig in the county medical office in Atlanta."

A shot of Wild Turkey sat in front of me, and I lifted it.

"To the dead," I said.

"To the living," Sarah responded.

I swallowed the whisky, shifting in my seat. "So why come here?" I squinted. "Atlanta's a modern city. Bustling. Good place to be in your thirties."

"Don't get me wrong," she said. "I loved Atlanta. But the department was a factory. Clock in, clock out."

"Dead-end job?" I said.

Sarah nodded, then caught the joke. Hit me on the arm again.

"The job was good," she said. "I won't lie." She stopped, and her voice lowered an octave. "But things didn't go as I'd planned."

I waited, but she didn't say more.

There was a part of Sarah that was exposed. She was cautious, as if she hid some secret. But at the same time, she left the scab of it open, for me to see.

"In any case, when I saw the spot open here," she said, "I thought to myself, I can be a tiny part of a big system in Atlanta, or play a bigger part in Mason Falls. I drove here and looked around. It reminded me of where I grew up. Good place to meet someone. Start a family."

I suddenly thought of Lena and Jonas. Of our plans for the future.

I downed the rest of my shot and stood up.

"I should go," I said. "Back to the case."

Sarah looked up. "Did I say something wrong?"

"No," I said. "Really."

I threw a twenty down on the bar, and Sarah placed her hand on my forearm.

"How old was he?" she asked. "Your son?"

I felt the back of my neck get warm. "Eight," I said.

"This case must've been impossible."

"Yeah." It was the first time I'd acknowledged out loud how much Kendrick and Jonas seemed connected.

Sarah leaned in and kissed me on the cheek.

I smiled and walked her back to the station parking lot. Went inside alone. Settling in the conference room, I put together my notes to close the case out.

I began with everything Abe had found on Cory Burkette, starting first with his criminal record.

I found a typed interview that Abe had done with Dathel Mackey, who worked at First Baptist and cooked and cleaned for the Webster family.

Q: Did Burkette spend a lot of time with Kendrick?

A: It was more of the other way around. That kid followed him everywhere. I think Cory might've been teaching him too.

Q: Teaching him what?

A: To ride. Cory had a motorcycle.

I grabbed the paper with the final text Kendrick had sent as the sleepover ended.

2nite is ending early. U said you'd show
me when rents r asleep.

Maybe "show" wasn't something sexual. Maybe it was Burkette teaching Kendrick how to ride his Suzuki. Then again, maybe teaching him to ride was how he'd earned Kendrick's trust. Before abusing it.

Around ten p.m. my boss called. "We're doing a little presser around lunchtime tomorrow," Miles Dooger said. "Wear a clean shirt and tie."

"Sure," I said.

Miles waited for me to fill the silence, but I didn't.

"It's the best of all worlds, P.T.," he said. "The mother and father have justice, and no one wastes the taxpayers' money going to court."

"You mean no one finds out about the lynching?"

"You think those parents need to know that?" he asked.

I thought of my own son. Knowing every detail of how he'd drowned hadn't helped me move past it.

"No," I said.

I hung up and laid down on the couch in my office, closing my eyes.

In police work you see all kinds of photos that are untenable for regular folks to stare at. And the reality is, you get used to them as a detective. "Desensitized" is the word Miles uses.

But the images of Kendrick's burnt face and body were different. Every time I saw them, I noticed some new horrific detail.

I focused on the darkness inside my eyelids and tried to rest.

In my dreams, I was an eagle, flying over the land. I saw the Spanish moss swaying in the wind on Unger's farm. I saw the tree burning and steered west. Still a thousand feet above the ground.

"Dad," Jonas's voice said. "Look closer."

I angled my body down, diving toward the loblolly. As I got lower, Kendrick's face melted, and I jolted awake with a start.

I wandered across to the conference room. The crop duster. We hadn't followed up with him.

Out in the bull pen, I heard a noise and looked over. Through the open door of the conference room, I saw Alvin Gerbin, our crime scene tech.

"Hey, P.T.," Gerbin's voice boomed. "Sorry, I

didn't think anyone was here." Gerbin had taken off his signature Hawaiian shirt and had on a wifebeater T-shirt underneath. His man boobs showed prominently through the fabric.

I looked at my watch: four a.m. "What are you doing here?" I asked.

"I just finished processing evidence out at that cabin," he said. "I'm headed home to crash."

Gerbin set six or eight clear bags into a file box on his desk. Inside one of the bags was a cell phone.

"Anyone go through Burkette's stuff?"

"Not yet," Gerbin said. "Chief told me there's no need to rush it. That with all the overtime this month, it's gotta get in line with everything else."

"You mind?" I asked, pointing at the phone in the evidence bag.

Gerbin shrugged. "Hell, it's just the two of us at four a.m. Gonna land on your desk or Abe's sooner or later."

I gloved up and turned on the phone. A locked screen came up.

"Hold on," I said. I grabbed the file we had on Burkette. Located his social security number and tried the last four digits as the password.

Locked still.

I found his prison ID number in his file. That had been his identity for eight years.

The phone unlocked, and I started moving through pages of apps.

I looked at his texts and found the one Kendrick had sent. I searched backward through chat, but found nothing that suggested a sexual relationship.

I looked at Burkette's photos then.

There were shots of his motorcycle. Then one of a spinning ride at the county fair. Then of animals. Lots of animals at the fair.

"You come from a farming family, right?" I asked Gerbin.

"Future Farmers of America. Born, raised, and proud," he said.

I saw photos that Burkette had taken of the main stage, where prizes were awarded. Biggest gourd. Best apple pie.

"You go to the winter fair last weekend?" I asked. "See who won what?"

"Never miss it," Gerbin said. "I mean, it's not like the one in summer, but still. Saturday night under the big top. The awards."

Saturday night?

Saturday night Burkette was at the county fairground?

I stared at a photo of a pig with a blue ribbon on his neck.

The fairgrounds thirty miles from Harmony? The same Saturday night that Kendrick was abducted and killed?

I thought about the conversation I'd had outside the cabin with Burkette. I'd asked him about

Virgil Rowe and he had seemed confused. He'd thought he was a member of First Baptist, not a fellow neo-Nazi.

Was it possible we had it wrong?

That the two men *didn't* know each other? And that Burkette wasn't involved in Kendrick's murder?

I found a selfie of Burkette with the prize pig at the fair. In the background, I could see the moon just coming out. It was enough to guess that it was around seven or seven-thirty p.m., putting Burkette a half hour away from Kendrick at the time of the abduction.

I walked into the conference room, still holding the phone. Looked at the pictures of the hundred-dollar bills I'd found inside the matchbox in Virgil Rowe's place.

The word "Rise" had been written on one of them. And on a Post-it note: *P.B. 2 p.m.*

P.B. wasn't someone's initials. It was Paragon Baptist. Kendrick's school.

When Remy had interviewed the Webster family about Kendrick's schedule, the parents had mentioned Kendrick got out of school each day at two p.m.

I looked out the conference room windows. The dogwoods were blowing gently in the rainy night, dark shadows against a black sky.

Maybe the Post-it note was an indication of where and when to find Kendrick, but something had gone awry at two p.m. when Rowe was supposed to grab Kendrick.

I bit at my lip, thinking this over.

What if Virgil Rowe had followed Kendrick since two p.m., watching him go home? Then watching as he rode through the fields to his friend's house the next night? And maybe when Kendrick left the sleepover, Rowe was still in the field, waiting. He wouldn't need any text or information from Burkette as to Kendrick's whereabouts. He wouldn't need Burkette at all.

I selected the photo of Burkette at the fair. Forwarded it to my personal email. Then I went into the phone's sent mail and deleted it.

I walked out of the conference room and back toward my crime tech.

"Anything good?" Gerbin asked.

"Nah," I said, putting the phone back in the bag. "I'll leave Merle or Abe to look at it when they get around to it."

It was a quarter to five, and I needed some fresh air.

If Burkette wasn't involved in Kendrick's murder, then the events of the last day were more than bad. Remy getting caught on film had alerted the media to Burkette. And like most ex-cons, when his face hit TV, Burkette ran, hiding at his cabin until we eventually shot him.

The last thing the Mason Falls PD needed was us shooting an innocent man. But worse than

140

that was the effect of Burkette being innocent. It meant the real killer of Kendrick was still out there. And this meant our last good lead was to dig into Virgil Rowe again. Which would steer the case right back to me.

I drove home and crashed for an hour. But the dream about flying came back again, and I was startled awake. By six a.m., I showered and put on a blue linen suit and threw a tie in the back of the car for the press conference later.

I got on the road to talk to the crop duster. The case wasn't closed, and I needed a lead.

21

The Southeast Regional Air Facility was a local helipad and airport that housed single-engine planes, a couple aircraft tied to the nearby Marine Corps base, and two regional airlines, each of them flying short-haul passenger routes under the Delta banner.

The airport itself was a small terminal with a shiny metal roof shaped like a wing.

I drove around the terminal and headed to a hangar where the crop-dusting planes were housed, slowing my truck outside a chain-link fence and holding up my badge to a camera.

The gate stirred to life, and I saw a runway used for small aircraft in front of me. About two hundred yards ahead, a tiny white plane lifted into the air.

Brodie Sands was the crop duster who'd called 911 to report the fire in Harmony. From the short phone interview that Abe had done back when the arson-murder was just an arson, there was nothing to do here except to dot some i's and cross some t's. But I kept having visions of flying. Who knows? Maybe it was nothing. Maybe I was a bird in a former life. Or I needed a vacation.

I found a large metal hangar to my right and got out.

Inside, about ten planes were parked at angles to each other, to maximize the space.

A man in a yellow windbreaker lay on his back under one wing of a plane, his body positioned on a dolly padded with carpet. The words *Topeka Sands* were painted on the side of his red single-engine.

"Brodie Sands?" I asked, and the man slid out. He was in his late sixties, tall and bone thin, in corduroy pants, a windbreaker, and a baseball hat.

"Detective Marsh," I said. "Mason Falls PD. You got a minute?"

Sands directed me over to a ten-by-ten patch of green artificial turf, glued to the polished concrete in between his plane and the next one over.

"Welcome to paradise," he said, motioning for me to sit down. A handful of five-dollar lawn chairs were placed on the fake green grass.

"Mr. Sands, you reported a fire out at Harmony Farms three days ago."

"Yes, sir," he said, grabbing a chair.

I sat down next to him. The stubble on Sands's face looked like it could cut me. "Can you walk me through that morning?"

"Not much to walk through," he said. "I saw a fire. Took her down to get a better look and called in here." Sands pointed. "We have a little ATC upstairs. He connected me to you guys."

I blinked. "ATC?"

"Air traffic control," he said. "Granted, it's not a real ATC. But most of us are ex-commercial or -military, so we call it that."

"How 'bout we start earlier," I said. "What time you got up. What time you got here."

Sands nodded. "Up at four usually. Here by four forty-five. In the air over there, a little after six that day."

I flipped through my notes. Unger, the farmer, had left for his church service at five a.m. And the 911 call from Sands had come in at five-thirty.

Which put the fire starting around five-fifteen.

I let Sands keep going. He wasn't a suspect. Maybe he had no idea when he was in the air.

"And it's the same route every day?" I asked.

Sands shook his head. "No, some clients are three days a week. Others once a week."

"So you're flying along," I said, getting him back on track.

"Sure," he said. "I saw a little burst of light off Highway 903." Sands motioned with his hand in that direction. "I called the ATC, and they called y'all."

Paging backward in my notebook, I got to when the 911 call happened.

"Would it surprise you to know that you made the call at 5:32?" I asked. "That you were up in the air much earlier than you just said?"

Sands made a funny look. "Does that matter? I

checked in later that day with the ATC. They said the fire department got out there. Not much land was burned."

I looked from my notes to a giant aerial map on the wall behind us. Had Sands been under a rock? Did he not know about Kendrick?

On the map, I could see where we were now. Up and to the right was Harmony. Six or seven fields were highlighted in yellow marker.

"These yellow fields are your clients?" I asked.

"Uh-huh," he said.

My eyes followed an imaginary line from the airfield to the yellow areas. It didn't go over Unger's place.

Something wasn't right, but I needed a moment to think. "Can you tell me how it works?" I pointed to his plane. "The spraying."

"It's pretty simple." He motioned at a pipe that ran along the edge under each wing. "The sprayers are attached to the trailing edges of the wings, and the two pumps are driven by wind turbines. That way you're not stealing power from the engine when you spray."

I cocked my head. "I remember there was an issue a couple years ago about insecticide going off course," I said. "People were protesting you guys. We had to send two squad cars out here."

"It's called drift," Sands said, his voice a touch defensive. "That's why we fly lower now when we're spraying."

"Gotcha," I said. "So when you saw the fire, you must've been pretty low. I mean, you wouldn't want to *guess* that it was a fire, right? Send the fire department on a wild-goose chase?"

"I wasn't guessing, Detective. I done saw it."

"So in terms of height," I asked.

"I probably brought her down to forty feet."

I got up and glanced again at the aerial poster. The smell of grease in the open hangar reminded me of a Civil War armory I'd visited with Jonas. Hints of gunmetal mixed with the smell of rosemary blowing in from the fields nearby.

"Were you spraying at the Unger place?" I said. "Or flying near it on the way to somewhere else?"

"I wasn't spraying there, no."

"So why would you be down at forty feet then?" I asked. "I mean, it's clearly not on the way to these other fields in yellow."

Sands put his hands in his pockets. "Geez, I dunno. Maybe I *didn't* take it down that low. This cold medicine I'm on—it's making me as useful as a screen door on a submarine."

I stared at the map again. Sands was dodging my questions. Which made no sense. He had nothing to hide.

"Do you know Tripp Unger?" I asked.

"He's a former client," Sands said.

I hesitated. Looked over at Sands. "A boy's body was found in that fire, Mr. Sands."

"Excuse me," he said, his surprise genuine. "It wasn't one of Tripp's boys, was it?"

"You don't watch the news?"

"My TV broke a couple years ago. I go to the counter at the Waffle House if there's a Braves game. Watch it while I eat."

"Is there a reason you never mentioned to Detective Kaplan that Unger was a former client?"

"Didn't seem relevant," Sands said. "Tripp and me—we had a fallin' out. We've known each other since the sixth grade. Then he sued me."

"And?" I said.

"And nothing," Sands answered. "There's a whole lotta reasons a crop don't grow beyond what comes out of these little pipes. But insurance kicked in some cash. So did I. And we parted ways. That's the end of the story."

"Mr. Sands, timing's important here. See, ten minutes earlier, you wouldn't have seen that fire. But you mighta seen the perpetrator."

"But I didn't see nothin'," Sands said.

There was a connection here, but my head hurt. I should've gotten more sleep last night.

"There's something I can't understand, Mr. Sands." I shook my head. "And I mean, from day one."

"What's that?" he asked.

"It took the fire department fifteen minutes to get out there," I said. "And the body still hadn't burnt all the way. I've been trying to figure out how that's possible."

"Well, it was raining on and off." Sands shrugged.

"Sure, but that loblolly . . . it's a thick tree, you know? So it shelters most of that rain. Which would've kept the body burning."

Sands's eyes were on the floor, and I ran my hand along the body of his plane.

I was thinking of the smell I'd noticed when Remy and I had first walked the field. *Cow shit, meet rain,* Remy had said. Or something like that.

"There was a fire last year up near the hills," I said to Sands. "It destroyed a couple houses. But this farmer I met—he was beside himself on where his cattle were gonna feed. I mean he was a big man, but I watched him weep."

I pointed at Sands's plane. "But then one of you guys laid something down. Rain came the following week, and there were buds coming out of the ground ten days after that. I think he called it 'top dressing.' Does the *Topeka Sands* spray top dressing?"

Sands offered a pleading look. "C'mon, man," he said. "What is this—no good deed goes unpunished?"

I opened my case file, pulling out the photo of the tiny green crystals I'd seen around the loblolly. "Mr. Sands, I saw these on the ground by the body. And there was this smell."

He took off his baseball hat. Ran his hands through his stringy gray hair.

"So here's where I remind you this is a murder investigation," I said. "You oughta be real careful if you lie."

"I didn't see no kid," Sands said.

"But you saw the fire?"

He nodded. "I took her down to forty feet, and I thought, Tripp and Barb are probably gone to church. And some instinct kicked in."

"What do you mean—some instinct?"

"I knew I couldn't land. So I dumped thirty gallons of TD-71 to slow down the blaze 'til the fire department got there. And if Unger knew that, he'd go after my license—even if I'm doing him a favor saving his land."

"Go after your license—why?" I asked.

"I was up in the sky too early, Detective. You can't be flying 'til six a.m."

So this was why he lied about the time. It was against city rules to be spraying at that hour.

"But I promise," he said. "It's all natural slurry. Water and fertilizer. No pesticide."

This explained the odd burn pattern on Kendrick. The slurry had dripped through the trees and onto his burning body.

But something bigger was popping in my head.

"How many people know this sort of thing?" I asked. "About when you can and can't fly."

"Pilots." Sands shrugged. "Farmers. People in the industry."

My mind was advancing the clock. Thinking about an alternate timeline. Building a scene in which Sands never got there 'til six a.m. Or later.

"So if you hadn't put that fire out at five-thirty," I said, "it might have been raging by six."

"For sure."

Which meant the blaze might've devoured half of Unger's farm if Sands had flown at the time he was legally supposed to.

I started walking away. Out of the hangar.

"Are we good then?" Sands hollered.

I turned around. Walked back toward him. "No," I said, pointing at the map on the wall. "There's something else. What made you fly in that direction in the first place—if you weren't doing anything on Unger's farm?"

He bit at his lip. "It don't make sense."

"Try me."

"Something called to me," he said. "I heard a voice that sounded like my late wife."

I hesitated. "You're right. It doesn't make any sense." I walked back toward my truck.

"You gonna tell Tripp?" he yelled.

I didn't answer. I needed to talk to a friend at the fire department.

22

The Mason Falls Fire Department was housed in a historic building on Fremont Street, just behind a German deli that made the best Reubens in Georgia.

I had to be back for the press conference with Miles Dooger, but momentum was pulling me down a different path. A direction that proved out other possibilities. That Burkette, who Abe had shot, might've been innocent of Kendrick's murder. And that the fire might've produced completely different results if Brodie Sands hadn't put it out so quickly.

I got to the front desk and flashed my badge, heading up to the second floor to talk to Pup Lang.

Pup was the lead arson inspector for the city, and we'd become friends on a previous case. He was a transplant from the San Fernando Valley outside of Los Angeles and had left after twenty years there. His wife was originally from Marietta.

"What's up, buddy?" Pup said as I got to his office. He wore a short-sleeved golf shirt, slacks, and flip-flops. Wraparound Oakleys were propped atop his graying head, even as it rained outside.

"Pup," I said, "you know this mess I'm dealing with, right?"

"Sure," he said. "The kid found in the fire. But you got your man last night, right?"

"I dunno," I said. "I've been trying to figure out how the fire out there was burning so slowly."

"Yeah, us too," he said.

"Except now I know the answer," I said. "The crop duster who spotted it dropped slurry on the blaze."

"No way," Pup said. "My people talked to him. He never mentioned—"

"I know," I said. "But he just admitted it to me."

Pup took this in. Shrugged. "So he's a Good Samaritan, and you got better evidence because of it. What's the problem?"

I closed the door to Pup's office. "Kendrick Webster was lynched," I said. "I removed the rope before anyone saw it."

"Jesus," Pup said.

"So here's my question," I said. "If you're some shitbag who lynches a kid—why do you do it?"

"Well, I'm not from here like you," Pup said. "But history tells us it's a racist show of force. Intimidation. Scares the community."

I was pacing in the small area in front of Pup's desk. "But if I'm thinking properly," I said. "If that crop duster doesn't put the fire out, by the time y'all get out there—"

"It wouldn't have been ten acres burnt," Pup said. "More like forty."

"So the rope . . ." I put up my hands.

Pup nodded. "It would've burned up in the fire. No one would've seen it."

"Which," I said, "is counter to why you'd lynch someone in the first place, if no one's gonna notice. So if the crop duster hadn't flown over at five-thirty and your truck hadn't gotten there when it did—"

"You'd be using dental records to try and ID Kendrick," Pup said.

I ran a hand through my hair. The press conference was in less than an hour. The one where we told the community everything was solved.

"You know, back in LA," Pup said, "you see arson-murders once in a while. But usually it's a cover-up. Someone shoots someone. Burns the body in an apartment to try and hide a gunshot wound."

"I've heard that," I said.

"My point is," Pup said, "it isn't something I associate with small towns in the South. Has this happened here before?"

"I don't know," I said.

Then something pinged in my head. Something that the crazy drunk in the cell had said. About the elbows. About it not being the first time.

"I gotta look into something. I may be back."

I rushed out to my truck and drove back to the precinct, taking the steps up the back stairwell two at a time. I got in front of my computer and logged in to the program we used to research crime patterns.

ViCAP, or the Violent Criminal Apprehension Program, was the FBI's database of violent crime in the US over the last three decades.

I punched in some variables.

A victim between the ages of thirteen and eighteen.

An area with a population under two hundred thousand.

A fire that burned so much of his body that dental records were used to ID the vic.

I waited to see if anything similar had happened in the past, and I heard a beep.

I clicked on the single record. Shonus County. Arson-murder.

Shonus was twenty-five miles north of Mason Falls.

I downloaded the abstract and began reading it.

Junius Lochland had been seventeen when he was found dead in a field. I scanned down and saw that Junius was black, the grandson of a Baptist preacher.

But then my heart started racing.

Junius's two elbows were broken.

I stood up, staring at my computer screen.

There was a problem. The case wasn't current.

It was from 1993. Twenty-five years old. None of our current suspects were even out of junior high then.

My cell rang, and I picked it up without seeing who it was.

"You on your way, bud?" Miles Dooger said. "We're meeting the press in thirty minutes, and I need a word first."

I stared at the abstract from the '93 arson-murder. The case had been solved. A man had confessed to the crime twenty-five years ago and been sent to prison.

"Yeah," I said. "Be there in ten."

I found Patrolman Gattling on the way out. "Do me a favor, will ya?" I pointed at the printout of the crime from '93. "Find out if the guy who did this crime in Shonus recently got paroled."

"And then?" Gattling asked.

"Text me. And don't talk to anyone else about it."

23

The press conference was scheduled for one p.m. in an 1870s plantation home that had been converted into a hotel called the Planter's House.

Chief Dooger had asked me to meet him in a caretaker's cottage behind the hotel.

I parked and found the place. Some private cigar room out back. The ceiling was made of tin squares that had been painted a deep red. The walls had decorative oak molding from floor to ceiling.

"P.T." Miles motioned me inside.

My oldest friend and mentor on the force sat in the dark.

"Grab some wood," he said, motioning me into a leather chair with copper rivets along the arms. On the table between us was a bottle of Evan Williams 23. I'd heard of this variety, but never seen one in person.

"I wanted to meet privately before the presser," Miles said. "Let's start with a toast."

Miles poured the Kentucky liquor into two lowball glasses and lifted one. "To cases that don't require juries," he said. "The fastest and cheapest prosecution around."

I'd never heard anyone use this as a toast, but I lifted my glass.

My phone buzzed with a text as the warm liquid coated my throat. It was from Gattling, the blue-suiter.

Guy from '93 never paroled. He was
killed in a prison fight in '99.

"I know you're still going through the details," Miles said. "And no one's expecting you to answer a bunch of questions today. I'm just gonna say that Burkette was our number one suspect in Kendrick's death. There's still a lot of loose ends. Questions about how. Questions about why."

"Good." I nodded, glancing a second time at the text.

The killer from the '93 crime wasn't paroled and roaming around. He was dead.

This meant that if there was any connection to twenty-five years ago, it had to be a coincidence.

Miles noticed me looking at my phone.

"There's no update I should know about, is there?" he asked.

I thought of Abe's career. Of how it could be ruined if I opened my piehole about Burkette's shooting. If I threw out some crazy theory about a picture on Burkette's phone.

"No," I said. "No update."

"Good," Miles said. "Because I'll let you in on a little secret. This bottle"—he pointed at the Evan Williams 23—"was bought for both of us.

I met Toby Monroe in this room an hour ago. Talked him through what happened."

"Toby Monroe as in Georgia's governor?"

Miles smiled. "Said he's got his eye on you, P.T. Made me really proud. Proud to have you on the force. Proud to be the guy who taught you everything you know."

"I'm pretty sure you just taught me where the vending machine was," I said. "Where the bathrooms are . . . how to avoid filling out paperwork."

"We call that delegation." Miles laughed.

He pulled out a business card of his and flipped it over. A phone number was scribbled on the back.

"Governor wanted you to have this," Miles said. "In case y'ever need anything."

I looked at the business card.

"His private line," Miles said.

"Wow," I said, pocketing it.

Miles winked at me then, raising his glass. "And as for Mason Falls, let's just say there's a good chance the next state police lab might be built off I-32."

I toasted to that, knowing Miles had been working his ass off to get that lab here. The local economy could use it.

We got up after the next drink and walked around to the front of the hotel. A college kid was playing "Jingle Bells" on the lobby piano, dressed in a suit that was two sizes too big. We entered a ballroom. A podium stood up front, a single chair to its side.

Miles stood in front of the podium and made a small statement, talking about the menace that entered our community and how proud he was of how the police handled the investigation.

He mentioned me and Abe by name, but left out Remy, who was at home ever since the YouTube video had surfaced.

"Chief Dooger," a guy from CNN said. "Does the department reflect the race of the communities it serves?"

"I believe so. We had three detectives on this case. Two of them were African American."

Reporters took notes. Drilled Miles from a dozen different angles. When they got to me, I didn't give them much to bite on, because there wasn't much I could say yet. As the press conference ended, reporters continued with Miles, and I walked out the side door to my truck.

I was tired and wondered if I really had to keep looking into the cases. The crime in '93 had been solved, and it wasn't in my jurisdiction.

Who cared how Burkette and Rowe knew each other? They were both white supremacists, and one of them had killed Kendrick. Miles was right. Silent justice was often smarter than what we could dole out in a courtroom.

I steered myself back toward the cigar room

behind the hotel. I was betting the bottle of Evan Williams was still sitting on the table.

So what if Burkette was at the county fair at the time of Kendrick's abduction? He still could've taken the information from Kendrick's text and sent it to Virgil Rowe. Tipping Rowe off to the boy's location. Maybe Burkette took the pictures at the county fair with the prize pig purposely for that reason—to establish an alibi for himself. After all, who takes a selfie with a pig?

"Detective Marsh," a voice said.

I turned and saw a patrolman. Young guy. Slicked-back hair. I'd seen him around, but didn't know his name.

"We got a woman who needs to talk to you."

"What for?" I asked.

"Yeah, uh . . ." He stumbled on his words. "She came for the press conference, but had some sorta seizure in the ladies' room."

He pointed at the hotel. "She's better now, but refused an ambulance. Asked for you by name."

I headed back to the lobby where I'd come in a half hour ago, and the blue-suiter steered me into one of the conference rooms. A black woman sat on a couch.

She was in her seventies and dressed in an island-themed dress that my wife would've called a muumuu. It was green with orange butterflies and flowers.

But what was most striking were her eyes.

The vessels in her left eye were popped, and black mascara was mixed in with something dark and reddish below both eyes. It looked like blood. She had a stinger of a red bruise on her chin too.

"My name is Dathel Mackey, Detective," she said. "I work for the Websters at First Baptist."

This was the woman from Abe's notes. From the Q&A I'd read last night.

"How can I help you, Ms. Mackey?"

She unfolded a flyer from her pocketbook. It was the same one that Remy had seen on the Websters' fridge.

"I saw an evil man the night of this talk," she said. "And it wasn't Mr. Burkette."

"Can you describe the man?"

"He was white," she said. "Big black beard down to his collarbone. Big teeth. Good-looking like you. In his thirties."

Big teeth?

I picked up the scent of kitchen spices as she spoke. Of nutmeg and ginger. "And you think what?" I asked. "That he's connected somehow to Kendrick's death?"

"Are you a believer, Detective Marsh?"

"I grew up going to Sunday school."

"When I was fifty-one, I took a pilgrimage to Trinidad. I got separated from the group and was kidnapped," she continued. "They thought I had money. Held me for a week. Beat me something awful."

I shook my head. She wasn't a small woman, and there was an intensity right below the surface.

"I came back with the gift of sight," she said. "The man I saw is a hunter. Hits women. Tortures animals."

As she spoke, a tear of blood dripped from the corner of her right eye. I noticed bruises on her arms and neck. Probably from falling during seizures.

"Are you all right, Ms. Mackey? Your eye." I pointed.

"The gift comes with a cost," she said.

She leaned into me and whispered so the patrolman couldn't hear.

"When I close my eyes, I can see the rope, Detective. The one you found around Kendrick's neck."

I stared at her. Dumbstruck.

Impossible, Purvis said.

"Don't worry, hon," she said. "I haven't told the Websters. What could be worse for a parent to learn?"

I hadn't breathed in about ten seconds, and I exhaled. Told the patrolman I could talk to Ms. Mackey on my own.

"So when I saw this man," she continued. "I could sense the pure evil in him."

Virgil Rowe, the arsonist, didn't have a beard, but I pulled his picture out of my satchel anyway, to be sure. "Is this the man?"

162

"No," she said. "The hunter I saw, Detective . . . maybe I could describe him, and you got someone who can make a picture for me?"

"Sure, we have a sketch artist," I said.

I hesitated. "I got an odd question for you, Ms. Mackey. We found a pair of Kendrick's underwear out in the shed where Burkette was living. Did you ever see Cory Burkette around young boys?"

"Not in the way *you're* thinking," she said. "But I do all the laundry, Mr. Marsh. Mr. Burkette's, right along with the family's. So I wouldn't take too much stock if you found underwear in that shed."

"Meaning what?"

"It's highly possible I just sorted one of Kendrick's underwear out in Mr. Burkette's dresser. It's happened before. Socks too."

I shook my head again. Another vote for Burkette's innocence.

"So this guy you saw," I said. "It's been a couple days. Do you think you remember him well enough to describe his face and eyes? Or did you see him again today, during your seizure?"

"Today I saw something different," she said, wiping the blood from the corner of her eye.

"Today it was a different boy," she said. "Muscular and darker. Someone was burning him too. But it wasn't nowadays, Detective. In the midst of the vision I saw a year. A month. It was November 1993."

24

I grabbed a pack of Marlboro Reds from off
the passenger seat of my truck. Put one in my
mouth. Shaking.

1993. Another boy burning.

This is how cases are solved, Purvis said.
Conversations like this.

I looked into the back of my truck. No Purvis.
Only Purvis in my head.

I hopped in the driver's seat and pointed
northeast, starting up SR-914 toward Shonus
County, where the '93 murder happened.

Did the wrong guy go to prison twenty-five
years ago and die there?

Or was there a copycat killer who knew
enough about the old crime to replicate it in
Mason Falls?

The road became one lane in each direction. I
turned the music off and drove in silence, the late
afternoon sun falling in slivers through the trees
across my face.

Thirty minutes later I was standing in the lobby
of the Shonus County Sheriff's Department.

The place looked like it had been furnished
with a Home Depot charge card. There were
two cheap waiting chairs with no padding and a
counter made of particle board.

Captain Andy Sugarman was white and in his forties with wide shoulders. He stared at the folder that had the ViCAP printout. "The detective on this case died eleven years ago," he said. "He was my mentor."

"I'm sorry," I said.

I reminded Sugarman we'd met once before, a few years back, at a conference, but he didn't seem to recognize me. I also gave him a rundown on what happened with the fire in Mason Falls. I left out the lynching.

"And what makes you think there's a connection—with all the time that's passed?"

"You mean other than both victims being black, the sons of preachers, the two fires, and the elbows being broken?"

"Well, the elbows—that could happen during a fire," Sugarman said. "It's part of the body's response to heat."

"Sure." I nodded.

"And the preacher thing . . ." Sugarman looked around to see who was within earshot. "Hell, you can't throw a rock 'round here without hitting a black kid whose daddy or granddaddy's a preacher."

"So I guess I'm looking for some professional courtesy," I said. "I'd love to read the case file."

"You realize our case ain't open, right?" Sugarman said. "It's solved. Guy went to prison. Admitted he was guilty at sentencing."

"Listen," I said. "I'm not crazy or nothing. I just want to dot all my i's and cross my t's."

Sugarman nodded. He asked for "a couple-three minutes" and came back with a copy of the file.

"It took me a bit—but I remember you now," he said. "From that conference. You presented a case. Some big murder. You were hot shit back then."

Back then, Purvis huffed.

I wondered if he'd looked me up while he photocopied the case. If he saw what happened to my family and felt bad.

"Go ahead and ask whatever questions you got," Sugarman said. "If you get any lip from anyone, you holler and tell 'em Sugar's coming. They don't help you—it's like they ain't helping me."

25

Out in my truck, I studied the file. Junius Lochland was seventeen when he was found dead in November of 1993. He was a local triple-threat athlete—track, basketball, and football—a star at Shonus High.

Two sets of photos dominated the file. "Before" shots that showed Junius clearing hurdles and catching balls. And three or four "after" photos, where his body was a quarter of that size, little more than a burn stain on the ground.

"What happened to you?" I said aloud, turning the pages and reading about the last night of Junius's life. The seventeen-year-old apparently made a habit of jogging in the evenings before bed. One night, he simply disappeared. Four days later, a cross-country runner found his burnt body while running by a field that had recently caught fire.

In the M.E.'s initial report, the elbows were listed as an antemortem injury, just like in my case, but the whole section had been struck—a horizontal line typed through the findings.

Stapled to the page was a note about the elbows breaking under the temperature of the fire. It was on a different letterhead than the rest of the files. Stamped by the state of Georgia.

I got out of my truck and looked around the back of the police precinct for the telltale ramp that signaled the M.E.'s office somewhere in the bowels of the building.

As I looked around, a red streak moved across the purple sky. I'd never seen anything like it. I blinked to study it, but it was gone.

I found the ramp to the M.E.'s office and knocked on the door.

"Hello?"

A short, chubby man with gray hair wandered out. I held my badge in one hand and the case file in the other.

"Are you the medical examiner?"

"All day long." He smiled.

His name was Brett Beaudin, and he was dressed in an XL polo over khaki pants. His Texas accent reminded me of Gerbin, my own crime scene tech, except with a feminine lilt to it. As he walked me into his office, I told him I'd talked with Sugarman about the '93 murder.

"That was an awful summer," Beaudin said. "My second year on the job."

I looked around his office. The walls were lined with cork, and he'd tacked medical studies and pictures to them until you could barely see a piece of open wall.

"I remember the day I drove out to that property. It was humid as hell."

"This was a call for the arson-murder?" I asked.

168

"And not a small fire either," he said. "Someone had used kerosene as an accelerant. Thirty acres burned."

Kerosene. The same accelerant found in Virgil Rowe's garage. And at the fire on Unger's property.

"The victim's elbows . . ." I flipped to that page in the report. "There's two different findings."

Beaudin grabbed the file. "Yeah, so this was a point of contention actually. I signed off on the elbows as an antemortem injury. But somewhere along the line, that got changed. The chief back then went to a specialist at the state who said no."

"So you thought it was what at first? Torture? Someone had broken Junius's elbows?"

"At first," Beaudin said, his hands on his hips. "But the guy from the state was a fire expert. Had a helluva lot more experience than I did back then."

"And what about soot in his lungs?" I asked.

"Well, we didn't have all the fancy tests we have now, but it wouldn't have mattered. To test whether there's soot in the bronchi, you need some bronchi to be in the remains."

I nodded. The victim's body had been too burned. Which would've happened with Kendrick if the crop duster hadn't put the fire out.

"Why don't you tell me what you're after, cowboy," Beaudin said. "I can give you an opinion, at least."

I pulled my own case file from my satchel. I walked him through it, and he nodded as I told the story.

"The hard part is the time that's passed," he said. "What's the angle? Someone killed a kid up this way in '93 and then took a break for a quarter century? You know better than me how unlikely that is."

"Yeah," I said. He was right.

I was thinking about the one detail I'd omitted. The lynching.

"Was it close by?" I asked. "Where he was found? I'm curious if there's trees there?"

"Trees, yeah sure," he said, putting a hand on my shoulder. "I drive by it on the way home every day. You want to see it? It's like a forest out there."

26

As we drove out, the evening sky was a beautiful purple. The whole of Shonus County was more rural than I'd imagined, and we moved through an area where a grouping of giant oaks formed a canopy over the road. It cut out the city lights almost entirely and blanketed us in darkness.

"It's up here," Beaudin said, motioning as we crossed over a small bridge. I slowed and parked where he told me to, along the side of the highway. From there, we walked on foot.

A line of Leyland cypress trees was planted, about fifty feet from the highway. Beaudin moved ahead of me, along the road. "You married?"

I figured where he was going. It was two days before Christmas, and here I was, wandering rural Georgia with him.

"I was," I said. "No longer."

"Kids?"

"Not at present."

"It was right there." Beaudin pointed at an area about thirty yards off the road. "But it's private land."

I smiled at him. "Well, we're just looking right? Not gonna steal anyone's fruit."

I walked over to the tree-lined area, and Beaudin followed me. I have the build of a tight end—tall but stocky—and I lowered my head under some of the smaller trees.

"This boy Junius wasn't the only one who went missing that summer, P.T." Beaudin flicked his eyebrows. "There was a girl too. Also black and around Junius's age."

"What happened to her?"

"I dunno." He shrugged. "Police eventually called it a runaway. I think the bigger concern was if she was sick. Infected with something. She'd been to the hospital the day before."

"For what?" I asked.

Behind us, I heard a noise. A truck moving through brush.

"She'd had bloody noses," he said. "Some pain in her chest."

The bloody nose detail popped for me. I thought of the kids in Mason Falls with typhoid.

I turned to ask Beaudin about this, but the truck accelerated, kicking up dirt as it cut through the tree line. It had fog lights mounted on top and came at us, fast.

The truck slid to a stop about twenty feet away, and the lights were blinding. A dirt cloud laid thick in the air.

"Put your hands up high, yo," a voice said through a bullhorn.

"Jesus," Beaudin said. "Damn rednecks."

Then I heard a shotgun cock, and we raised our hands.

"I'm a police officer," I said.

"And I'm an American," the voice came back. "Y'all know you're on private property?"

The headlights shut off, but through the fog lamps, I could see a Bushmaster AR-15 mounted to the top of the pickup. The Bushmaster is a semiautomatic, and mounting one to your truck is illegal in Georgia.

"I'm gonna pull out my badge real slow," I said.

I did this, and a skinny guy in a tank tee jumped down from the truck. He was no more than nineteen.

As he put his hands on my wallet, I spun him around, pulling out my Glock and shoving it against his temple. I had him down on the ground in two seconds. "If there's any more of you," I hollered, "I got a gun to his head."

"It's just me," the skinny guy said.

"You're under arrest."

The kid started laughing then, his whole attitude a half-bubble off plumb.

"What are you giggling about?" I said.

But the kid just kept it up, even as his head was shoved in the dirt.

"You got no clue who you're messing with," he said.

27

It took Captain Sugarman twenty minutes to get to us, and when he arrived, he was frazzled.

"You gotta get your cuffs off that kid, P.T." He leaned into me.

"He's in violation of Georgia state law," I said, pointing at the semiautomatic. "On top of it, he's pulling this militia rank and serial number shit. Won't tell me his name."

Sugarman steered me away from where the kid was cuffed. "His name is Tyler Windall," he said. "Hell, P.T., I *know* the militia he's part of. Y'ever heard of Talmadge Hester?"

"As in Hester Peaches?"

Sugarman nodded. "They own about ten farms here. Half the real estate in downtown Shonus. And the land you're standing on. Dumbshit over there is one of their peckerwood security patrols."

I smiled. "I was fifty feet from a public highway."

Sugarman shook his head at me. "And those sumbitches own that fifty feet."

I looked to Sugarman. What the hell did I care about some redneck kid? I wanted to meet with the family of the kid who died in '93. Pissing off Sugarman wouldn't do me any favors.

"What do you want me to do?" I asked.

Sugarman looked back at Tyler. "We can't release him. He'll go around bragging about bestin' some out-of-town cop."

Sugarman walked over to Tyler. He replaced my cuffs with his and stuck Tyler in his black and white. "Why don't you come with me, P.T. We'll run him up to the Hesters."

Another squad car came by and grabbed Beaudin, the M.E.

After that, I followed Sugarman up a winding road. The moon was full, and it lit up a plantation house in the distance. As we got closer, I stared at the tall white columns that made up the front of the place. They were hung from top to bottom with sparkling white Christmas lights, and cars were parked along the roadside for a good five hundred yards from the house.

We parked in front, and I looked up at the mansion. The place was giant—ten bedrooms probably—and gorgeous. Orchestral music was playing in the distance. A holiday party under-way.

A beefy woman in a maid's uniform let us in, and Sugarman asked me to wait in a parlor room while he went with her down the hallway.

The inside of the room was decorated in what locals called the antebellum style, with chunky ornate moldings running the perimeter of the ceiling and walls covered in paintings of Confederate soldiers.

A few minutes later, Sugarman walked back in with a man in his seventies.

"You must be Detective Marsh," the old man said. He had thick gray hair parted on the right, and he wore a white suit with a white tie and shirt. "Talmadge Hester," he introduced himself. His voice was soft and encouraging, like an actor in a commercial telling you to retire to Georgia to golf.

"Mr. Hester," I said. "My apologies for showing up unannounced and at this hour during the holidays."

My phone vibrated in my pocket, but I ignored it.

"Not at all," the old man said, motioning me into a den across the hall. We passed a woman in a blue Victorian gown with puffy sleeves and a low neckline. "We throw a little costume party every year at this time," he said. "So no one's asleep just yet."

The den was similar in style to the parlor room, except it had a large oak desk at the far end. Confederate officers probably drank whisky here with debutantes. Back before they were called debutantes.

Leaning against the desk was a man in his early forties. He was stocky and tan, and he wore an outfit I can only describe as the casual wear of an 1860s soldier. The family resemblance to the old man was uncanny.

"Mr. Marsh, this is my son Wade." The old man motioned. "Mr. Marsh is a detective from Mason Falls and had a run-in with an overzealous employee of ours."

Wade put out his hand, and I shook it. "Can I guess which one?" Wade smiled. "Was it Tyler?"

"Sugar's got him out in the car," I said, trying to use the shorthand of Sugarman's name, to make it seem like we were all buddies.

"Tyler attached an AR-15 to his 4Runner," Sugarman said. "P.T. bumped into him along Highway 908. He announced he was a cop, and Tyler didn't seem to care much."

In the distance, I could hear a full orchestra, most likely on the back lawn. They were playing "Dixie," and I got the feeling we had slid back in time.

"Was there something you were looking for out there?" Wade asked. "Along the highway?"

My phone vibrated. "Just some background," I said. "I'm investigating a crime from twenty-five years ago."

The older Hester looked impressed. He pointed at the thick packet of files that I carried with me, rubber-banded together. "This is like one of those cold case shows on TV?"

"Something like that." I smiled.

I noticed a frame on the antique credenza beside me. The picture had been taken at a golf course and showed Wade and Talmadge Hester, between them Governor Toby Monroe. The same guy my boss had met with this morning.

"Well, we have a great respect for local law enforcement," Talmadge Hester said. "So anything we can do to help . . ."

"Were you here twenty-five years ago?" I asked.

"We were here two hundred years ago," the younger Hester said, pointing at a painting of a general above the fireplace.

"Do you remember the boy whose body was found in '93?"

"Of course," Wade said. "We went to the same high school. It was a tragedy."

"Were you friends?"

Wade smiled. "We didn't exactly . . . run in the same circles. But that boy could sure shoot a basket."

"So you remembered he was an athlete?"

Wade shrugged. "Shonus was favored for state that year. Lucky thing was—our boys still won somehow. Had some kind of magical run without him."

My phone buzzed again.

"Do you need to get that?" Wade asked.

"Do you mind?" I said.

"Not at all." Wade opened a side door for me, and I stepped into a walled-in garden. The phone had gone to voicemail by now, and I checked my messages.

"P.T.," the voicemail said, and I recognized a deputy's voice. "This is Fin McRae. We got your father-in-law at MotorMouth off SR-902. He had a couple drinks and got into a bar fight."

"Jesus," I said aloud. I turned on the flashlight on my phone to jot down the patrolman's cell number, and the brightness lit up the garden.

An ornate sculptural piece was welded to the far wall, its curved rusty filigree spelling out a single word:

RISE.

The same word that had been written in Sharpie on the hundred dollar bill I'd found in the matchbox at Virgil Rowe's.

I turned my phone on to illuminate it even more.

"Everything okay?" Wade asked, stepping out into the garden.

"Yeah," I said. "Just admiring this."

"That old thing." He snickered. "It's been hung there since before I was born. I've caught my shirt on it. Tore my pants. When my daddy passes, I'ma rip it off the damn wall."

He leaned closer, twirling his index finger around at the house. "The facade looks good, Detective, but underneath, the place is falling apart."

I walked back in with Wade and looked around, taking in the details more slowly this time.

My eyes moved across each framed photo that lined the desk.

179

There were ground-breakings. Deal signings. The Hesters holding up giant checks for charity.

One picture piqued my interest.

It was a church service at Sediment Rock, the same place that Tripp Unger had gone the morning Kendrick was burned on his farm.

Behind the group in the picture, a sign read *First Son of God, Easter 2015.*

First Son of God. Remy had asked Unger what church he went to. It was the same name.

If I believed the local M.E. instead of the guy from the state, then the two cases had the elbows in common. A black teenager. The same accelerant. And now two farm owners, forty minutes away from each other, both who attend the same church?

I remembered what the crop duster had said of people who'd know the law on when a plane could be up in the sky. Farmers and pilots.

"Well, you certainly have a beautiful home here, gentlemen." I smiled.

"That's nice to hear," the older Hester said.

Two thoughts flew through my head. The first was that the Hesters had some interesting connections to the two cases—now and in '93. The second was that they had juice and a lot of it. If I came at them, it had better be with proof.

I turned, holding up my phone. "Unfortunately, gentlemen, I've got an emergency to attend to. Maybe it's best we just let Tyler go with a warning. And get that weapon off his truck."

"Consider it done," Wade said. As he moved closer, he looked to see what picture I'd been staring at. Then he glanced at my stack of files, trying to read the tabs on the side of them.

"I hope you find what you're looking for," he said. "With Junius."

"Appreciate that," I said.

Outside, Sugarman and I walked down the curving driveway. "You all right?" he asked.

I nodded. A man was piling equipment into the trunk of a sedan parked behind my truck. I couldn't make him out, but I heard the word "spelunking." It's a funny word, and it made me think about the word "Rise" from the sculpture.

Was it possible there was some connection— between the word "Rise" on the money and "Rise" on this old metal sculpture?

"My father-in-law is having some problems," I said to Sugarman. "I gotta hightail it back home. Thanks for your help tonight."

I got in my truck. Heard the trunk slam down on the sedan behind me.

I pulled around Sugarman's patrol car to speed out, but hit the brakes.

A man crossed in front of my F-150 and glared at me. He was the type of guy we call a "big'un" down south. Nearly seven feet tall, I guessed, and three hundred pounds.

I pulled past him and sped back toward Mason Falls.

28

MotorMouth was a biker bar set on a strip of gravel off State Route 914, just inside the Mason Falls jurisdiction. I didn't see a squad car when I pulled up, so I parked beside a row of choppers and got out.

Inside, the place was flooded with greenish-blue light, and an old Harley Panhead was hung from the ceiling. Couples in leather crowded the place. My father-in-law, Marvin, was nowhere in sight.

"Machinehead" from Bush blared through speakers: *Breathe in. Breathe out. Breathe in. Breathe out. Breathe in.*

Old Marvin liked to drink. There was a time when he drank at home, back when his wife was still alive. And then there was a time he drank on the road. Like the night my wife and son were killed.

In the last few months, he did his drinking at the Landing Patch. That's what had brought me to that strip bar in the first place. I was doing therapy, trying to resist beating the shit out of Marvin, sitting there in the parking lot. Watching him go in. Wondering if he came here because of the location, right beside the Tullumy. Right where his daughter and grandson had gone in the drink.

But tonight, he'd come to MotorMouth instead. To some random leather bar. Why?

I found a bartender. "MFPD." I badged him. "Was there a uniform in here earlier. Settling some fight?"

He pointed out the back door. I moved out of the place and across a dirt overflow parking lot. Signs stuck on cars and bikes advertised a Harley-themed New Year's Eve party.

A black and white was parked under a tree on the far side of the lot.

Patrolman McRae saw me and got out. He was short and stocky, with a bald head. He'd been on the force about six years, and for a little while we'd been in a poker game together.

"I'm sorry it took so long, Fin." I put out my hand.

"No problem," he said, shaking my hand. "I had some paperwork to finish. The snoring's been what's bothered me most."

I peered into the back of his patrol car. My father-in-law was passed out across the seat. He wore jeans and a white dress shirt, the sleeves rolled up to his elbows. His head rested against the side window. Little gray hairs sprouted from his dark brown ears.

"What happened?" I asked.

"If you believe what Marvin said, someone was talking trash about *you*."

"Me?" I blinked.

McRae nodded. "Marvin asked them to step outside and promptly got his ass kicked."

I didn't believe a word of what my father-in-law said.

"Listen, P.T.," he said. "I'm not one to tell you your business, but your father-in-law said you hadn't talked to him in three months."

I didn't want to hear what McRae thought of me, but I also knew he was doing me a solid by not arresting Marvin. "It's a long story, Fin," I said.

"It's also the holidays," he said. "Why don't you take the old guy home. Get him into bed."

I got Marvin out of the squad car. Stood him up. His eyes flickered opened. "Paul," he said to me.

Steering him across the lot toward my truck, I put Marvin in the passenger seat.

"I didn't do it, Paul," he said as I fired up the engine. "There was a car. It came along the highway."

I'd heard this before. That Marvin hadn't been behind the wheel of his car, pushing my wife's car with his, the night she died.

"I can't talk about it," I said.

When I got to Marvin's house, I saw he was asleep again and grabbed his house keys.

I opened the door and looked inside. The hall was full of framed pictures of Lena and Jonas, and it smelled like my wife. Like her house had smelled when we'd first met. When things were easy.

I blinked. Held my eyes shut. Then opened them and hurried to the bedroom. Pulled back the sheets on Marvin's bed.

As I passed the spare room on the way out, I saw pictures of cars taped up all over the wall. They were cropped photos of the fronts of sedans from the '90s.

"Son of a bitch," I said, feeling the anger rise inside me.

The old man had only been charged with a wet reckless, back on December 21 of last year, even though his blood alcohol level was right at 0.08. Most of this was based on Marvin's account of what had happened, which the DA believed. That he had been called by his daughter Lena, whose car battery had died. That he'd found her stranded off I-32, just south of the bridge. And that he was talking to her, leaning against the driver's-side window, when a car came along and rammed into the back of his own parked car, pushing it into hers and off the road.

Lena's 2001 Jeep had picked up speed as it careened down the hill. Within seconds, it had been dumped into the cold waters of the Tullumy River and carried downstream.

I stared at the pictures taped to the wall. Close-ups of the front grilles of cars.

When we'd inspected Marvin's Chrysler 200

last year, we'd found a broken rear taillight and a dented fender, both with white paint on them. Marvin had argued it was from the car who had hit the back of his sedan. He'd also told anyone who'd listen that he would know the front of that car if he ever saw it again.

I walked out to the truck and opened the passenger side.

I had a much simpler theory on how I'd lost my wife and son the week before Christmas last year. It was the story of a drunk father who already had that white paint on his smashed-in bumper. Who misjudged his speed while trying to push-start his daughter's old Jeep while he was loaded drunk.

I poked at Marvin. "Wake up," I said.

He stared at me. "Paul."

"Don't say it," I said. "Just get in the house."

I helped him into bed. As I pulled up the covers, he grabbed my arm.

"The guys who beat me up," he said to me. "They said you had become a drunk like me. But that you were still bumbling around and finding shit you should stay away from. That if you didn't quit, they'd put you in the ground."

"What did you say?"

I shoved him backward, and his head banged off the headboard.

"They said you were—"

"I'm nothing like you," I said. "You're a drunk and a fool. We're not the same."

I stared at him. Was someone threatening me? Was it possible?

Then I remembered who I was talking to. A liar. "You killed your daughter, Marvin."

Tears ran down his face. "I swear," he said.

I turned and left.

29

I got back to my house by midnight and sat on the front porch.

Purvis wandered onto the lawn and squatted, taking his best crack at killing the crabgrass that was growing up around the real grass.

The December night air was cool, and I thought about the Hesters and this crime from 1993.

Was it possible that someone from the old case was tied to the death of Kendrick Webster? Was it possible that someone had bullied my father-in-law into a fight by using my name?

I kept hearing Marvin's voice in my head. "They said you were a drunk like me."

I got up and walked into the house. Opening the cabinet to the right of the fridge, I grabbed a bottle of Johnnie Walker. Dumped it into the sink.

Two bottles of wine sat behind it. I poured them out too.

"Good," I said aloud.

I looked around. The house was an open floor plan, with the kitchen and dining room combined into one big space.

Atop Lena's antique oak dining table were piles of mail I hadn't gotten to. Mostly overdue bills.

I heard a noise behind me and turned. It was

Purvis, walking into the kitchen. He looked past me, to the empty bottles on the counter.

If you're gonna do something, do it right, Purvis huffed.

I turned and moved into the dining room. Looked in a brown bag under the table. There was a half-finished bottle of Belvedere. Along with it, a fifth of Bacardi. Down the drain.

I went out to the garage and found a shit brand of tequila. Gone.

A bit of Knob Creek. Drained.

I found a six-pack of Miller and did the same. A bottle of Cuervo on a shelf in the bedroom. A half bottle of Dewar's had rolled under Jonas's bed, where I slept some nights.

I watched the browns and clears swirl over stainless steel, and the scent of it rose into my nostrils. The smell alone was intoxicating.

Kamchatka. Patrón. Some vodka with Russian writing and no English words. I carried each one into the kitchen. Hesitated over some really good rum, but dumped it too.

The smells filled the whole house, and when I was done, there were ten cans of beer and twenty empty bottles of liquor on the counter.

Putting them into two garbage bags, I brought them out to the trash. Grabbed Purvis and walked him without a leash down the street.

A few doors down, a neighbor's house abutted a small pond, and I looked out at the fecund water, wondering if I could make it a day without liquor. The air coming off the pond smelled like stale bread and duck shit, and the winter pansies around the edge looked like faded tissue paper. The plants were being eaten from within, the result of lace bugs or bad sun tolerance or some soil-borne fungus that was just as much a part of the ecosystem as the plants themselves.

Walking back, I climbed into bed with Purvis.

I shivered most of the night, too tired to get up and see if I'd left a window open or if I was coming down with a cold.

By six a.m., I could no longer deny that I wasn't sleeping, so I got up and showered. Put on a sport coat and shirt over gray slacks. My hair can start looking like a perm if it rains a lot and I don't brush it, so I tidied up a bit. Shaved too. Then headed out to see Tripp Unger at Harmony Farms.

I got near Unger's property and slowed my truck.

We'd placed a patrol car there four days ago to keep media away.

I pulled next to Officer Winston Lamar's car, and he rolled down his window.

Lamar was a blond in his early thirties with spiked hair. Red acne dotted his chin and forehead.

"How you doin', blue?" I asked.

"Double time for the graveyard." He shrugged. "Can't complain."

"You've been checking in with the farmer?"

"Yeah, but it's pretty uneventful," Lamar said. "Some new equipment got dropped off at five a.m., but I knew about it. The farmer's wife drove down around midnight and told me to expect it."

"What kinda equipment?" I asked.

"There was a backhoe," he said. "A trencher. Couple others. He's got some of it going already." He motioned up property.

I thought about Unger. A few days ago he'd been so broke he couldn't pay attention, and now this?

My mind was expert at worst-case scenarios, and I imagined one. A farmer who needed money. Who sold the story of a black boy, burned to death on his property.

I moved past the cruiser and up the gravel road.

Passing Unger's house, I saw a giant machine swiveling around. It was a yellow backhoe with a black stripe down the side. It was double mounted with a scooper on each end and a cab in between.

It was starting to sprinkle, and I parked in a swath of mud. Unger waved, shutting off the backhoe.

"Detective," he said. The farmer stepped out of the backhoe's cab. I told him I had a couple follow-up questions.

"Shoot," Unger said. He wore a checkered tan flannel under a puffy orange vest.

"Do you know Talmadge Hester?"

"As in Hester Peaches? Sure," he said. "We're not close, but the Georgia farm industry ain't that big. Why?"

"It's probably nothing," I said. "But do they go to the same service as you do out at Sediment Rock?"

"Yup."

"And what about last Sunday, when the fire was? Did you see the Hesters?"

"Well, Talmadge is there *every* Sunday. These days he's got his oldest, Wade, working with him. So I saw him and Wade."

I thought about the crop duster who Unger had sued. "And y'all get along—you and the Hesters? They wouldn't have reason to set a fire here?"

Unger smiled. "In the farm business, I'm what you call small potatoes, Detective. I don't think they consider me much at all."

"Got it," I said.

"Truth is, we hardly talk at church," Unger said. "I'm an usher, so there were some issues with his boy a couple times. Being disruptive. Coming drunk to service."

"This was Wade?" I squinted.

"No, the younger Hester son. Bushy brown beard. Around your age."

Dathel Mackey had talked about seeing a

bearded man at First Baptist the day Kendrick disappeared. "The hunter," she'd called him.

"I think his name is Matthew," Unger said.

I jotted this down, glancing at where Unger had been digging. The farmer had trenched a hundred feet in length, first with the backhoe, and then a thinner, deeper channel with the micro-trencher.

"What is that—eight or nine feet?" I asked, staring into the trench.

"Ten," Unger said.

Too deep for seed, Purvis said.

I looked from the trench to Unger. "My partner and I mentioned the other day that some folks from TV might come at ya. Offer you cash to tell them what happened here."

Unger put up his hand, seeing where I was going. "It's not what you think, Detective. A couple fellas came by after you left. But these guys weren't reporters. They've been laying pipe across half this valley over the last month. They finally decided that to go around my property was too expensive."

"What are they putting inside the trench?" I asked.

"Some broadband fiber." Unger shrugged. "They wanted to bring in their own crew, but given the fire and all, I didn't want anyone on my land."

"Well, good for you," I said. "I know you guys have had a tough time of it. This sort of thing help out?"

"Let's just say I'll make my yearly nut in four days of trenching," Unger said. "And then the same every year after."

I whistled. This was some windfall.

He explained to me how he'd be able to farm his whole land now. Even the burned area.

"I took a walk down there this morning to check out the soil," Unger said. "You know, that boy wasn't the only casualty. A lamb was burned."

"One of your animals?" I said.

"Nope. And normally I'd guess it wandered onto the property, but the next farm over with livestock is six miles. So it don't exactly make sense."

Unger pulled out his phone and showed me a picture. It was the burnt body of an animal, but there was something wrong.

I stared at it. Not sure what to make of what I was seeing.

"Is its head missing?"

"Yeah," he said. "Odd, right?"

I drove back to the precinct then. I didn't even bother going upstairs to my office. I had a patrolman at the intake desk print me the info on the younger Hester brother.

Matthew Hester. Thirty-two years old. Brown hair. Blue eyes.

In his DMV photo, Matthew Hester had a shaggy beard that hung down past his chin. I looked at his description. Five foot ten. Hundred and sixty pounds. From the picture, a wiry athletic build.

If Matthew Hester was involved with Virgil Rowe or Cory Burkette, it would tie together a number of things. The two areas, Mason Falls and Shonus. The two time periods, '93 and now.

I grabbed my phone and texted Remy, even though she was officially on leave.

> You around? Want to bounce some ideas off of you.

I checked my in-box in the mailroom while I waited for a response. I saw that Captain Sugarman from Shonus had sent me a file I requested.

It was on Brian Menasco, the kid convicted of the crime in 1993. The kid who'd gone to prison for the arson-murder of Junius Lochland. Menasco had himself been killed in a prison fight a few years later, never completing his sentence, so the file was pretty thin.

Detective Berry walked by, a Starbucks coffee in hand. He was dressed casually, a golf shirt clinging to his rounded belly.

"Been looking for you," he said. He made sort of a dumb smirk. "We were about to put out an APB."

"What do you need, Merle?"

"We got a lady upstairs. She came in to see

Abe, but he's been in with the head shrinker for two hours for the shooting. I put her with a sketch artist."

Berry was normally Abe's partner, and this was good form, to cover for him.

"Thanks," I said. "But I might just be able to show her a picture instead." I held up the photograph of Matthew Hester. "This is the black lady? Seventy or so? Works at First Baptist?"

Berry shook his head. "No, this is a Latino gal in her sixties. Lives in the numbered streets. Saw someone skulking around the night your neo-Nazi got beaten to death."

Jesus, I thought. It was Martha Velasquez. The woman who'd seen me enter Virgil Rowe's.

"She's here right now?"

"Sitting up in your office with a sketch artist," Berry said. "That's why I joked about putting out the APB."

"How's that?" I asked Berry. Not following him.

"Well, the drawing's only halfway done," he said. "But it looks a lot like you. Me and Vannerman in patrol were saying when we find our guy, we should put P.T. in the lineup with him. For kicks, you know."

"Sure," I said. "That'd be funny."

Hilarious, Purvis said.

My phone buzzed. Remy texting back.

Come on by.

I glanced down. Made sure my heart pounding wasn't obvious through my shirt.

"There's something else." Berry fished through his notes. "Here," he said, finding a file. "Abe was checking neighboring cities on arrests. Guy with tattoos that read *StormCloud*. This came in from Macon PD."

Berry handed me a rap sheet, and I stared at the name on the outside cover.

"Donnie Meadows," I read.

He looked at me, and I shrugged.

"He's got StormCloud ink on his left biceps."

I flipped the folder open and stared at Donnie Meadows's booking photo.

Meadows was the big'un that I'd seen outside the Hester place last night. He was part of StormCloud, the same hate group that Virgil Rowe belonged to.

"You know him?" Berry asked. "Some kind of giant. Seven feet tall is what it says."

The file described Meadows as being of mixed race. Half Samoan and half German. His head was shaved and he had a wide bulbous nose with flared nostrils. In the photo, he didn't look like someone you messed with.

"I've seen him around," I said.

I'd left the Hesters in Shonus County, curious about a connection between 1993 and now, other than the coincidence of both Unger and them attending the same church.

Now someone outside their mansion belonged to the same Nazi group that Virgil Rowe did?

I was onto something. I just didn't know what it was.

At the same time, I was skating dangerously close to being linked to Virgil Rowe's murder myself.

"I'll see you upstairs," Berry said. "The woman in your office . . . ?"

I felt the urge to run. To get in my car and drive out of Georgia as fast as I could.

Just as much, I needed a drink.

But something else was banging around in my head. The word "giant" that Berry had just used. I'd heard the same reference two days earlier—in the jail cell here in Mason Falls—from that crazy loon.

"Yeah," I said to Berry. "I'll be right there."

Berry left, and I popped down to the basement where the holding cells were. Found the patrolman in charge.

"There was a guy here," I said. "Kinda went crazy on me. Reached through the bars and tried to grab me. I think his name was Bernard Kane."

"Sure," the patrolman said.

"I need to chat him up real quick."

The patrolman grimaced. "Bad news, P.T. We

did our seven a.m. check, and Mr. Kane was dead in his cell."

I blinked. "What?"

"He hung himself. His people came an hour ago and got the body."

"You sure it's the same guy?" I asked. "Sport coat? Jeans? Didn't smell good?"

The patrolman nodded.

"What do you mean they got the body?" I asked. "There'd be an autopsy. An investigation. We'd pull camera feeds—"

"The family insisted," the patrolman said.

"Who cares what they insist?"

The patrolman held up a hand, as if to say, *Let me explain.*

"Their lawyer shows up with some paperwork, P.T.," he said. "It apparently holds the department free of any blame in Kane's death—in exchange for releasing the body right away. The chief checked with counsel at the city, and they said we'd be idiots not to sign it, especially given the guy died on our watch."

I backed up against the wall. "You keep a log on who visited Kane?"

"Sure," the patrolman said.

He pulled it out, and I saw the time the lawyer came. Seven-twenty a.m. *How'd he have the agreement ready that fast?*

I turned to the previous page. The same name was written in the log the night before, when

Kane was alive. Lauten Hartley. The same lawyer had visited him.

What the hell *was* this? And how did it relate to Kendrick?

30

Remy leased a two-bedroom condo just west of downtown. It was owned by a businessman who'd transferred to California for a three-year rotation and wanted a quiet tenant he could trust. He'd hit the jackpot with a female police detective, and leased it to Remy for half market.

She buzzed me into the building, and I got into an elevator that had a chandelier in it. Hit the button for the third floor.

As the elevator moved, I wondered whether I should tell Remy about being at Virgil Rowe's the first night.

I needed to tell someone, and Remy was my friend. My partner.

The elevator opened. The hallway smelled like fresh paint.

"Hey there," Remy said, opening her door.

She wore running pants and an old sweater. I was unused to seeing her dressed down.

"How you doing, partner?"

"I'm bored." Remy led me into the dining room. It had black wooden beams crossing the ceiling and wallpaper with a decorative silver leaf pattern. "Give me something to do."

I grabbed a chair and opened my satchel. Gave Remy a rundown on what she'd missed in the past

201

day. There was the shooting of Cory Burkette, which she'd heard about on the news. And then me finding the pictures on Burkette's phone that put him thirty miles away from Kendrick on the night of the boy's disappearance.

"Damn," she said, realizing what this could mean about the guy Abe shot. "Does anybody else know this?"

"Just us," I said.

I filled her in on Dathel Mackey, my trip to Shonus, the Hester family.

"So we kept thinking Virgil Rowe and Cory Burkette knew each other through StormCloud," Remy said. "But we never confirmed that."

"Exactly," I said. "But that's not true for some of these new players. We know who knows who."

Remy took out a pad of paper and wrote some names down. She put them in circles as she talked.

"So Virgil Rowe is buddy-buddy with this big'un, Donnie Meadows. They both have StormCloud tats."

"Right."

Remy drew a line between the circle that read *Meadows* and a new one. "Donnie Meadows is buddy-buddy with Matthew Hester. Or *some* Hester."

"We can guess," I said. "He was at their house last night."

Remy's hand ran up and down a line of rivets

on the chair. "Still doesn't prove anything on our case," she said.

I kept going, telling her about the metal sculpture inside the Hester house that spelled the word "Rise."

"And the same word was on the money?" she asked.

I nodded, and we talked about this. If it meant that the Hesters might be the type of people who put up the money for Virgil Rowe to kill Kendrick.

"You said there was a girl with typhoid that went missing twenty-five years ago?" Remy asked.

"I don't know if she had typhoid. The coroner just said she had bloody noses."

"And what'd you make of that?" Remy asked. "Because there's some journalists suggesting these kids from Paragon Baptist could've been targeted. The water infected."

"Journalists or bloggers?" I asked. Knowing Remy knew the difference.

"Blogger," she said. "Singular actually. One guy."

"I dunno," I said. I stood up. Paced while Remy read through the rest of the file.

I was frustrated. Stuck. And scared that my badge was about to be yanked. I went into the kitchen and stared at an open bottle of Chardonnay. I grabbed a cup and filled it with water instead.

I thought about the sketch artist, drawing my face right now. About my inability to make connections on the case. Was I less of a detective than before? Was it the drinking? The grief? Or was it the fact that I might've killed Virgil Rowe? All of the above?

"There's something I need to tell you," I said from the kitchen.

Before I could finish, Remy walked in with one of my files. It was Junius Lochland's murder book from 1993. She had a confused look on her face.

"This Menasco guy," she said, turning to a particular page. "He's the dad of the kid who got convicted of the '93 arson-murder?"

"Yeah," I said. "The kid himself is dead. Killed in some prison fight. So I asked Sugarman for his dad's info."

"Is this a current address?" she asked.

I looked at the file.

Will Menasco; 265 Lake Drive; Schaeffer Lake, GA.

"I think so," I said. "Why?"

"An old boyfriend of mine rented a place through Airbnb at Schaeffer Lake. It's *more* than upscale, P.T. Every home on Lake Drive is worth two or three million bucks."

I saw where she was going.

"So these Menascos are dirt-poor twenty-five years ago," I said.

"Look." She pointed. "They used a public defender for their son. He gets found guilty, and suddenly they live with millionaires?"

I took my phone out and went to a real estate site. Punched in Will Menasco's address. A value came up: $2.8 million. Bought in 1994 for $1.1 mil. The same month as the boy's trial.

"Think it was a payoff?" I asked Remy.

"It's possible," she said. "Their son takes the fall for something he never did. The parents make off with the cash—"

"And the real killer's still around twenty-five years later," I said.

Remy nodded. It was a theory.

"What did you want to tell me?" she asked.

I thought about the night I'd beaten up Virgil Rowe. I still couldn't remember a thing after I threatened to blow his fingers off. Maybe I'd just walked out.

Maybe.

"Nothing," I said.

Remy looked at me, and for a minute I thought she knew.

"P.T.," she said, "you drinking every night during a murder investigation? It's not a good look."

I swallowed. Nodding.

"And you *not* drinking?" Remy continued. "Staring at that wine bottle? Your hands shaking like a June bride in a feather bed? It's not a good look either."

"What do you want me to do?" I asked.

"You can always sit this one out," Remy said. "You have that right, you know. To say, 'Sorry, guys—this one's too close to home.'"

I stared at her, but said nothing. Because we both knew I wasn't gonna sit this one out.

I grabbed my file and left.

31

Kendrick screamed, but air barely entered his lungs.

Flames leapt from the ground to his body. They met the kerosene, and his skin bubbled.

Black marks dotted his pupils, and he wriggled his body back and forth.

In the distance, he could see the older man from the cave. Walking down from the road.

Smoke billowed through Kendrick's vision, but he saw fireflies dancing in the night air. Coming to rest all around the man's arms and head.

Kendrick squinted, looking at the man's feet. They weren't touching the ground. He was floating.

"Fortune can be won back," the old man hollered. "Fortune is everything."

Kendrick could hear a buzzing sound somewhere above him. Far in the distance.

The man rose high up in the air. Out of Kendrick's line of sight.

And the flames covered Kendrick's chest until he could no longer breathe.

32

Schaeffer Lake was an hour from Mason Falls. I'd stopped by and grabbed Purvis, who'd promptly fallen asleep in the back seat of the truck. As I got closer, I thought through the details of the old case.

In 1993, twenty-six-year-old Brian Menasco had been picked up along the side of Highway 908, disoriented and wandering in burnt clothes. With a forty-acre fire nearby, he'd been arrested for arson.

When Junius's body was found two days later, the arson was upgraded to arson-murder. A trial followed, with the jury out for only eight hours.

My GPS told me I'd arrived at the Menascos, and I slowed my F-150 outside of a gray ranch-style home with paint peeling off the trim.

Through the pines to the right of the place, I could make out the greenish-blue water of the lake behind it.

Schaeffer Lake was half natural lake and half reservoir, created by the completion of the Stanley Dam in the 1950s. It was popular with boaters and jet skiers, and had over a hundred finger inlets rich with largemouth bass and blue-gill.

I rang the doorbell, but no one came. After a

minute, I saw a faded sign below the bell that directed packages to the lake side of the house. I threaded through a trail of weeds and found myself along a dirt shore. The property was overgrown, but even larger than I'd guessed from the street. A sprawling six acres, set along an inlet in the lake.

A wooden dock jutted out into the water. A man sat on a lawn chair.

"Hello there," I hollered.

The man was in his seventies and wore a checkered blue flannel.

I moved closer, walking onto the dock. It was made of cedar, and the decades had turned the wood gray, the water rotting it from below and the sun bleaching it from above. The dock had no railings around it, and you could walk right off into the water.

"I'm looking for William Menasco."

"You found him," he said. The look on his face was somewhere between "Who the hell are you" and "Who gives a shit."

"P. T. Marsh." I put out my hand.

The old guy didn't shake but pointed at a chair nearby. He was skinny, full of wrinkles, and had jeans hiked a good three inches above his waist.

"You some real estater, P.T.?" he asked. " 'Cause I ain't selling."

I smiled, shaking my head. Far out on the lake, I saw a man standing on a paddleboard. The water was calm, and the man had an oar in one hand.

I flashed Menasco some tin. "I'm a detective, sir. I wanted to talk to you about your son, Brian."

The old guy's look turned to annoyance. He had small dark eyes, set closer together than an earthworm's. "Brian's done passed," he said. "Twenty years ago next month."

"I know," I said.

"He wasn't in no shape to go to prison," the father said. "It's a community of its own, you know."

I cocked my head, not exactly sure what that meant.

"You gotta get on with everybody," Menasco clarified. "Or you get fuckin' killed. Brian never got on with no one."

Menasco reached down to a red Igloo beside his chair. The kind that held a single six-pack. He took the can of Bud that he'd just finished and tossed it out into the water. Grabbed another one.

"You fuckers charged my boy with conspiracy." He looked over at me. "You ever heard of a man who can't make no friends being charged with conspiracy?"

I didn't answer him. Out on the lake, the man on the paddleboard leaned over and jabbed with his oar into the water. Maybe he was fishing and it was a spear.

"I work in Mason Falls, Mr. Menasco. Do you know the area?"

He took a deep pull on his new Budweiser. "I drove a truck for thirty years. You blindfold me, and I'll find Mason Falls and half the other shit towns in this state."

"I'm looking into a murder that has some similarities to the one that your son went to prison for," I said. "I've got a black kid who was kidnapped and burned to death. He was fifteen, and his elbows were broken."

Menasco put down his beer, and I noticed an empty can of potted meat beside his chair, a plastic fork inside it. My daddy used to call the stuff redneck caviar.

"We had a suspect we liked for the crime," I said. "He's an ex-con, and looks good for it, but I don't think he did it."

Menasco turned. "Is that supposed to make me think you're the good guy? You're the cop who would've helped my son out if you were here back then?"

"No, sir."

"I don't know nothing about Mason Falls and a kid there," Menasco said.

"The local cops in Shonus," I said. "Did they look at anyone else back in '93—other than your son? Anyone who'd still be alive? I got their case file, but it's pretty thin. Maybe you heard rumors."

"Brian was a firebug since he was a kid," the old man said. "But he was gentle like his momma. I couldn't never take him fishing on account of him being so damn squeamish about hooking a shrimp for bait. He was a loner, but if you got the match out of his hand, he was harmless."

"So the broken elbows on Junius Lochland . . ."

Menasco shook his head. "At first, the papers made my boy into some evil genius—and violent. Then they come to their senses. Realized that Brian couldn't never have done that. So at the trial they changed their story. Brian just knocked Junius out. The fire broke them arms."

I thought about my conversation with Beaudin, the M.E., about the two different reports. Beaudin's original thought was that Junius was tortured.

"So no other suspects that you know of?" I asked.

He shrugged. "No."

"Mr. Menasco, does the word 'StormCloud' mean anything? They're a neo-Nazi group."

"I just done told you my son wasn't like that, Marsh. Half the guys I drove with were black. We played cards at my house every month."

"What about a family called Hester?" I asked. "They owned the land where Brian was picked up."

"Everyone knows Hester Peaches," he said. "So what?"

I stared at the old coot. I was running out of options, and I couldn't go back to Mason Falls empty-handed. Berry was probably looking at a sketch of me right now.

"Mr. Menasco," I said, "Brian had a public defender. Is there a reason you didn't hire a lawyer?"

Menasco pointed around. Almost smiling. "You mean why didn't I cash all this in to help my boy?"

I nodded.

"It didn't exist then," Menasco said. "The jury went into their room to talk, and the city attorney told us it'd probably be a day or two. My momma was sick, so I drove up to Kentucky to see her. I took her to play the ponies. Walked out two hours later with $1.5 million."

A crack inside my brain like thunder. "What?"

"Back-to-back superfectas," he said. " I took the winnings from the first race and rolled it into the next."

I shook my head. The odds on getting the first four horses in the right order was insane. Doing it two races in a row—impossible.

"This was the same day Brian was sentenced?" I asked.

He nodded. "I tried to use the cash on an attorney for my boy, but it was useless. By the time I had the money in hand, the public defender had told Brian to admit to killing Junius, to get a

213

lighter sentence. There was no going back from that."

The old guy finished his beer and did the same trick, tossing the can out into the lake.

We watched the empty take on water, slowly sinking to the bottom, where I was guessing there were about five hundred other cans of Bud. Maybe some Miller High Lifes. Some cans of Schlitz.

Life was full of ironies. Strange reversals of fortune. Coming into money a day late was Menasco's. But hearing his story four hours after talking to Unger about his windfall from the broadband fiber—it was too much, even to a cynic like me.

I stood up. "I'm sorry about your son, Mr. Menasco."

"There's no giving it back, Marsh. When you get the luck."

I squinted at him. It was an odd phrasing—"the luck." But it wasn't just that.

It was the same expression that drunk Bernard Kane had said to me in the jail cell.

"What do you mean?" I asked.

But Menasco just shrugged, opening his cooler for another beer.

I stared hard at him. "You said 'the luck.'"

"I don't gotta talk to you, pig."

I knocked the can of beer out of Menasco's hand. Leaned over and grabbed him by his flannel, my hands near his neck. "I'm in a fight for my life here, you old fuck. You said '*the luck*.' Now explain."

Menasco's eyes were big. "There was this old boy who ran the freight dock at work," he said. "He was a real prejudiced motherfucker. Never talked to me 'til Brian was charged. Then he'd come by like we was best friends. He told me it was gonna happen before it did."

"He told you about Brian and the fire—before it happened?"

"No, no. He told me I was gonna win at the racetrack before I did. Said I was chosen to get 'the luck.' For what Brian had done. He's the one who said it that way."

"Chosen by whom?"

"I dunno." Menasco shrugged. "He babbled about some group. The Order. He told me the day before I won the money, Don't be afraid to play the cards or the ponies. Buy a lotto ticket. Put down a wild bet. You'll find that the scales get evened up. That the Order takes care of you."

A lotto ticket? Purvis said inside my head.

Someone from Harmony had won the lottery the day of Kendrick's murder.

I let go of Menasco's shirt.

"He called it 'the Order'?"

The old guy nodded slowly.

"This was some group here in Shonus?"

215

"I dunno, Marsh," he said. Looking tired. "I dunno."

I had gotten everything I could out of the old guy. Now I needed to keep moving. If I could break one little detail, maybe I could trade it in. For my own future.

33

I was in my truck and heading back to Mason Falls when my phone buzzed. A number I didn't recognize.

"There's a girl," a woman's voice said.

It took me a second to realize it was Dathel Mackey, the old woman from First Baptist. Behind her I heard some odd noises.

"Ms. Mackey," I said. "Where are you?"

"In the woods," she said. "I was having trouble sleeping, so I went for a walk. Now it's done gone all rainy."

I heard what sounded like thunder. A growling noise that I associated with the expansion of air. Of someone being too close to lightning.

"Why don't you get home, and I'll come by," I said. "I've been fixin' to show you a photo of a man. See if he's the bearded fella you mentioned."

"They grabbed a girl now."

"What?" I said. "Who?"

"They're taking a lamb and burning it—"

"Did you say a lamb?" I hollered. I wondered if maybe she was seeing the past again. Maybe the girl who'd gone missing in '93. The girl with the bloody nose.

"The bearded one. And his friend, the big fella."

I heard thunder again, and the phone went dead.

"Shit," I said. I pulled over and checked my reception.

Full bars.

I tried the number, but it rang out. No voicemail set up.

I needed to find Donnie Meadows, and I called Abe, knowing that he was on desk duty after the shooting.

After a minute of small talk, I could tell that no one had connected me to the sketch yet. I wasn't dead in the water.

I told Abe I was following up on an open lead. Asked if he could look up past addresses for Donnie Meadows.

Finding none, Abe looked up the big'un's mother and father. Oddly, the only address listed was the Hesters' plantation house.

"No shit," I said to Abe.

"Yeah," he said, reading it back to me. The same house where I'd seen women and men in Confederate gear yesterday.

I changed the direction I was driving in and pointed my truck east, along a state highway that led through the backwoods. Toward the Hester estate.

"Listen, P.T.," Abe said. "I was about to call you on something else. You coming back here?"

My pulse sped up. "I wasn't counting on it. Why?"

"You remember Corinne Stables?"

"Sure, the stripper," I said.

"Well, I got an alert she used her credit card at the bus station. Looks like she's about to leave town."

"I'll come back," I said. "Pick her up myself."

"No need," Abe said. "Patrol's five minutes away. You keep heading to the Hesters'. The blue-suiters are bringing her to me. I just wanted you to know."

I hung up and exhaled. At the first crime scene, everything seemed to be pointing toward me.

I put my foot on the accelerator, and the truck moved past eighty. *On to the Hesters,* I thought. *Make something happen, P.T.*

The afternoon sun was dropping in the sky, and peach trees covered each side of the road. I wondered if they all belonged to the Hesters.

When I got to their mansion, I left Purvis in the truck sleeping and went inside. The maid quickly found Wade. He was dressed in the latest country club wear, an aqua polo tucked neatly into seersucker pants. A blue canvas belt with illustrations of whales and clipper ships held it all together.

"Well, normally the police don't come by to say 'Happy Christmas,'" he said. "But I bet my daddy two hundred dollars last night. I told him—we're gonna see more of that Marsh fella."

I smiled. Wade moved like a chicken thief. He slid when others walked. "Maybe you go double or nothing, and I'll come back tomorrow," I said.

Wade chuckled, leading me into the same room we'd talked in the night before. "What can I help you with, Detective?"

"Donnie Meadows," I said, holding up a photo. "Does he work for you, Mr. Hester?"

"It's a big operation, Detective Marsh. For any employee, I'd have to check with Human Resources."

"He's an unusually large man, Mr. Hester. Seven foot one. Weighs over three bills. I think you'd remember him."

Wade glanced at the picture a bit longer this time. Handed it back to me as he sat down on a small couch.

"Cigar?" he said. He took a Cuban from a nearby box and cut the end off of it. "What's your interest in him, Detective? Does Mr. Meadows have a Bushmaster mounted on his truck too?"

"I'm not sure about that," I said. "He *is* an ex-con, though. Been arrested multiple times."

Wade lit the cigar. Began puckering and puffing. "Well, we're a tolerant people. Give folks second chances."

"Mr. Meadows has a tattoo of a neo-Nazi group called StormCloud on his arm," I said. "The same tattoo is on a man associated with our open murder in Mason Falls."

Wade's forehead wrinkled. "I heard on the news that you solved that murder."

"Well, you can't believe everything you hear on TV," I said.

"What exactly are you after, Detective Marsh?"

"I think Mr. Meadows can clear up some holes in our case. Get some justice for a boy's parents."

Wade pointed his cigar at me. "So I'm gonna hazard a guess here, Marsh. I'm betting you saw Mr. Meadows while you were pulling out last night."

I nodded.

"So your question of whether I knew him was of the rhetorical variety?"

"Last night I didn't know who he was," I said. "Is he an employee? A friend?"

"He's a friend of a friend," Wade said.

"And is he here now?" I asked. "I just have a couple questions. Five minutes, max."

Wade suddenly shrugged. "And that'll settle things for you? To talk to him?"

"Probably, yeah."

"Wait here then," he said, and left the room.

I sat down on the couch and closed my eyes for a moment. I was exhausted and didn't know where to go next.

Purvis chirped. *You don't think he's actually gonna drag the seven-footer in here, do you?*

I pictured Corinne, back at the precinct.

Abe liked to sweat suspects. Even witnesses.

He'd leave them in a box for an hour before he said a word.

But he wouldn't wait on Corinne. He'd book her for conspiracy to commit murder, cuff her to an interrogation table, and she'd sing like a squeaky hinge.

The maid who let me into the house came into the room, holding a brass platter with a kettle.

"Coffee?" she said. She was a big woman and taller than me, with olive skin and meaty arms.

My hands were shaking from lack of sleep, and I threw back a cupful, knowing I needed a shot of caffeine.

After about ten minutes, Wade returned, but he told me that Mr. Meadows was not on the property.

I changed my tack. I was tired of exchanging softballs with this guy. "Is it your brother Matthew that Donnie Meadows knows?" I said. "You said he was a friend of a friend."

Wade walked toward the entrance to the study, where the maid had laid down the kettle. He closed the door and poured himself a cup.

"I heard about your wife and son," he said to me. "After you left last night, Daddy and I looked it up."

I hated when strangers brought this up.

"I'm sure losing his family can push a man to desperation. To a place where everyone looks like a suspect."

I stared at him. I wanted to hit him, hard.

"Does Captain Sugarman know you're here?" Wade asked. "Harassing good folks on the Lord's birthday?"

"No."

"And what about your own chief of police. Is it Miles Dooger?"

"I was in the neighborhood," I said.

"Well, we haven't done anything except be good friends to the community. And helpful to the police and governor. So I think it's time you left the neighborhood."

Wade walked over and opened the entrance to the hallway. I moved ahead of him, toward the front door.

"Some things aren't worth looking into, Mr. Marsh," he said. "The cost is greater than the investment."

"I guess I'm just one of those people," I said. "Stubborn."

"Nothing to lose?" Wade asked.

The way he said it, it was like a knife he was sticking into my side.

"Guess so," I said.

Then he almost laughed. "Well, that's where you've got it wrong, Marsh. Everyone's got *something* to lose."

34

Outside, I turned my cell on, and a series of texts came through.

Chief Dooger. Abe. Remy. All of them asking where I was.

I rang up Remy as I drove down the Hesters' driveway.

"They called me back to work," she said, sounding confused.

"Already?"

"Yeah, but there's something weird," she said. "I checked with my union rep, and he told me I was still on leave."

I thought of the Hesters and their connections. Of Wade asking about Miles Dooger, my boss. Had he left the room and not looked for the big'un, but instead made some calls? Was he trying to jam me up?

"Why don't you call the precinct?" I said to Remy. "Nose around a bit and see what's up."

Remy hung up, and I got onto the interstate, not entirely sure where I should be heading.

When she called me back, Remy's voice was shaky. "Let's meet," she said. "But not at the precinct. *Where are you, P.T.?*"

"A half hour away," I said. "What's going on?"

"You tell me," Remy said. "Apparently the

department received an anonymous tip. A picture caught on a cell phone of a guy outside Virgil Rowe's place the night he was killed."

I swallowed and steeled myself for the gut punch.

This was more than a sketch that looked like me. Someone had a photo?

"I guess it's grainy and dark, but they say it's you, P.T." Remy paused. "Did you kill Virgil Rowe?"

35

An anonymous photo dropped at the police station spelled bad news in a few languages.

A glass-half-full type would look at it simply as evidence of my innocence. The real killer must've been sitting outside of Virgil's place. They saw me exit and took a shot of me with their camera phone. Then they went in and strangled Virgil Rowe to death, knowing they had the ultimate alibi. A shot of someone else, a cop at that.

Glass-half-empty? *I* beat Virgil Rowe to death and walked out without remembering. Maybe a couple was sitting in their car—maybe on a date, who knows—and they took a picture and later recognized me from the news. Realized I was a cop and got scared. Turned in the picture anonymously.

I told Remy I'd explain everything, and we set up a place to meet outside the city limits. Right near the Landing Patch.

I tried to think clearly, but I suddenly felt like pure hell. I glanced in the mirror and my eyes looked bloodshot. I'd slept only six hours in the last two days.

By late afternoon I was out of Shonus County, but sweat was building up along my neck.

You haven't seen the photo, P.T., Purvis said. *Relax.*

I stared over my shoulder at my bulldog.

Another five minutes passed, and I felt worse. The lights from the other cars became blurs in the shapes of diamonds.

I looked in the rearview mirror. The same sedan had been behind me for five minutes. It had squared-off lights and was about ten car lengths back.

My throat was dry, and I felt nauseous. The steering wheel was heavy in my hand.

I looked down, and I was going only forty-five miles an hour. Somehow the sedan was still back there. The same distance away.

"New plan," I mumbled and changed course, switching roads and coming into Mason Falls from the south, along I-32.

I felt like something was in my system, but the only thing I'd consumed—

The coffee.

Was Hester that bold?

I pictured the maid. The beefy arms. The tall body and flattened-off face. Could she be related to Donnie Meadows? Abe had said a relative's address was listed as the Hesters' plantation home. I never asked him which relative. Could the woman have been Donnie Meadows's mother?

I thought about who else I trusted at the department and rang up Sarah Raines.

"Hey, how are you?" she said, her voice upbeat.

"Someone drugged me, Sarah. I can feel it in my system."

"Tell me where you are, P.T.," she said. "I'll call 911."

Another person asking where you are? Purvis said.

I bit my lip, not sure if I should trust her. "I'm heading to where it happened," I said. "To Lena and Jonas."

"Okay," she said, tentative. "I'm not sure what that means. What can I do?"

I cursed myself for not trusting anyone. For becoming such a recluse since the accident. Lena would've disapproved.

"Take care of Purvis," I said, "if something happens to me. Tell Remy to look where the accident was. Just tell her. No one else."

I hung up and started grabbing all my notes. My hands felt like jelly.

They were after me. The Hesters. The Order. Someone. Everyone.

Maybe I had proof of how they were all in it together and didn't even know it.

I looked back, and the sedan was still there. Hanging back.

I remembered Wade Hester and his old man, each of them staring at the packet of files I carried around.

My eyes were blurring, and I grabbed an

oversized evidence bag from my glove box. I started jamming all my notes into it. The printouts about Donnie Meadows. All my incomplete theories that I knew were so close but I hadn't yet connected.

I sealed the bag and sped up as I approached the bridge along I-32.

There was a curve coming up in the road. A curve where my wife's accident had happened. A quick bend in the road that would put me out of view of the sedan for two seconds.

I accelerated, looking at the place where I'd lost everything in my life. I tossed the sealed bag high in the air and into the bushes.

I needed to find somewhere quiet where I could sleep this off. Where if things calmed down, I could find Remy and sort through everything.

On the other side of the bridge I saw the glowing sign that I recognized. The Landing Patch.

Slowing, I hit the brakes and slid into a parking spot on the outskirts of the lot.

I stumbled out of my truck, wondering precisely what was happening to my body.

I looked around for my phone, but I must've dropped it. I could see the neon sign with the woman's legs opening and closing.

"Horace," I said, calling for the bouncer. "Horace!"

But no one was sitting at the door at this hour. It was too early to staff a bouncer.

A minute later a man with a thick brown beard approached. He was a few inches shorter than me, and his nose looked like it had been broken a couple times. He wore a red South Carolina Gamecocks T-shirt.

I squinted.

What the hell?

It wasn't Matthew Hester. The bearded man was someone else. Someone whose name I didn't know.

"Who are you the hell?" I asked.

My words didn't make sense, but he smiled, the whites of his big teeth surrounded by that giant beard. A forest with a wolf inside it.

It was so simple. The Hesters must have put something in the coffee and had me followed here.

I heard another voice then. Saying something about enemies and friends.

My head felt like a stone. "You know what happens?" I mumbled. "People fuck with guys mess cops up?"

Beard laughed, and I tried to turn, but the night was like a wall behind me. I realized someone was there, pushing me. The big'un, Donnie Meadows. That was the other voice.

Meadows shoved me into the front seat of my truck. He smelled like mint chewing tobacco.

"Can't drive," I said, but I heard the ignition start.

Then I heard Lena's voice. Echoing somewhere in the darkness. "Maybe it's time, P.T."

Beard said something about my notes. He couldn't find them. He asked the big'un if he saw them.

"I see a damn dog," Meadows said. "Some ugly-ass speckled bulldog."

I heard the cab open. A yelp as someone kicked Purvis out. Meadows said he didn't kill dogs.

The world opened in front of me.

"Truck is huge," I said. Which made no sense until I realized my seat was being slid backward. Beard was leaning over me.

I smelled moonshine and Listerine on his breath, and something burned in my mouth. White lightning, 160 proof.

The liquid filled my throat, and I gagged for a minute before swallowing. There were pills mixed in with it.

Purvis barked in the distance, and Beard hollered something at him.

The truck moved.

"No," I said.

But it was gaining momentum. Maybe being pushed by hand.

The headlights were off, and my eyelids felt heavy. Meadows had eased my F-150 around the bend just past the Landing Patch. The sun had dropped in the last hour, and I was pushed into a dark spot that couldn't be seen by an oncoming car.

"Sitting duck." I coughed, my body trying to get rid of whatever they'd put in me. Trying to throw up.

"Yeah, that's the idea," the big'un said.

Fireflies danced around the two men, hovering above their arms. They were like tiny assistants, helping them push me into a dangerous corner of the universe.

"Meadows." I pointed at him.

"He knows my name," the big'un said. "I want his gun."

"No, that stays here," Beard answered. He glared with his steely blue eyes at his giant friend. "Take the safety off and make sure it's loaded, because this is one reckless cop." He looked down at me. "Merry Christmas, asshole."

"Please," I said, but I was only speaking to the darkness. The men had gone, and I couldn't move.

I saw the obit: *P. T. Marsh. Widowed paranoid drunk detective. Corrupt cop who kills for strippers and talks to dogs.* And those were my winning points.

Then I saw a flash of light, and the ground beneath me dropped out.

Everything reversed. Sky was earth, and earth was sky.

Blood dripped across my eyes, and I saw the steel of a semi. A long white body. Mud flaps and tires flipped upside down.

Then fire and darkness. And my eyes closed. I heard the words that echoed back from December 21 of last year. Lena had called me.

"I'm heading home," she said. "I'll see you soon."

And then blackness.

36

I heard noises. Felt myself fly through the air. My shoulder and head hit metal, and blackness came over me again.

Then hands lifted me up. Carried me. My eyes felt swollen, and I heard the sound of a thousand boots marching. Of wars being fought and lost, and my body scraping against the ground.

I had thoughts, but couldn't form them into words.

I saw a flash of Remy's face and tried to speak. "Talk Sarah," I said.

Darkness alternated with light. The beautiful blue night sky of rural Georgia. The bright white of too many lightbulbs.

Finally my body wasn't being scraped anymore. The sensation of pain came, and I felt the stiff fabric of hospital linen.

I opened my eyes and closed them. Slept for what felt like days.

When I opened them again, I saw a man I knew mostly by reputation.

"Hello, P.T.," he said.

"Water," I whispered, and he grabbed a paper cup, filling it up from a plastic pitcher on the tray table.

I was in a hospital room. My head shifted right.

A window. Nighttime outside of it. Then left. A closed door. A white sheet was wrapped tightly around me. Shiny silver rails on each side of the bed.

The man poured the cup into my mouth, and I swallowed. Coughed.

An IV snaked its way into my arm. I closed my eyes and tried to remember. Tried to understand why the only person waiting for me was Cornell Fuller from Internal Affairs.

"I've been sitting here thinking—today's the day you're gonna come up for air," Cornell said.

I opened my eyes. Cornell was an odd-looking guy. People called him Big Bird because he was tall and walked funny. He had an odd, scruffy patch of wavy blond hair on his head.

"Rep," I said, my throat hoarse. Indicating I wasn't going to talk to him without my union rep.

"You'll get your rep," he said. "But you're in so deep, P.T., you're gonna beg for a deal with me first."

I blinked down hard, holding my eyes shut. I felt pain along my back and side, but I moved my fingers and toes. Then lifted my feet. Nothing seemed broken.

When I opened my eyes again, Cornell's chair was closer. He was holding a manila folder full of papers.

"Get outta here," I said.

But he didn't leave. He held up a photograph. My F-150, mangled in the middle of a road.

I closed my eyes, not wanting to see. But then I opened them, needing to see.

He pulled out another photo. A semi was on its side.

"The driver of this truck is in ICU," Cornell said.

"Don't remember."

Cornell laughed. "I guess that's kind of a side effect of being a mile high and drunk as shit."

The drugs. They'd put something down my throat and pushed my truck out into the road. Matthew Hester and Donnie Meadows.

Except my mind corrected itself. It wasn't Matthew Hester. The Bearded Man was someone else.

"And then there's this." Fuller held up another folder. "This is my timeline of you last Sunday. I got you out at the strip bar. Then driving into town around three a.m. Your buddy Horace at the Landing Patch already helped me connect some dots."

"Get out," I said. I found a call button near my hand and started pressing it, over and over.

Cornell stood up. "Strange thing is, Horace said you don't necessarily like the ladies at the strip bar. That most of the time you just bring a drink out to your truck. Sit there and stare over at the riverbank like some retard." Cornell put up his hands, palms out. "His words, not mine."

A nurse came in, and I told her I wanted Cornell to leave.

After she shooed him out, I sat up and felt pain. Pain everywhere.

"Hold on there, cowboy," the nurse said. She wore purple scrubs and had blond hair with blue streaks in it.

After five minutes I swung my legs off the bed. Touched the ground.

"Like it or not, I'm getting up."

"All right, well, let me disconnect you at least," she said.

I let my feet touch the ground. Pins and needles, but I was alive. I looked at my arms. Scraped and scabbed to all hell. Felt at the right side of my neck. Same thing.

I walked around the bed, but felt my eyes closing. I climbed back into bed, out of energy after a ten-foot walk.

The next day Remy arrived. Something was sedating me, and I had trouble concentrating.

"Don't tell Cornell Fuller shit," she said.

"The accident," I said. "I saw the pictures."

"Wade Hester," Remy said. "He got ill after you left. They had to pump his stomach. He's barely alive."

"He drank the coffee too?"

She nodded. "It all changed in the last day.

Cornell is grasping at straws now. Trying to get you to say something. Everyone knows that maid poisoned you for going after her son, Donnie."

I squinted at her. Was it over that easy? Even with the things I'd done?

"The stripper," I mumbled.

Remy smiled. "Yeah, I guess she was smarter than Abe thought. The bus he was tracking was a ruse. She was never on it. Probably bought the ticket and then left town in the opposite direction."

My eyes were closing now. Remy's words hard to understand.

"Wait a sec." I blinked. "So Wade Hester? The Hester family."

"Innocent," Remy said.

I shut my eyes. The Hesters had done nothing wrong. The crime in '93—they were as guilty as Tripp Unger. Someone else had just done something horrible on their land.

"What about the Order?" I asked.

"Yeah, I saw that in your notes," Remy said. "Sarah told me where to find them. What is that?"

My head hurt, and Remy adjusted the pillow for me.

"P.T.," she said. "What is it?"

"What's what?" I asked. The medication was kicking in, and I wasn't sure what she was talking about.

"Get some sleep," Remy said, dimming the lights. "We can talk tomorrow."

She kept staring at me though, and I recognized the worried look on her face.

"What's wrong?" I mumbled.

She just kept staring.

I ran a hand along my cheek. "Am I scarred or something?"

"I went to check on the trucker you collided with, P.T. He's doing better."

"Good," I said.

"Your father-in-law, Marvin, is in the room next door to him. Someone beat the hell out of him again. When you get out of bed next time, you should go down there."

My eyelids closed.

Wade Hester was right. I did have more to lose.

37

When I woke up, I found my way to the ICU floor and Marvin's room. It was the dead of night, and I pushed open the door and stared.

A strap was wrapped around Marvin's head and a tube attached to it. It met up with other tubes that snaked their way across his body and toward some machinery by the bed.

I felt nauseous. Angry. This wasn't a little bar fight at MotorMouth. A pump whirred up and down and another machine beeped.

I moved closer and stared at the bruising on his face. Marvin's jaw and nose looked broken. There were swollen marks of purple and black around both eyes.

I wanted to kill whoever did this, and I needed out of here. Out of the hospital.

I opened the small closet in Marvin's room and found the clear plastic bag that held his clothes. I put on my father-in-law's pants and tucked my hospital gown into them. Threw on his jacket.

Moving out to the hallway, I found an empty nursing station. An iPhone sat beside a computer, and I looked at the date. Realized I'd been out for five days.

I found an Uber app on the phone and requested a car.

"Angie?" the driver asked outside the hospital lobby.

I managed a half smile as I got in. "My wife called it in on her phone. She's Angie," I said.

When I got home, I moved into the bedroom and stripped off Marvin's clothes. Got into a hot shower.

When I got out, I put on some shorts and a T-shirt. I moved from room to room, picking up all the dirty clothes and piling them into the hamper, trying to make the place somewhat livable.

About fifteen minutes later, I heard a barking noise and opened the front door. It was Sarah Raines, and she had Purvis with her.

"Hey, buddy," I said, crouching down and hugging my bulldog. I smelled the forest on him. Some rosemary that he must've rubbed up against.

Sarah had on cutoff shorts and a T-shirt with a butterfly design.

"How'd you know I was here?" I asked.

"I went by the hospital. Your bed was empty."

I nodded, and my bulldog ran over to his bowl. Started drinking right away.

"Do you remember calling me?" Sarah asked. "You told me to find Purvis."

"Barely," I said.

"Well, I told IAD that you were drugged. It's on the record."

"Thank you."

"You also told me to send Remy to the scene of your wife's accident."

I stared at her. The evidence bag I'd tossed. Trying to connect the pieces made my head hurt.

"Should I come in?" she asked, and I explained that I was just cleaning up.

"I'll help," Sarah said, and she began picking up some things in the kitchen. A few minutes later she asked when I'd eaten last and made me some scrambled eggs.

It was the first real food I'd consumed since the morning of the accident, and I took a seat in the living room, scarfing it down quickly.

I remember lying down then, a feeling of fatigue coming over me.

I must've fallen asleep, because I woke up the next morning with an old blanket thrown over me and a note from Sarah telling me she didn't want to wake me.

Purvis was curled under my arm, his brown and white nub of a tail wagging. I pulled him close, and he made a huffing noise, nuzzling into me in a way that he hadn't in months.

"The people you've lost," I said, realizing that Purvis had been abandoned again. Left on the side of a highway.

In the next hour, I picked up the house a bit more, but found myself drawn into memories of my wife and son. I found my old laptop. Firing it up, I sat with Purvis and watched videos from a family vacation two years ago.

We were in Key West, Lena's favorite place, and my wife looked radiant in an orange and blue sarong over her bathing suit. There was an hour with her and Jonas at the water. Then on a boat. Jonas struggling with a fishing rod.

Purvis barked when he heard Lena's voice, and I rested my hand on the folds of his neck.

I got lost in memories for another half hour until something pulled me out. Something Lena said.

In the video, we were playing a board game in the hotel lobby, and Jonas was holding the camera. He was recording us.

"Be careful, Paul," Lena said to me. "You think you're winning, but I'm about to whoop your ass."

Lena winked then. "Or Daddy could win the game but lose something else later tonight."

I sat there stunned. Lena had called me Paul. She'd also said the word "whoop."

I took a hot shower and got dressed, trying to think of the advice Lena's twin had offered the day she'd told me of her vision. Exie had said it was about betrayal. That someone close to me was going to whoop me.

I pulled back the rug under my dresser and opened my floor safe. Inside was my personal .22 and some ammo. A pile of cash I kept on hand for emergencies.

As I lay on the ground closing up the safe, I saw the tail of a shirt lying under the bed, stuck under a sheet I must've kicked off during the night.

It was the flannel I'd worn the night I went to Rowe's. The one I thought I'd tossed in some trash can after beating him up. I took it to the laundry room and spread it out on the table. Flicked on the bright lights.

There was a smear of blood on the cuff of the right hand, but it wasn't much. And nothing else anywhere.

This wasn't the shirt of someone who'd beaten Virgil Rowe up. Who'd strangled a neo-Nazi? No way.

I went to the kitchen. Called a cab and took it over to my father-in-law's place.

When I got to Marvin's, the front door was wide open, and I stood in front of it, spooked. I pulled out my .22 and checked each room, one by one. No one was there.

A dried piece of cat poop sat in the middle of the kitchen floor, and I wondered how long the place had been left open.

And if so—what did that mean? Was someone searching the place? For what?

I grabbed the old man's keys and fired up the 1972 Charger that he kept in the garage and never drove.

Some things for a cop were a matter of instinct, and a lot of things hadn't been adding up.

I drove the Charger to the corner store and bought three burner phones, not knowing what was coming next or who I could trust.

As I got back on the road, I felt something I hadn't in a while. It would be easy to call it enlightenment, driven by sobriety or a near-death experience. But it was more than that.

Over the last year, my anger at losing Lena and Jonas had fueled a recklessness. A sense of apathy. Now I felt focused to find who was at the core of this. Who wanted me dead so bad that they'd drug me. And why? What the hell did I know?

An hour later I was at the police mechanical mod yard. This was the place at MFPD that patrolmen brought their black and whites to get fixed or upgraded. It also served as an investigative area for IAD and was the final resting place for my Ford F-150.

I stared at my truck. The passenger side was completely smashed in. The roof dented about eight inches. The front headlights smashed.

My friend Carlos walked over. He had shoulder-length dark hair that was wrapped in a thick red rubber band. He wore a one-piece mechanic's jumpsuit with a tag that read *Ray*.

"I could lie to you that there's a body shop out there that's gonna make you whole again, brother," Carlos said. "But you ain't gonna be driving her no more."

Tim McGraw cooed from an overhead speaker.

"I loved that truck," I said.

Carlos kissed his St. Christopher medal. "Rest in peace. Travel well to the junkyard."

I turned to Carlos. "Listen, I don't know if you heard. The word's out that yours truly was drugged. Which makes me innocent."

"I did hear." Carlos leaned in. "Question is, was it good drugs?"

I ignored Carlos's joke. "We got a lead on one of the two guys who did this to me," I said. "But I need a break on the other. Good thing for me"—I tapped at my head—"this thing's a steel trap, even under the influence."

Carlos got serious. "You remember something?"

Carlos had recently been promoted on the crime scene team. And although he pushed this laid-back vibe, he was smart as hell and even more meticulous.

"The guy pushed my seat back, C.," I said. "So his prints must have gotten onto the driver's-side slider."

Carlos put on some gloves.

"I'll look." He opened the truck door. "There's only one problem. This ain't my truck. And it ain't your truck no more. This is IAD's truck. So if I touch it without Fuller knowing, I'll get Big Bird's beak up my asshole."

I nodded. Nobody wanted the wrath of Internal Affairs.

I needed a name on the Bearded Man, but I wasn't clear on my status as a cop. My gun and badge had been confiscated after the accident. Then again, no one had formally taken them away or charged me.

"Listen," I said to Carlos. "I don't want you to feel obligated to help me—just because when your *sister* was in a jam last year, I helped you."

Carlos looked at me. "C'mon, man."

"Just got her unbooked," I said. "You know how hard it is to *unbook* someone in today's criminal justice system?"

"I get the sense you're about to explain it to me."

"I'm not," I said. "I'm just reminding you that we're friends, and I'm not a guy who uses that word lightly. And, Carlos." I pointed at my truck. "This guy didn't hurt my feelings. He tried to murder me."

Carlos exhaled loudly. Looked around.

"I'll tell you what," I said. "How 'bout you print the slider and text me the guy's name. You can tell Big Bird at the same time. And no one will know where I got the info."

"How's that?" Carlos asked.

I pulled two of the burners from my pocket. Handed one of them to him. "The number on this one's programmed into that one. They're disposable, man. I get the text. I toss the phone in the river. You toss yours in the recycling bin, and no one's the wiser."

He glared at me.

"I need this," I said, and turned to head out without waiting for an answer.

There were machinations at play that I hadn't figured out yet. Someone was controlling part of the chessboard, and I could only see one step backward and one forward. I needed to move diagonally. Think more creatively.

I texted Remy, letting her know the burner was the best way to contact me.

Could use your help. U up and about?

I tossed my phone on the passenger seat and thought of what William Menasco had said about "the luck." He'd mentioned a group called the Order.

I'd never had a chance to look into them before I got drugged.

Could the Order be more than a Nazi group related to StormCloud? Could it be some cult group?

I needed help from an expert, and I had one in mind. A researcher I'd known half my life.

38

By four p.m., I'd arrived at the University of Georgia campus and parked in a lot off Sanford Drive.

Candy Mellar had been a friend of my mom's and oversaw Special Collections at the university library. She'd been there since 1983. She was an expert on the occult, and we'd worked together on a previous case.

My phone dinged with a text from Remy.

> Taking a couple days off. Rain check on joining you.

The message spooked me.

My partner balking at finishing an investigation?

Could this be about Virgil Rowe's murder? Or IAD?

I knew a picture of me leaving Rowe's house had been turned in and a sketch of me drawn. Could there be more to IAD's investigation of me still going on? Could Remy have been lying to me at the hospital when she said I had nothing to worry about? Was she told by IAD to keep me at arm's length?

I moved past LeConte Hall and toward the library.

At the time of my poisoning, Remy had been suspended for pulling her piece on church grounds. But at the hospital she'd had her badge clipped to her waist.

I thought about what I'd do if I ran Internal Affairs and was hunting a cop. I'd go to the suspended partner, make her a deal that put her back onto the detectives' squad—and all she had to do was keep an eye on me. And touch base regularly with IAD.

I texted Remy back, asking what she was up to.

Heading out to Dixon in 15.

Dixon was where Remy's grammy lived, and the woman had been good to me. She'd literally moved into my house for two weeks after my wife and son died.

I rang my partner up. "Is everything okay with Grammy?"

"She's fine," Remy said. "It's her cousin. He's a minister, and there's some issues with his granddaughter. She's sixteen and was dating a college guy."

"The girl run off with him?"

"That's what it looks like," Remy said.

I hesitated. Could this be a bullshit story?

"Why didn't they call the locals?" I asked. Meaning the Dixon police.

"It's unincorporated, P.T."

"So the sheriff then?"

"You know how people up there feel about police," Remy said. "They called Grammy. Who called me."

I *did* understand. The locals in the hills didn't call the cops, and for good reason. They'd been the victims of police abuse too many times.

"Keep me posted," I said and hung up.

I knew the campus at the University of Georgia well. My mother had taught in the Humanities Department when I was younger.

I found the library and asked for Candy.

"P.T.," she hollered a minute later. Candy was over seventy, and her ash blond hair was tied back in a ponytail. She met me in the library lobby, a giant expanse of a room. Gave me a hug.

"I read your email," she said. "Couldn't tell if you're investigating some old fraternal order or some contemporary Nazi group."

"That's what I'm hoping you'll tell me," I said.

Candy smiled. "Well, c'mon then." She moved ahead of me up a set of stairs to where her office was. She was slender, always wore a loose dress, and ducked her six feet and three inches under low door frames. I remember my dad saying she could hunt geese with a rake.

I sat in Candy's office, and she punched away at her keyboard. All around her were quotes and affirmations, tacked up on corkboard. *Trust the Universe* and *Have an Attitude of Gratitude*.

"There's a whole mess of occult groups that sprung up in the late nineteenth century," Candy said. "Golden Dawn, OTO, SRIA. We call 'em Freemason rejects."

"So you've heard of the Order?"

"No," she said. "And just looking one more time to be a hundred percent sure, the answer's still no."

I slumped in my chair.

"What case is this related to?" Candy turned to me.

I explained about Kendrick. I even told her about the lynching.

"I had this theory that the murders were recurring," I said. "Same race. Age. The broken elbows."

Candy sat forward. "What do you mean, broken elbows?"

"Both kids had their olecranon process broken. In both arms. I imagine they were tortured. Their bodies posed backward or something."

Candy stood up and flipped open a cabinet. Took out a laptop that looked like it had seen better days. She started searching through it, this time not in the university search system. "There's a book," she said. "A ledger of sorts."

"From the Order?"

"I don't know about the Order," she said. "Maryanne, who had this job before me—she'd request donations from old Southern families."

"Donations of books?"

Candy nodded. "Some guy's wife shipped us a crate after he died. Maryanne called this one book the Southern Marquis de Sade. Lunatic ravings. Horrible pictures. We couldn't put it into circulation."

Candy got up, and I followed her, moving eight stories down the back stairwell into what she called "the stacks."

"There's drawings of girls with their hands behind their backs, P.T. Their elbows broken."

The bowels of the building smelled like dirt, and a handful of lights were turned on. Candy unlocked a door that read *Private Collections* and found a cardboard box. Grabbing a large leather-bound book from the box, she paged forward at her usual ninety miles an hour.

She stopped on a page covered in graphlike vertical and horizontal lines, and I stared at a symbol hand-drawn in a box. It was the all-seeing eye from the one dollar bill. The same symbol I'd found carved into that tree by the irrigation ditch.

Instead of a pyramid below the eye, there was a plantation house.

And above the eye, in a curving shape, was a single word.

RISE.

The same word as on the money. And the sculpture at the Hester house.

"Shit," I said.

Candy paged forward. "Looks like the group was some fraternal order, made up of men from twenty-five Southern families." She pointed. "The ledger isn't just *one guy's* diary either. There's entries from his great-great-grandfather. Look at the year, P.T."

I read the entry marked June 23, 1868.

I brought in a bucket of well water and poured it on Rowen's dead body, laid out on the fine linen of the dining table. I used a sponge to wipe away the dirt, watching as the homespun linen below him took on the color of burnt hay and the smell of mud.

After cleaning his skin, I took Rowen's body out to the back garden.

The War for Southern Independence had ended, and I stuck my shovel into the ground to bury my son.

Lately when I spoke to the earth, a voice came back, echoing in the air around me.

If I concentrated hard, I could make it rain some days. Focus even harder, and locusts would cover the sky.

"Tell no one," Annis had warned me. "Whatever you're learning out there in the dark from that slave woman you've captured—desist from it."

But as I stood alone, I couldn't help but close my eyes and concentrate.

"Rise," I said to Rowen's dead body.
But nothing happened. Not yet.

The entry ended, and I looked at Candy.
"Creepy," she said.
"No kidding," I agreed.
She turned to the next page, and we saw a scrawl of words . . .

Andine Emphavuma
Endibweret Serenee Mdima

Below it read other words, this time in English. I couldn't tell if it was a translation of the above or not.

Bring me the Power
Bring the Darkness to Bear

"You said twenty-five families?" I asked.
Candy nodded.
And crimes twenty-five years apart, Purvis's voice echoed in my head.
She paged farther into the diary, and we saw some of the founding members' last names.
"Looks like some guy named Bayard Oxley was the founder," Candy said. "There's other names in here. Stover. Hennessey. Kane. Granton."
"Kane?" I blinked.
"That name mean something?" Candy asked.

"It's the same last name as some crazy drunk we had locked up. He was innocent, but knew about Kendrick's elbows being broken. Told me it's how *they always do it*."

"You think he's part of this?"

"He's dead, Candy. He hung himself in his cell."

Candy turned a page. In one of the drawings, I saw an illustration of a girl with her hands bound behind her back. In another, there were notes about animal sacrifice.

"Deer heads cut off," Candy said. "Lambs on altars."

I told Candy about the beheaded lamb remains that Unger found in the fire. Of Dathel Mackey's vision of a lamb being sacrificed.

Candy handed me the book. Pointed at an entry dated November 9, 1968. Fifty years ago.

> The two names were given to us today. Sheila Jones and Jerome Twyman. We will send the boys after them, and life will begin to improve again. Amen and Rise, Olde South, Rise.

The entry was short and was the last one written in the ledger. I wondered what that meant—*the two names were given to us*.

"Let's say I wanted to see if these were real people," I said to Candy, motioning at the mention of Sheila and Jerome. "And if anything happened to them in November or December of '68. You got old newspaper records?"

"We're digital back to 1975," Candy said. "Before that—microfiche."

She brought me two flights up, to an old microfiche station. I'd used one of the machines years ago—these giant ancient devices that read negatives from old newspapers.

Candy placed a film cartridge into the machine, and I sat down. Into focus came a newspaper from the '60s, the *Marietta Daily Journal*. I turned the dial, and images of old dailies zoomed past us—day after day—big reproductions from November of 1968.

As I moved faster, the pages became a blur of black and white.

I stopped at a page that listed a story about Sheila Jones. She was black, seventeen, and had gone missing. The date was November 16, 1968.

"Page forward, and see if they find her," Candy urged.

I swiveled the knob forward. Stopped at a front-page article.

A fire in a sewing machine factory two days later. Sheila's body had been found in it.

"Arson-murder," I said. "Fifty years ago."

Within the same day's news, Jerome Twyman went missing. We looked around more, but couldn't find any evidence of his body being found—either alive or in another fire.

I hesitated a moment, talking out loud. "So two kids in 1968. A boy and girl. Then twenty-five years later, in '93, Junius Lochland."

"And now Kendrick," Candy finished my thought.

I moved the dial back and forth to find more about the lost boy in '68, but found nothing. I stopped at an entry in the newspaper.

"You went too far," Candy said.

I stared at the lead article. It was a day after the fire in November of 1968.

Freak Snowstorm Leaves Cliff Monroe Sole Candidate

The article was about a debate between two gubernatorial candidates in December of 1968. Halfway through the event, the roof of the building collapsed under the weight of an unexpected snowstorm, killing both candidates.

The situation left the third-party candidate sitting pretty to win governor.

He was an unknown from a rich family, and his name was Cliff Monroe. The father of the current governor, Toby Monroe.

"Toby Monroe is the same guy who met with my boss," I said. The guy who had his eye on me.

"And something fortuitous happened to his family," Candy said. "Around the same time two kids went missing."

I turned to Candy, who still held the ledger. "When you said influential families who started the Order," I asked. "Was the name Monroe on that list?"

Candy opened the ledger and paged back and forth. She stopped on a particular page.

"It is."

I stood up from the microfiche. The Hesters. The Monroes. People in positions of power and wealth were sprinkled all around this case. People I couldn't bring in.

And in the middle of it—powerless black teens.

My mind flashed to that first night in Shonus County. The local coroner was telling me about a girl who had gone missing the same week in 1993 as Junius Lochland.

"Look earlier than 1968, Candy, will ya?" I asked. "See if there's other kids mentioned."

Candy found another page: 1943.

Twenty-five years earlier.

One boy and one girl. Again, a description about receiving two names, and sending "the boys" after them.

I stood up. "This case isn't about neo-Nazis, Candy. It's something older, deeper."

Candy stared at the ledger, paging through it to different sections. "These last names, P.T. They're heads of industry in this state. Big corporations."

"I know," I said.

"Big library donors."

"I never got it from you," I assured Candy.

But there was something else. Something moving through the machinery of my mind.

"Two kids in '43. Two in '68. Two in '93 per the coroner in Shonus. But now we just have Kendrick."

"You think there's a girl out there?" Candy said. "That someone already grabbed?"

"There's missing kids reported every day, Candy." I shrugged. But then I thought of something else.

I called up Remy on her cell. "You get ahold of that boyfriend?"

"An hour ago," Remy said. "But, God, P.T., he's got no idea where Delilah is. Says she left his place two days ago and was headed home. He's gotta be lying, right?"

"Rem," I said. "This girl Delilah—did you say she's the daughter of a minister?"

"Granddaughter," Remy said. "Why?"

I thought of the words in the ledger.

The two names were given to us today.

"Stay where you are, Rem. I'm coming to you."

39

There was no excuse for it. For losing their catch like this.

"The boss is gonna beat the hell out of us," the bigger man said.

"No, he ain't," the man with the beard said. "Because he ain't gonna find out."

The smaller man had about twenty feet of industrial cable in his hand. As they walked through the scrub brush, the rocks around them grew from boulders into craggy formations.

Between two large rocks was an entrance to a cave, about eight feet wide, a crooked O, set at an angle into the rocks.

"What's that for?" the big guy asked, pointing at the cable.

His friend held it up. "*This* is to keep our girl here from escaping."

They climbed into the hole and the smaller man stopped. From inside, he threaded the cable through metal eyeholes chiseled into the limestone. The park service had installed the hook-and-eye system after some college kids got lost or hurt in the caves.

During the off-season, park rangers would run one long chain back and forth through the hooks, closing off any access to the caves.

But the two men had cut those chains a week ago when they got here with the boy.

"I've been down here sometimes and seen visions," the big man said.

They turned and started walking through the tunnel.

"Lightning underground," he continued. "Blood in the water. Shadows moving across the walls."

The big guy dropped down through the hole in the ground and found himself in a long tunnel, angling deeper into the earth.

"Let's split up," the smaller man said. He went to the left while his partner moved right.

But neither of them noticed a pair of blinking eyes ahead of them in the mud.

Gotcha, the girl thought. And she ran as fast as she could the other way—toward the cave entrance.

She heard the men behind her, but she didn't care.

She was faster and would be out that hole and into the night before they could touch her.

But as she reached the entrance, there was something blocking it.

She grabbed at the metal cord blocking the exit hole and screamed for help. But all she could hear was footsteps behind her.

40

Remy and I were in the old man's Charger and headed to Dixon. As I drove, I filled my partner in about the Order and what Candy had found in the library.

Remy showed me pictures of Delilah Ward. She was fifteen and wore a pink jogging jacket. Her hair was tied up in a bun with a chopstick.

I looked to Remy. My partner had always been there for me, and I still hadn't come clean with her.

"Listen, Rem," I said. "We never talked about the picture. The one turned in to the police."

"Well, I've seen it by now." Remy shrugged. "And I'm not saying all you white guys look the same, but honestly, it could be any tall dude with wavy brown hair."

"But the person who turned the photo in—they said it was me, right?"

"There was a note inside with your name on it," Remy said. "Came in addressed to the chief."

The real estate around us shifted from poor to destitute. Small wooden houses with corrugated aluminum over the windows dotted the pastures.

I thought of the flannel I'd found earlier that day with almost no blood on it.

"I didn't kill Virgil Rowe," I said to Remy.

"But you were there?"

"Yeah," I said, reflecting on all that had gone down in the last ten days. "You remember that shrink I went to—after Lena and Jonas died?"

"Sure," Remy said.

"I had a lot of anger issues with my father-in-law, and the psychiatrist talked to me about this thing. She called it 'painting the hallway.'"

"What is that?" Remy asked.

I switched lanes and moved around a U-Haul.

"It's like putting yourself in a bad circumstance and then observing yourself dealing with it."

"Okay," she said.

"So I started tailing Marvin," I said. "I wasn't even sure why. Maybe I was trying to keep myself from beating the crap out of him. Painting the hallway. Or maybe I just wanted to see what he did every day. How he made it through the day without them."

"Where'd he go?" Remy asked.

"The Landing Patch," I said.

"At his age?"

"He wasn't getting any lap dances. It was just a bar close to where it happened. Just the other side of the bridge from the accident."

Remy got quiet, and so did I. "So I was smoking a cigarette in the parking lot one night—with Marvin inside—and I met this girl."

"Corinne?"

"Crimson was her stage name. And she had these bruises—up and down her legs. She was getting the shit beaten out of her. So I promised to come by and give her old man a talking-to."

"Why didn't you call it in?"

"I dunno." I shrugged. I mimicked a call. "Hi, this is P.T., I'm in a parking lot with a stripper who doesn't trust cops. Please come."

Remy nodded in understanding. "But Rowe was alive when you left?" Remy said. "That night?"

"For sure," I said. "I hit him in the nose, and he bled bad. I put my Glock against his kneecap and threatened to kill him if he hit her again."

Remy took this in and motioned me to make a turn onto a small state road that took us higher in elevation. Up into the hills.

"No more secrets?" she said.

"None," I promised her.

"Good," she said. And that was Remy. All forgiven in one word. It's why she's one of the best people I've ever known.

I passed an exit with a faded sign that advertised a commercial crawfish pond. In the distance, an oil rig was being constructed out in a field. It was a strange sight in a state that had never produced a successful petroleum project. Then again, the area had been down so long that anything looked like up, and desperation often masqueraded as hope.

My face tightened. "I'm stuck on something else, Rem. And it's not a small thing."

"What is it?" she asked.

"The picture of me outside of Virgil Rowe's—did anyone pull footage to see who dropped it off at the station?"

"It wasn't like that," Remy said. "An envelope was handed to Abe in the parking lot. Addressed to the chief, but handed to Abe. There's no camera out there. We assume it's the same envelope that was found an hour later in the chief's in-box."

"Sure—but who gave it to Abe?"

Remy directed me toward a gravel road.

"That's the thing," she said. "Abe was in such a mess from the shooting that he didn't pay attention. Some white guy is all he remembers. Handed him an envelope, and Abe put it in Miles's in-box."

On the radio, a bluegrass song by Alison Krauss played. We drove along a wooden bridge, almost at Remy's relative's house.

"What's wrong?" Remy asked.

A cylinder fell into place, locking down something in my mind. Who exactly had "whooped" me.

"So these two guys who tried to kill me—Meadows and the Bearded Man—they were what? Lying in wait for me to show up at the Hester estate?"

"That's our theory," she said. "That's how they followed you so easy."

"But how did *they* know I was coming?" I asked. "Up until forty minutes before, *I* didn't know I was coming. I was at your place while you were suspended. Then up at Schaeffer Lake. And," I pointed out, "I must've been in and out of the Hesters' in ten minutes."

"I don't understand," Remy said.

"Well, were they just waiting there? Was it a coincidence for them that I showed up?"

"Do you have another explanation?"

"I do," I said. "I made one call thirty minutes out. Told one person I was headed to the Hesters'."

"Who?" Remy asked.

"Abe."

"What are you saying, P.T.?"

"He's the only one who knew," I said. "He's also the guy who shot Burkette out at that cabin. Two times, when we all agreed to take him alive."

"No way," Remy said. "Not possible."

"And have you noticed an absence of something, Rem? The picture of Burkette at the county fair with the pig that proves Abe shot an innocent man. It hasn't come forward. Abe's had that evidence box for almost a week now."

"He's been busy," Remy said.

"Abe's also the guy who showed up with a picture that didn't exactly look like me—even

267

though it *was* me? And he's got no idea who gave it to him?"

Remy didn't say anything for a bit.

"Remy, do you remember that journalist Deb from Fox who scooped us?"

"Sure."

"She ambushed me the night we found the cable. I got a ride back to the station, and you were out at that irrigation ditch where we found the bike."

"So?"

"So she knew about our room—closed off, covered in craft paper."

"Every cop in the house saw that paper on the windows."

"But she referred to the *timeline on craft paper,* Rem. The timeline was on the *inside* of the room. Only you and me and Abe saw that."

Remy swallowed. "You gotta go to Chief Dooger."

"Not 'til we bring everyone in," I said. "This guy with the beard who tried to kill me. Donnie Meadows. Even Abe."

"And think about that as you say it," Remy said. "A black cop working with neo-Nazis to kill a black kid?"

I stared at my partner. "If this goes back as far as I think, Rem . . . they could be throwing money around. For all we know, they got something on Abe."

Remy motioned for me to make a right, and I

turned down a dead end, pulling to a stop outside the home of Grammy's cousin.

We got out, and the mood was thick. A girl was missing. And a man we worked with—one of our own—might've turned bad.

The home in front of us was a small one, built from discarded wood and aluminum. On the south side of the house, someone had spray-painted the whole wall. The painting had the body of an angel but the head of a goat. Its outstretched wings were dripping with red paint—drawn to look like blood.

"Jesus," Remy said, walking over to it.

There was a black man, maybe eighty and dead skinny, sitting atop an oil drum in knee-high grass near the side of the house.

"Has this always been here?" Remy asked him.

" 'Bout a month now," he said, his eyes not lifting from the half-empty forty of Olde English wedged between his legs.

I stared at the mural, and then turned toward the front of the house.

"Rem," I said. "There's something we haven't talked about. These reversals of fortune. The lottery win in Harmony after Kendrick was killed. The four-horse superfecta for William Menasco. That telecom company paying Unger a windfall a day after the murder."

My partner opened her iPad. "I'll give you one more. While you were in the hospital, I checked out the guy who won the lottery. His daily truck route went right past Unger's farm. But that morning, he woke up late. He would've seen the murder, P.T."

"But he didn't," I said. "And he got rewarded."

"You think it's this group?" Remy asked. "The Order?"

"The Order can't determine a four-horse win in back-to-back races. They can't make that guy wake up late."

"So what then?" she asked.

"I dunno," I said. We stood there in silence. If this was something we couldn't touch, how could we prove it?

"You and me," I said to Remy. "We gotta find evidence. Not some woo-woo theory. We need to cuff someone."

We walked up the steps to the house.

Inside, Grammy grabbed me into a giant bear hug. "There's my boy," she said.

Grammy was tall like Remy, but wide-bodied and strong, her hair wavy and gray. She wore a burgundy dress with big ivory earrings in the shape of crosses.

"How are you making it through the holidays?" she asked.

"Not that well," I said, feeling a wave of honesty.

She ran a thumb along a scab on my forehead from the accident. "C'mon in, hon."

A few minutes later we had moved into a small living room.

I sat on a metal folding chair, across from the missing girl's little sister, Leticia. The couch the girl sat on had rips in it, the arms of it threadbare.

Leticia explained that she'd originally lied for her older sister, to cover up that Delilah was staying with her boyfriend on campus.

"But then you got a phone call?" Remy asked.

The girl nodded, explaining a call from a screaming voice that sounded like Delilah.

"Tell Miss Morgan and Mr. Marsh exactly what you heard," Grammy said.

"Delilah called on the phone right there." She pointed. "First I had to say yes to the call. Then I heard her voice."

I looked at my partner. Had Delilah called collect?

"She was out of breath and sounded scared," Leticia said.

I turned and glanced at an old rotary-style phone hung on the wall nearby.

"And what did she say?" Remy asked. "The exact words if you can remember."

"She yelled that there's two of them. White guys. And one of them tried to tie her arm behind her back. To break her elbows or something."

I looked at the girl. She was young. Her hair was in pigtails with pink ribbons. "Leticia, did

271

she say it *that* way?" I asked. "Tied her arms behind her back? 'To break her elbows'?"

The little girl's eyes were wet. "Yes, sir," she said.

"And how long was she on the phone with you, hon?" Remy asked.

Leticia looked around, hesitating.

"Tell her," Grammy urged.

The girl wiped at her eyes, steeling herself. "She only talked for a second. But I listened for a long time. The phone clanked—and then it clanked again. I could hear screaming. I got scared and ran to my room."

"You did good, honey," Remy said. She turned to me then. "P.T., could I talk to you for a second?"

We moved into the kitchen, but I knew what Remy was gonna say.

"These are the same guys."

"Sure," I said. "Problem is, we don't know where Meadows is. And the other guy—"

I stopped. Realized I hadn't checked my burner since I'd left the university. To see if Carlos from the lab had sent me anything.

"The other guy—what?" Remy asked.

"Hold on." I grabbed my burner phone and found a text from Carlos.

I opened an attachment, and the face that came up was the Bearded Man. The guy who'd helped Donnie Meadows push my truck into the middle of I-32. Who'd tried to murder me.

272

He had a long face with an angular nose and blue eyes. A dark brown curly beard covered most of his lower face. His hair was wavy and unkempt.

Elias Cobb. Caucasian. Thirty-two years old.

"You recognize him?" Remy asked.

In his booking photo, Cobb wore StormCloud ink, a big tat across his neck and chest. "Yeah," I said.

I wanted to get this guy. To take him to a swamp and weigh down his body with milk jugs full of concrete.

Cobb's address was listed as south of downtown.

509 13th St. #219.

"If we go by the book," I said to Remy, "we could blow a whole day. Watching Cobb . . . getting warrants."

Her eyes met mine. "You got another idea?"

"Well, I don't have a badge right now," I said. "So I got lots of ideas."

41

Remy dropped me in the alley behind 13th Street, and I made my way along the backs of buildings until I found the place. A beaten-up brick apartment building with a door that led in from the back alley.

I stepped into a small lobby. The area smelled like a wet dog, and green Astroturf was peeling up in the corners.

The main purpose of the lobby appeared to be housing the residents' mailboxes, nearly all of them shoved full of flyers and door-hangers. A trash can held even more junk mail, along with a pizza box and an empty six-pack of Rolling Rock.

I threw my satchel over my back, leaving both of my arms free. I grabbed the pizza box and tucked my .22 under my shirt.

Upstairs I knocked on the door to apartment 219.

"Domino's," I said. Holding up the logo in front of the eyehole.

A woman opened the door. She was heavyset, with long black hair and a flowing dress with orange paisleys. Her skin was so red it looked like she used sandpaper as a washcloth.

"I ain't ordered no pizza."

"Well, I don't have any," I said, tossing the box and shoving my foot in the door.

"He ain't here," she said. Nonplussed.

"I haven't said who I'm looking for."

"You're a cop or a PO, and y'all ask the same question."

I pulled out my .22 and pointed it at her head, pushing the door open.

"How 'bout now? He here now? Does his PO do this?"

She was tough, but scared, and she shook her head slowly from left to right.

I pushed my way inside and closed the door behind me, her eyes registering fear as I locked the dead bolt.

"We alone?"

She nodded, and I pulled her close as I cleared the place, my fist holding on to a handful of her hair. "Stay with me, sister," I said. "He pops out of a door, and you're a dead woman."

I pushed her into the bedroom. No one there. Then the kitchen. An old farmhouse sink was piled a foot high with filthy pots and pans.

As we moved out of the kitchen, she grabbed a skillet and came at me. I blocked it with my forearm and twisted her arm behind her back. Shoved her against the wall.

I hadn't noticed until then, but she was missing a tooth. Where her right incisor should've been was just a reddish-black socket of blood.

"Tell me where the fuck Cobb is," I said. "Him and that goddamn giant."

"I don't know," she said.

I bent her arm farther back and felt her wince.

"I got no idea," she hollered.

I spun her around so we were face-to-face. "Then you're worth nothing to me."

I put the barrel of my .22 in her mouth.

She twisted her head to get the barrel out from between her lips. "Wait." She started crying. "He's with those rich people."

"I need a name."

"I think it's Jester? Or Hesmer?"

"Hester?" I asked, pushing the gun against her cheek now.

Her head bobbed up and down.

"Where?" I said.

"They're in Shonus."

I pressed the barrel harder to her face.

"He thinks he's one of them," she said. "Them against the blacks."

My mind was spinning, confused.

Wade Hester had almost been killed the same night I got poisoned. Remy said he was innocent.

I knew I couldn't trust her not to call Cobb, so I dragged her across the room. Used a zip tie to fasten her to the heater pipe in the bedroom. I stood up.

"What the fuck," she cried. "You gonna leave me here?"

I turned on the TV. Tossed her the remote. Grabbed a bag of pork rinds and two beers from the fridge. Gave them to her. "If you're not lying, I'll be back tomorrow and let you go."

A minute later I popped out of the back alley and walked casually to the street. Got in the Charger.

"Was he there?" Remy asked.

"His girlfriend was," I said. I turned to my partner. "The Hesters—we figured they were clean, right?"

Remy nodded. "Wade was almost in a coma from the same poison that got you."

I needed to connect something. For this to make sense.

"That's not what the girlfriend says."

Remy looked confused, and I fired up the ignition, calling Captain Andy Sugarman, the cop up in Shonus County.

"P.T.," he said. "I'm surprised to hear from you."

"How's that?"

"I heard they pulled your ticket."

"Almost," I said. "Your boy Wade Hester saved my job. Him throwing back a couple cups of that coffee after I left," I said. "It put that maid of his on the run and tied her son, Donnie, in a neat little bow for us."

"What can I do for you then?" Sugarman asked.

"I felt bad about Wade. Calling to check on how he's doing?"

"Okay, I guess," Sugarman said. "But I think the whole thing caused a split between the old man and him."

"He tell you that?"

"A deputy of mine," Sugarman said. "He talked to one of their security patrols. I guess Wade moved to their house on the river. Told security to stay away. His old man to stay even farther."

I hung up and thought this over. Maybe the younger Hester didn't know what was going on with the Order. Or maybe he'd *chosen* not to know, until his father's bullshit almost killed him.

I got onto SR-914 toward Shonus. I could've asked Sugarman where the Hesters' second home was, but I didn't want him to know I was nosing around in his backyard.

I asked Remy to pull up a map of the area on her iPad.

"Any street that runs along the Opagucha River?" I asked.

"Two of them," Remy said. "Windy Vista and Highland."

I called our office and got ahold of Donna, my friend in admin. Asked her if anyone named Hester owned property on either road.

"Are you supposed to be working, P.T.?" Donna asked.

"I'm not," I said. "I'm checking out real estate. Thinking of changing occupations. Think you'd

278

buy from me if I was a realtor and you saw my face on a bus bench?"

"Not a chance," Donna said. Then she told me the address.

42

The Hester place was quiet as Remy and I approached. A long curving road led up to a five-bedroom house set along the Opagucha River.

I flicked off the lights and put the Charger in neutral, coming in quiet.

At ten o'clock, most of the lights in the house were off. We knocked on the front door, but no one came. Finally Remy and I pushed our way through a path of elderberry trees planted along the left side of the place.

The Opagucha was a thick black line curving perfectly around the house at night. A swallow-tailed kite flew a pattern above the river, its long narrow wings and forked tail black against the purple sky.

I adjusted my eyes and found Wade Hester at the end of a wooden dock. His feet were in the water, but his body was slumped over in a sitting pose. If you tapped him from behind, he'd probably drop like a rock off the dock and into the water.

"Rem." I pointed, and my partner hustled over, moving through the brush beside the house and onto the dock.

As we got closer, we saw two bottles of Captain

Morgan empty beside him. Wade Hester was dressed in a white T-shirt and pajama bottoms—a far cry from last week's aqua polo and seersucker pants.

"Jesus," I said, pulling him back from the edge and using my phone's light to check his eyes.

"Wade," I said. "It's Detective Marsh from Mason Falls."

"He barely has a pulse," Remy said.

"G-yod," Wade mumbled. "You again? Don't you quit?"

I moved the phone light from left to right, and his irises barely dilated.

"I seen stuff," Wade said. "Just leave me be."

"Let's get him inside," I said.

I put a hand under each armpit, and Remy grabbed his legs. We carried Wade into the house and found the bathroom.

"Into the tub."

Remy turned the cold water on, and Wade's eyes blinked a little bigger.

"Ice," I said, and Remy left for the kitchen.

I crouched beside the tub, plugging the bottom so it started to fill up and wet his body. "I need your help, Wade."

"It's too late," he said.

I looked under the sink and found a bottle of hydrogen peroxide. Looked at Wade and hustled out to where Remy was.

The kitchen and living area were one big room, with white wicker furniture covered in blue cushions.

Remy was yanking the rectangular plastic tub from the freezer that collected the ice.

I ran hot water into a cup and poured in a capful of the peroxide.

"Dump the ice on him."

I fished through the cabinets until I found some dried mustard. Dumped some into the cup, along with a splash of Tabasco.

I mixed it with my finger and ran into the bathroom. Remy had poured the ice on top of Wade, and he was sitting higher. Waking up.

"We need your help," she said.

"I didn't know we were . . ." Wade said. "My father. My brother . . ."

Wade shook like a dog shitting peach pits, half from the ice, half from the liquor.

"There's a girl that's missing, Wade." I raised my voice. "She's not dead. She got away."

"What?" He glanced over. His eyes were glassy.

I put the cup to his lips and force-fed it down his throat. Held his mouth closed as he swallowed.

"We need to know where they bring the kids," Remy said.

Wade's throat spasmed, and he started to vomit—all over his clothes and the ice. It was a familiar smell to me. Rum. Mixed in with some pasta he'd eaten.

When he was done, I held up my phone with Cobb's picture. "Elias Cobb," I said. "Where is he?"

"I didn't know they were gonna poison you."

"I don't care!" I said, willing him to focus on me. "Cobb has a girl. You can make this right, Wade. You can *save* her."

"She's probably dead already."

Remy stood up and grabbed my arm. "You're yelling at him, P.T.," she whispered. "And you're shaking like a leaf yourself."

I looked down at my hands. Remy was right.

"I got this," she said. "Trust me."

I took a step back, standing outside the bathroom door.

"The girl got away, Mr. Hester," Remy said, showing him a picture of Delilah. "She got away from Meadows and Cobb."

A small light appeared in Wade's eyes.

"So now it's up to you," Remy said.

She used the cuff of her shirt to wipe Wade's mouth, cleaning him up.

"I know you feel bad," she said. "And that's 'cause you're a good person at heart." She patted Wade on the chest. "Now you have the power to do something about it and save a woman's life. You want to do that, right?"

Hester looked at Remy and then out at me.

I nodded that she was right.

"There's a state park," Wade said. "It's off I-32 down by you." He looked at Remy now. "They do things in those caves to your people. Horrible things."

43

Cantabon was a small state park, not far from my father-in-law's place. It had hiking trails and underground caverns that filled with water from the Tullumy River.

As Remy and I drove there, my mind made a connection. The first night, outside the Hesters'. I'd heard a bit of a conversation while I was leaving.

"Spelunking," I said to Remy. "They were loading equipment into a sedan outside the Hesters'. One guy I never saw. That was probably Cobb. And that's where I saw the big'un, Meadows, the first time. The guy loading the trunk said the word 'spelunking.'"

"The cable," Remy said. "That's why they had it. The pulley system was for cave climbing."

We drove the next few minutes in silence, with me cranking the speed up and each of us thinking only one thing: *Let Delilah still be alive.*

"You've been to this place before?" Remy asked.

I nodded, bringing the Charger up to ninety on the open road. "We used to park a patrol car up there during the summer when I was a rook. Kids would get drunk. Make out in the caves."

"I never had that duty," she said.

"The state took it over before you could," I said. "Some kid got hurt one night. Now they cordon off the parking lot. Big orange signs in the middle of the road heading in. Even chains over the cave holes. Kinda killed the place."

"So if Delilah is athletic and got away," Remy said, "there's places she could hide?"

"That's the hope."

Remy looked at me. "These guys already set you up once, P.T. How do we know Wade's not lying?"

"No way to know," I said. "But I don't think he cares anymore. That was someone ready to kill himself, Rem."

"Sure, but if you believe the girlfriend, Cobb's working with the Hesters. It could be a trap."

Remy was right. I thought of my rookie year at Cantabon. I'd been dating Lena at the time, and the park was desolate at night. Crappy cell reception. I'd be up there by myself and would call Lena from a pay phone by the restrooms.

"Delilah's little sister," I said to Remy. "She said she heard the phone clank and then clank again. She got scared and ran up to her room. You think she left the phone hanging on her side?"

"Maybe," Remy said.

"There used to be a pay phone out at Cantabon. If the younger sister heard two clanks, Delilah might've left it hanging."

Remy looked at me. "You think we could trace it?"

"We can try."

"Who do we call?" She hesitated. "If Abe finds out—"

"No problem," I said.

Miles Dooger wasn't just the boss in Mason Falls. He was also my friend and first supervisor.

"Miles," I said when he answered. "It's P.T."

But Miles wasn't thrilled to hear from me.

"You get my message?" he said.

"No," I said. "I lost my cell."

"P.T., did you unhook your IV and walk out of the damn hospital?"

"I got a ride home."

"A ride?" he said. "Is that what we're calling it?"

I waited to let him get it out.

"I got a call from Internal Affairs," Miles said. "I had to go down and check the hospital cameras myself. Then pull DMV records and harass some poor guy who works for Uber. You had me doin' real detective work."

"I'm sorry," I said. "I saw my father-in-law, and something snapped. I couldn't be there anymore."

"So you're at home now? Getting some rest?" he asked. "No, you're not, because I went by your house."

"Listen, Miles," I said. "I need a favor."

287

"*You* need a favor? You *owe* a favor."

But I knew he'd come through. When Lena had passed, his wife, Jules, had brought over food every other night for a month, filling the freezer with pink and purple Tupperware.

"Well, I need *another* favor then," I said. "Remy and I were up near Dixon. It's a long story, but she's got a family friend in some trouble. I need to run down a phone number, and I don't want to go through our people."

"Why the heck not?"

"Can you trust me?" I said.

"Not lately."

"There's a girl up here. Black teenager. A couple white guys grabbed her. She's the granddaughter of a preacher, and someone mighta broke her elbows."

"Bullshit," he said.

"No, man. It's true."

"Did they call the police?" Miles asked.

"No," I said. "And they're up here in the hills. Don't trust cops. They called family. That's Remy."

"The rook?" he said. Not wanting to go all-in on information from a rookie detective.

"*Boss,*" I said. I was working just as hard to get him focused as I'd done with Wade. "I think we pull this number and we'll know right quick if it's related to our case or not."

At last he agreed to help, and I told him

Delilah's home number and the time of the call. "I'ma text my buddy Loyo at the phone company," he said. "You remember Loyo?"

"Sure," I said. Miles still had his connections. Old-school guys he came up with back when I was younger.

"Give it five minutes, and he'll call you back at this number."

I hung up, and we continued to haul ass toward the park.

When we got to the street that led into Cantabon, the big sign saying the park was closed had been moved from the middle of the road. Someone had slid it over to the right lane.

The phone rang, and it was Loyo.

"I got your phone call," Loyo said. "Seven minutes long. Collect, from a pay phone."

"Where'd the call originate?" I asked.

"Cantabon State Park," he said. "The parking lot."

I hung up. "It's not a trap," I said to Remy. "Let's go!"

44

A lone Chevy pickup sat in the Cantabon parking lot. The night air was cool, the moon nearly full.

I stared at the truck's plate. We'd already checked what Cobb drove, and this was his. Remy peered in the windows of the cab, her flashlight moving across the front and back seats.

I popped the trunk on my father-in-law's Charger. In a box of auto supplies, I found a switchblade and flipped it open.

I walked over and jammed the knife into the front tires of the truck. Then the back.

Remy's eyes followed me. "Jesus," she said.

"There's a hundred ways out of these caves. I don't want Cobb and Meadows popping out one hole while we go in another."

Remy's flashlight stopped on the front dash of the truck, and I stared over her shoulder. A diagram was drawn in thick black ink on white paper.

In the picture, a figure of a woman was on her knees, her arms tied behind her. Someone had used a red pen to draw blood all over her—a chaotic angry scratching that had torn a hole in the paper.

I put the switchblade in my back pocket and

motioned Remy over to a trailhead. Time was running out.

"What are you thinking in terms of backup?" Remy asked.

She was talking about Abe again. And anyone else dirty who might answer the call. "We might have a legit reason to call in someone who's not from Mason Falls," Remy said, pointing at the state park sign. "It's their jurisdiction."

"True," I said.

"But the state will take a half hour to get here," Remy said.

"Call 'em." I motioned, and Remy took out her phone.

I started down the trail while Remy called the state police. About a hundred feet down, the scrub brush ended, and I turned on my flashlight, finding the mouth of a cave.

"Is that the entrance?" Remy asked, coming up behind me.

"There's a bunch of places to enter." I shrugged. "If she ran from the parking lot, this is the closest."

I crouched, flicking on her flashlight. The hole was a crooked circle, about ten feet all around. Without a flashlight, the inside was pitch-black.

A cable was strung across the hole.

"This is the thing the state police puts over the hole?" Remy asked. "To keep kids out?"

I looked at a link of chain on the ground nearby. "No." I pointed. "That is."

I went back to my father-in-law's car and grabbed a tool. Cut the cable strung across the hole.

As we moved into the cave, the rocky land below us angled downward. The air inside smelled musty. After a minute, we came to a hole in the ground.

"Watch out." I motioned, pointing at the cave floor that dropped out in front of us.

I lowered myself down, into another tunnel.

As Remy and I made our way through the cave, I thought of Delilah. If she was hiding from Cobb and Meadows, she'd also be hiding from us. If we yelled out her name, we could compromise her safety.

We kept moving, but decided to use one flashlight only. The area ahead of us looked like a mining tunnel, taller than it was wide. As we walked down it, the ceiling dripped with water.

I heard a strange echo and turned, pointing the flashlight to my left.

There was a large boulder in the cave. It sat awkwardly, half wedged into the floor.

I moved closer, thinking of the nights I'd worked out here a decade ago when I was on patrol. The caves had charmed me, and I'd come back on the weekends five or six times. Made my way through during the day.

"I've never seen this," I whispered to Remy.

My partner put some weight against the boulder, and it rocked back and forth, revealing a hole in the ground below it.

"You think this stone normally blocks that hole?" she asked.

"Yeah, but not up on its side like this or I'd remember."

I thought of Meadows. He'd have the strength to move the rock. Maybe he got lazy and left it like this.

I pushed against it, and the boulder rolled onto its face, clearing the opening.

I lowered myself down the hole and let go, a three- or four-foot drop until I hit bottom inside another tunnel.

The look of the cave had changed.

A long tunnel, maybe six feet all around, lay out in front of me. But the passageways weren't formed by water. This new tunnel had been carved into the limestone, and overhead there were faded red bricks shaped into curving support arches every ten or fifteen feet.

"C'mon down," I said.

Remy dropped behind me, and our eyes met. This place was man-made, and ten feet below the other cave. The dark areas were pitch-black, and you could hear water dripping all around you.

We walked slowly, and the character of the cave changed even more.

The tunnels were crowded with tangled under-brush—dead wood mostly—gnarled branches that had been placed in the cave by hand.

The pieces of trees were curved like animal antlers and had been placed in the cave. They forced us to slowly move left and then right to get down the tunnel, pointing our flashlights waist-high so we wouldn't catch our clothes on the branches.

We moved into a circular room and found the skulls of animals placed on sticks coming out of the ground. The smell of burning kerosene and rotten meat was in the air, and the darkness around the narrow beams of our lights was suffocating.

Remy pointed her flashlight around. Someone had spray-painted the words *Poison the Water* in fluorescent green on the walls. I thought of the kids with the bloody noses. Of the conspiracy blogger who wrote that the children at Paragon Baptist had not accidentally gotten typhoid.

I recognized the skull of a cow, but there were smaller animals too. A cat maybe. A rabbit. A lamb.

"What the fuck is this?" Remy asked.

We heard muffled voices in the distance, and I put a finger to my lips, moving through the circular room. Coming out of it were five or six tunnels, each turning in different directions. In a few of them old furniture was piled. Warped two-by-fours were stacked atop wooden dressers. A child's mattress and a handful of old dolls.

"Should we split up?" Remy whispered.

I shook my head no and motioned her down the first tunnel.

As we got closer, I heard a voice and we flicked off our lights, moving faster in the dark with Remy behind me, holding on to my belt.

"Prepare the body," a man said. The voice was husky and nasal, and I moved toward it.

"Prepare the body," another voice repeated.

A ripple of light moved across the standing water and through my legs, heading to the voices. It disappeared as soon as I saw it.

"Fuck," Remy whispered. "You see that?"

Then the tone of the first man's voice changed, less ritual and more concern. "I think she passed out," he said.

"Well, wake her ass up. If she's dead, he ain't gonna be happy."

Up ahead the tunnel opened onto a large space filled with calf-high muddy water. I saw Donnie Meadows in blue mechanic's overalls, but he couldn't see me. I craned my neck farther and saw Elias Cobb, the Bearded Man.

My mind flashed to the night I'd seen them last.

"Merry Christmas, asshole," Cobb had said to me, just before pushing me into a dark area on I-32 to die.

Meadows was crouched close to the ground, and Cobb used a Maglite to illuminate the area.

Delilah lay on the ground on her stomach in front of Meadows. The big'un pulled her right hand behind her back and held it there. Then pulled at her left. He had white nylon rope looped around his forearm.

I inched my way forward, my hand moving down to my .22.

The big'un's head looked like it had been shaved recently and was starting to grow back. Black peach fuzz covered his dome. He had blood on his face, but he didn't appear to be cut. It looked more ritualistic. A reddish-black smear on each cheek.

I steadied my weapon atop a rock that faced the two men. I was too far away and my hand was shaking, so I inched closer. Quietly.

Meadows pulled hard on Delilah's left hand, and the girl either woke up or stopped playing dead.

She flipped onto her back and came around with her right. Slapped him across the face.

"Bitch," Meadows said, dropping both knees onto her stomach as she tried to wriggle free.

The girl gasped at his weight, and Meadows flipped her body back onto her belly in one quick move. He grabbed her two arms and dropped them into a knot he'd prepped.

"Let's see how this feels," he said, ready to yank them backward and shatter her elbows.

I flicked on the flashlight. *"Police! Hands in the air!"*

Cobb took off down a tunnel at the far end of the cave, and Meadows dropped the rope, running after his buddy.

Remy and I splashed into the big room where the men were a minute earlier, heading toward Delilah.

A shot rang out, and a flash lit up the cave. I dove into the wet muck for cover, and time seemed to slow down. A second shot came and then a third.

"I'm hit," Remy grunted, the noise of the gunfire still echoing off the limestone.

I ran my hand across Remy's arm in the darkness. She winced as I touched her biceps, and I felt blood moving out of her. A small stream, but steady.

Remy's breath was shallow.

I crawled over to Delilah. Untied the rope from around her hands. "You okay?" I whispered.

The girl nodded, but said nothing, and I flicked on my flashlight, looking around.

My .22 was gone, down into the mud. I searched through the silt, but found nothing.

The splashing of boots subsided, and I lifted myself up, taking off my MFPD jacket. I bit a hole into the arm of the windbreaker and tore a strip of it off. Moved over to Remy and wrapped the strip of fabric tight around her arm, right where the bullet had cut into her.

"Jesus." Remy winced, but I ignored her, tightening it hard. Then ripped a second strip and did it again.

I stared at the darkness where Cobb and Meadows had gone.

We could wait for the state police to come and see this place. The tunnels were probably full of evidence of human and animal sacrifice.

But that wasn't gonna happen.

Cobb and Meadows had wheeled me out onto the highway to kill me. Now they'd shot my partner. Almost killed Delilah. There was no way I was letting them get away.

I handed my car keys to Remy. "I'm going after them," I said. "Get Delilah out. If you don't see me up top, leave and get to a hospital."

Before she could argue, I took off, hustling down the tunnel where Cobb and Meadows had gone.

As I ran, the water on the ground disappeared, and the earth angled upward. I could tell I was moving northeast, curving back toward where Remy and I had come in.

My heartbeat and breath echoed in my head, and I passed charcoal drawings on the walls.

One depicted an avenging angel. A drawing that looked like the one we'd seen beside Delilah's home. Another was the all-seeing eye, similar to what was carved in the tree where Kendrick had been abducted.

"You crazy bastards," I muttered, moving faster.

As I reached the end of the tunnel, I saw a bit of moonlight through a hole. Cobb was squeezing out of the cave through an open space. An opening I would have more trouble getting through, with my height.

I rushed over, but Cobb was gone, off into the scrub brush.

"Shit," I said, suddenly worried that Remy and Delilah would run into him in the parking lot.

I lifted myself up, using the same foothold that Cobb had used.

As I did, a weight hit my side, and I landed in a pool of mud.

I looked up and saw Donnie Meadows on top of me. He planted his knees on my stomach and pushed my head backward under the water.

I struggled, trying to punch Meadows, but I was on my back and barely keeping my head above the surface.

I started taking in water and mud. I reached my hands around to hit him, but Meadows was too big. His body was too far from me, his reach too long.

"Fuckin' die already," he said, his voice guttural and thick.

My head went under, and I held my lips closed.

Even as I struggled, a thought came to me. Nothing means anything except strength. Right and wrong, justice—these were all well and good. But if Meadows was stronger, I'd drown, just like Jonas and Lena had.

Meadows was slamming my head backward against the ground, and black smears were shooting across the insides of my eyelids.

I felt something hard against my back and reached around, my hand fumbling along the cave floor.

My father-in-law's switchblade had fallen out of my back pocket.

I brought it around, striking Meadows in the gut. He let out a noise, and I lowered my aim. Slicing at him again and again, each time aiming for the femoral artery with Marvin's hunting knife.

Meadows thrashed around, reaching for my hand. But I slashed at anything that moved, and his screams echoed off the cave walls until the place went silent.

His body went slack, and he slumped onto me, the initial hit taking the breath from my chest.

I pushed his weight off me and lay there in the dark, exhausted in the pool of red mud. I was done. "No more," I said aloud. "No more."

But a minute later I remembered Cobb had gone out the hole and was headed toward Remy. I lifted my body up and climbed out—into the night air.

When I got to the parking lot, Remy was there

with Delilah. The teenager reeked of urine and mud, and her eyes were black holes with no emotion.

"Cobb's truck was gone when we got here," Remy said. "They got away."

I looked to where the Chevy pickup once was.

"Not they." I gave Remy a look. "Just Elias Cobb."

Remy glanced back to the cave, following me.

"Cobb must be riding on rails with four flat tires," I said. "He's not gonna get far."

"Go," Remy said. "We'll wait for the staties."

I got in the Charger, not sure where I was headed. About two miles down the road, I saw a giant chunk of tire. Then another in the dirt nearby—heading onto some private land.

A single mailbox was set in the dirt, and a metal cord that looked like it blocked the entrance lay on the ground.

I'd seen this place before. A big plot of empty land with some old buildings on it. The part that backed up to the interstate had electrified fence for miles.

I flicked off my lights and drove slowly, the gravel road widening to a giant open plot of scrub brush.

Far up ahead of me, I saw Cobb's pickup.

45

left the Charger and went on foot, crouching as I moved through the waist-high scrub brush— six or eight steps at a time—toward the truck.

Ahead of me by about two hundred feet was the pickup. I could see a figure standing near the hood of the vehicle, a lit cigarette in his hand. He had the parking lights of the truck on, nothing else. The night sky had grown darker, and the air smelled like hickory.

I stopped moving and slowed my breathing, lying down in the brush.

Beyond the truck, I saw shipping containers all around the quarter-mile-wide swath of dirt. Each container was a few feet over from the next, and door holes had been sawed into the sides of them.

I'd seen this type of setup before. A police training course outside of Charlotte on door-to-door warfare.

But this was not police land.

I started moving. Eighty feet from Cobb and the truck. Fifty feet. The scrub brush moved from waist-high to thigh-high, and I lay down again.

In the still of night, I could hear Cobb's voice.

"Well, why the hell not?" he said. "I'm here at their place. They know *me*."

I craned my neck to see who he was speaking

to, and a glint of metal shone beside Cobb's face: his cell.

"Well, who the hell do they think did the heavy lifting on all this shit?" he asked. "And now they don't want to let me in? Really?"

The conversation went quiet, and Cobb cursed, putting the phone away. I glanced around the land a second time, wondering whether it was owned by the Order.

A spotlight came on in the distance. Far beyond the shipping containers was a tower, three stories high. The light shone across the tops of the containers and lit up the pickup truck.

Cobb put his phone on the hood of the truck and raised both hands high. Someone was looking him over. He knew not to come closer without permission.

The light flickered out then, and I considered the situation. Kendrick had been killed by Virgil Rowe. Then Rowe had been killed by Cobb and Meadows. Cobb left Meadows in the cave with two cops.

Whoever held the payroll behind these murders might be directing each person to eliminate the next at the right time. And Cobb was the last man standing. If he died, we'd have no one to question.

I started to text Remy to tell her where I was. But at the top of the phone, I saw the date glowing. December 31, 1:20 a.m.

Just one day left in the year.

I thought about the pattern of deaths every twenty-five years. Of all the near frantic activity in November and December.

What if the Order failed to kill the girl, and the pattern broke?

What if this was the last day for them to fulfill their ritual?

I had lived in this part of the country all my life. I'd seen peculiar people. Fabled wonders. I'd witnessed roadside religious miracles that I couldn't explain, and unimaginable situations like my wife's death.

Was I refusing to believe this?

Something impossible, but right in front of me?

That some group had been around for a hundred and fifty years, sacrificing black kids? And that in exchange for this act, they created wild reversals of fortunes for themselves and their members? And even for those tangentially involved? Like Unger at the farm with the underground cable, or the guy who won the lotto?

Then something hit me.

If the Order welcomed Cobb in, he'd tell them Delilah was alive. Which would give them the next twenty-three hours to find some other innocent black girl to torture and murder.

I had to get to Cobb before they took him in.

I texted Remy a quick message, telling her I needed help.

10–78. Land nearby. Follow tires.

I took off then, moving at a sprint through the dark.

The night air was cool, and my shirt was soaked with a mixture of sweat and Donnie Meadows's blood.

I moved fast. Heel toe. Heel toe. Thirty feet out.

Cobb was smoking again. Leaning against the hood of his truck. His back to me.

Twenty feet out.

At fifteen feet, Cobb turned and saw me, but I was too fast. I hit him with all my weight.

I had three inches and forty pounds on him, and his phone flew through the air as he landed under me. Without my .22, I had to take him down with pure muscle.

I held his throat with my left hand and hit him hard with my right. Once across his jaw. A second across his nose.

I felt blood under my fingers on the third punch, but he got his hands under me, sticking his lit cigarette into my abdomen.

I yelled, and he pushed my body off his, getting up.

He looked around, disoriented. Then ran around the front of the truck, toward the passenger side.

Did he have a weapon inside?

I dove across the hood of his truck, my right

hand grabbing his shirttail and yanking him backward before he could open the passenger door.

He landed atop me, but I pummeled him in the kidneys. Once. Twice. I could hear him whimper, but I kept it up. Thinking of Kendrick. Of my son and wife. On the fifth punch, the spotlight on the tower flickered on, and I pushed him off me, instinctively moving to the darkness and leaving him on the side of the pickup that faced the tower.

I scrambled around to the other side of the truck and yanked open the driver's-side door. Hit the locks button so Cobb couldn't open the door on his side.

"He's a cop!" he yelled in the direction of the tower. "Kill him."

"They're not gonna help you, Cobb," I hollered. "They're getting rid of everyone who knows anything."

Cobb took off suddenly. Not toward the tower, but sideways. There was something there in the dark. A rusted tractor that was part of the training course. We could see each other now, him behind the old piece of farm equipment and me behind his truck.

The tower light went off.

"They're coming to kill you, pig!" Cobb screamed, his body hidden behind the tractor.

"They're coming for both of us," I said.

He took off again, running at an angle back toward an old camper shell set into the dirt. Cobb was behind me now, and I couldn't see him. If he kept working his way back to the road where I'd driven in, I'd left the keys in the Charger. He could drive off and leave me here.

"Shit," I said, taking off toward the tractor and sliding into the dirt behind it. From the camper shell, Cobb saw me.

He began to make his next move through the dark, but stopped.

That was when I saw where he was looking.

It was a four-point buck. A beautiful male deer, standing in the open area that Cobb was about to run toward.

The majestic animal could see Cobb, but didn't appear scared. It almost looked domesticated, walking slowly toward him.

Cobb stopped moving, and some synapse fired in my brain.

"Get back," I yelled, but it was too late. I heard the zipping noise. Then saw an arrow land in Cobb's chest, right at his heart. Another one entered the buck, felling him.

I took off toward the camper shell, sliding behind it. Cobb's body was on the ground a few feet away. I reached out and grabbed him by his shirt, pulling him behind the shell.

The arrow was stuck deep into his body, and I knew not to pull it out.

He had blood smeared across his teeth, and more came out of his mouth, mixed with bubbles.

"Who paid you, Elias?" I said. "Who's behind this?"

"Na-nev," he mumbled, blood across his teeth.

"Don't protect these bastards." I pounded on his chest. "They let that buck out as cover. They wanted you dead and quiet."

"Fuck, fuck." His breathing became labored.

"Who sent you to kill Kendrick?" I pushed him. "Who's behind all of this?"

"Lots of good men in the Order," he stuttered. "Even some of *you,*" he said, grinning at me, before his whole body convulsed.

The anger was building inside me. But there was still someone out there in the night. Deadly with a bow and arrow.

"Mason Falls Police," I shouted. "Get on the ground."

I heard a commotion behind me. Three or four police cars pulling in with lights and sirens.

"Detective Marsh," I hollered back to them. "I got a man down. I need an ambulance!"

The lights from the squad cars came on. So did the tower light from afar. The place was suddenly lit like dusk.

A man dressed in full camouflage and face paint was some thirty feet from the camper shell that I was crouching behind.

The man's knees were on the ground, and a bow lay beside him. His hands were laced behind his head.

"You're on my land," the camoed archer yelled. "I thought I was shooting that buck. It was an accident."

I looked down at Cobb, dead. I took in the odor of his blood.

Who was I if I couldn't stop this? If I couldn't make this right?

I always told myself I wasn't prejudiced. I'd married a black woman. Was raising a half-black son. But I saw the divide. Eating at restaurants with Lena. Feeling eyes on me at the park with Jonas. When will we learn that it's not about being color-blind? It's about respect and humanity, pure and simple.

Cobb had bled out, but his body was hidden from the guy kneeling. The archer didn't know if he'd killed him or not.

"Cobb's still alive," I yelled as loud as I could to the patrolmen behind me. "He's talking. Someone write this down!"

I racked my brain for the names from the ledger Candy had found in the university archives. "The Stover family," I yelled. "The Hennessey family," I said. "The Monroes. Is someone writing this down?"

A blue-suiter was moving past me and approaching the archer, a pair of cuffs in his hand. The patrolman stared at me talking to myself while Cobb lay dead as a doorknob, his body propped up in my lap, behind the camper shell.

"Order of the South," I yelled. "Granton family. Shannon family. Kane—"

As I said the name Kane, it finally hit me what went down with the drunk. The lawyer had come the night before to the jail. Bernard Kane must've told the lawyer what he'd said to me about Kendrick's elbows. About *all* the kids' elbows. The lawyer had ordered Kane to hang himself.

The archer started talking.

"*Andine Emphavuma,*" he suddenly yelled in some foreign tongue. "*Endibweret Serenee Mdima.*"

These were the words from the book, and a chill ran along my spine. The archer was beckoning power from the darkness. I saw a touch of fog move quickly along the ground in the distance.

He was also shifting his body, slowly kneeing himself over toward his bow.

Go on, I thought. *Go for it.*

I wanted to face off against whatever power he thought he had.

"Cobb's partner was Donnie Meadows," I yelled. "He got paid in cash. The Oxley family. The—"

It happened almost in slow motion then.

The archer went for it. Stopped chanting and took matters into his own hands.

Grabbed for his bow and got to his feet.

"Get down," I screamed to the blue-suiter near me, but it was too late.

An arrow zipped into the patrolman's stomach.

The patrolman fell toward me, and I was weaponless. I pulled the patrolman's Glock from his holster as he landed.

I rose up behind the camper shell, just as the archer pulled back his bow a second time.

The arrow released. Coming right toward my chest.

I felt my index finger tap the patrolman's Glock. Once. Twice. Center mass.

I tried to shift my body away from the arrow, but it was headed straight for me.

The archer's body flew backward from the hit, landing in the dirt.

I stood there. Looked down at myself.

I lifted my right arm away from my chest, to see if the arrow was in me and I just hadn't felt it yet, from all the adrenaline. But it wasn't. It was on the ground, about ten feet behind me.

The patrolman shook his head, lying injured next to me. "That hit you," he said. "I saw it."

I felt along my right side, noticing my shirt was torn, but nothing more.

"No," I said to him.

I moved around the camper shell and kicked

the bow away from the archer. On his shirt was stitched the name *F. Oxley*. A descendant of the man who'd founded the Order.

His chest was seizing up, and I crouched beside him. The ground all around him was flooding with blood. One of my shots had hit him directly in the heart. Another in the neck.

"The girl's alive," I whispered in his ear. "By the time we sort you people out, it'll be New Year's Day. Your little club is over."

He grabbed my arm, his blue eyes wide. "You think you fixed something? You weakened a nation." He started coughing blood. "The industry. The luck. The dirt—"

An ambulance slid beside us, and two paramedics rushed out. Pushed me out of the way.

But Oxley was gone, his injuries too massive.

I stood up. Took a few paces toward the tower in the distance and the spotlight. "I know all of your names," I yelled. "And what you've done. I have your ledger."

I turned and walked back to the old man's Charger. At angles to it were two cop cars. One from the state and one of ours.

Standing near ours was Abe Kaplan. His hair was all mussed. It looked like he'd been woken up to come out here.

The words from Cobb were still banging around in my head. *Good men in the Order.*

312

Even some of you, he'd said. *Cops,* I thought.

"P.T.," Abe said.

I clocked him across the jaw.

Abe took a step back. "What the hell?"

A state patrolman in blue just stood there. Not sure what to do.

I pointed toward the tower. "Those your friends? You know this place?"

"What?" Abe squinted.

"You get off killing kids, Abe?"

"Fuck you, P.T."

"If you were here earlier, you could've shot Cobb yourself—just like you shot Burkette at that cabin."

Abe's fist hit my jaw before I saw it coming.

I tasted blood on my lip and tackled him. We rolled into the scrub brush until he was on top of me. Holding my shoulders down.

"That was a clean shot at that cabin," he said. "So whatever story you're making up in your head—you better quit it right now."

A patrolman pulled us apart.

"The night I drove to the Hesters'," I said. "Nobody but you knew I was going there. They knew I was coming and poisoned me."

Abe looked confused, his hair full of dirt. "What?"

"And the picture of me outside of Rowe's," I said. "What did the Order offer you? Money? Protection?"

"I got no clue what you're—"

"The journalist who knew about our timeline in the war room?" I said to Abe. "Are you saying you didn't talk to anyone?"

"I talked to you," he said. "And I report up the chain. You know that about me. I'm military through and through."

I turned and walked off. Still pissed.

Abe followed me. "Where the hell are you going?"

"Who'd you let into our war room—other than me and Remy?"

"No one," he said. "Seriously. You. Me. Remy. Stash."

I stopped, and Abe stared at me for a minute before shaking his head. "Screw you, P.T.," he said, walking over to the ambulance.

I sat down in the driver's seat of the old man's Charger and exhaled, my shoulders slumping against the black vinyl.

It was over. Finally over.

What we couldn't do for Kendrick's family, we'd done for Delilah. Found the bastards before they killed another kid.

My phone rang, and it was Remy. "Did you find Cobb?"

"He's dead," I said flatly.

A strange buzzing settled around me. In the last hour I'd killed two men. And I didn't have a badge.

314

"They want to talk, P.T.," Remy said. "The state guys."

"Yeah," I said. Realizing that the cops here had seen this go down. But Meadows was dead in that cave with no witnesses. "I'm on my way," I said.

46

I drove the few minutes back to the Cantabon parking lot, which by this time was filled with state patrol vehicles.

Delilah was dressed in a hospital smock and covered in blankets. She clutched Remy's cell phone, talking to her little sister while seated on the back lip of an open ambulance.

My partner's arm was patched and in a sling.

A state cop introduced himself as Lawrence Neary. He was slender, with gray spiky hair and a mustache. He wore the rank of a senior investigator.

"We just pulled Mr. Meadows from the cave," Neary said. "That was one big boy soaking in a pool of his own blood, Detective Marsh."

"Yeah," I said.

Nothing more unless he asks, Purvis urged.

"Is there a reason you called us when you got here, Detective? You know, your own people would've gotten here faster."

"It's your jurisdiction," I said. "I worked the area as a rook. I remember the year we handed it over to the state."

Neary nodded. "Can I ask how you took 'im down? You're a big guy, but Meadows must've had ten inches on you."

"Luck, I guess," I said. "Meadows slammed me against the rock floor about ten times. I remember blacking out. In one of those moments I felt the knife in my back pocket. Until then I'd forgotten about it."

"Well, twenty-six slashes later, he's not getting back up."

I bit my lip. In my mind I'd cut Meadows four or five times, searching for his femoral. Not twenty-six.

Neary peppered me with other questions he'd need for his report. I told him how Remy and I had found Kendrick in the field, just hours after finding Virgil Rowe. How Meadows and Cobb had hired the arsonist to burn Kendrick alive.

I left out parts that I couldn't explain. Parts that involved magic and wonder.

"Can I ask you a favor?" I said to him.

"Name it."

"We're still sorting out a couple questions," I said. "How information got out of our department. You mind leaving a car with Delilah overnight? For her safety . . ."

Neary agreed. "If there are some loose ends and you need a clean team on this, P.T.," he said, "you just let me know."

Then he asked if Remy wanted to take Delilah back to her family.

We drove in silence, with Delilah in the back

317

of the Charger with Remy. Occasionally I'd hear her sniff, and Remy would pull her in close.

Back at her house, Delilah's family expanded quickly. Cousins came out of nearby houses. Friends arrived from church.

Bowls of salad and macaroni were laid out on an end table. Piles of sandwiches on a dining table.

In the kitchen, Remy's grammy gave me a big hug.

I stared out the window at a dead tributary of the river. Dried twigs piled a foot high along each side, and I couldn't help thinking about which things in life made sense and which didn't. My wife's SUV had been swept down a different branch of this same river. She was gone, but I was still here.

Kendrick was gone, but Delilah had been saved.

I walked out into the field and crouched in the high grass.

I thought of Lena, full of goodness, and Jonas, an innocent. Had I killed the two men tonight to settle a score? And what the hell was I doing? Putting a gun in Cobb's girlfriend's mouth? Who was I now?

I fell to my knees. All that sadness masquerading as anger melted, and I broke down. A whimper turned into a sob. Before I knew it, my head was buried in the saw grass, and my shoulders shook like I was having a seizure.

When the tears stopped, I stood up and wiped at my face, heading back to the house.

I sat on the porch, my foot resting on an old soccer ball hidden in the thick kudzu that was pervasive in Georgia.

I would have to go talk to Miles. Abe was my former partner. But there was only one path with a dirty cop: cut out the cancer.

Delilah walked onto the porch with Remy, the young girl's hair wet from a long shower.

"How are you holding up?" I asked.

She shrugged but didn't speak.

"You're a brave girl, Delilah," I said.

"I was scared," she said. "But then I heard *you guys* were coming. At that point I was just holding on. Trying to buy time."

I scrunched up my brow, not following her.

"Sorry," I said. "What do you mean, you heard we were coming?"

"About five minutes before you got there, the really big man got the heads-up that you were on your way to the cave. Said they might have to move me to some other location nearby. 'Change how it's always been done.'"

Remy's eyes met mine. The words "how it's always been done" were creepy enough, but it wasn't that.

How the hell did they know we were coming?

Wade Hester could've had a change of heart and called Meadows. But Remy had sent a state police car up to Shonus to check on Wade. They'd found him passed out on his couch. Front door unlocked and sleeping the liquor off.

"You heard them say those words?" Remy said. "The cops are coming?"

Delilah nodded, and we asked her more, but that was all she knew.

I'd been leaning against the edge of the porch, and I stood up. Feeling something tighten in my stomach. A spasm. A wave of nausea.

I wiped at the blood that lined the corner of my mouth, right where Abe had clocked me.

I'd gotten it wrong.

"A military guy. Through and through," I whispered. The expression that Abe had used. A sentence about chain of command.

"What is it?" Remy said.

"Stay with Delilah," I said. "Until I figure something out." I turned and headed out to the Charger.

"Where are you going?" Remy asked.

"I'm not sure yet," I said.

But it was a lie. I sped out of Dixon and on toward Mason Falls.

Over the bridge at the Tullumy River I passed the Landing Patch. A couple minutes later I found a dirt road that led up to a ranch-style home.

47

I parked the Charger outside the home of my boss, Miles Dooger. On the front lawn, two reindeer made of string lights stood sentinel.

After a few minutes of knocking, Miles met me at the front door. He was dressed in sweats and a Harley T-shirt that barely covered his gut.

"I need to bounce something off you," I said.

"It's two a.m., P.T."

I shrugged, and Miles waved me inside.

We walked into a wood-paneled study with dark curtains covering the windows. Since he didn't ask about the mess at the compound, I was guessing he hadn't been briefed yet.

"Did I wake Jules up?" I asked.

"She's at her sister's with the kids."

Miles offered me a drink, but I passed. He poured two inches of The Macallan 25 single malt in a lowball glass and sat down in a leather recliner.

I was hyper. My mind running faster than my mouth.

"This case has been tough for me," I said. "And the poisoning and accident—it caused me to think about some things I've been avoiding."

Miles rested the Macallan on the curve of his

321

stomach and took off his glasses. "That's good, right?"

"I guess." I nodded.

I walked over to a bookcase full of sports mementos. There was a signed picture from the '80s of Hawks' forward Dominique Wilkins. A baseball set in a clear cube featuring autographs of every player from the '95 Braves.

"Two hours ago, I was damn near convinced that Abe was a dirty cop." I touched the corner of my mouth. "This isn't from the accident. Abe's got a solid right hook."

Miles smiled at me. From the other room, a cell phone rang.

"There was a moment, Miles," I said. "Abe and I went at it. And I asked if he'd broken our rule and let anyone else inside the conference room where we'd put up our timeline on Kendrick's death."

"And what'd he say?" Miles asked.

"He said he'd just let a few people in the room. Me and Remy. And Stash."

"Stash?" Miles cocked his head.

"I know," I said. "I didn't make much of the word. It's been hard to make much of anything lately. I've been distracted. This whole mess started on the anniversary of Lena's and Jonas's deaths."

"I'm sorry you had to lead this," Miles said. "But we needed you."

"Miles, those guys in the cave at Cantabon,

322

where Loyo traced that call? They knew we were coming."

"What do you mean 'they knew'?"

"The girl heard them talking," I said. "So I started to question myself. I've been thinking all week how unreliable I've been. From the beginning of this thing—showing up to help that stripper."

"You've been reckless all *year*, P.T. You're *lucky* you got friends on the force. Guys who watch out for you."

"Like you?" I asked.

"Like a lot of us."

"But then when it happened to my father-in-law," I said. "His house. No forceful B and E. Just someone in there. The door wide open. It got me thinking about who's got keys to both houses."

"What'd you come up with?"

"Me," I said. "I keep this spare set of keys in my locker at the station. It's Lena's key ring. Got recovered from her car in the river. They were in her purse, Miles. You remember? The arguments I got into with you about the keys?"

Miles's mouth turned up a bit. He hated when I brought up the investigation into my wife's death because he knew I was unsatisfied with the results. Marvin was never held at fault, and no car that hit Marvin was ever found. A crime with no criminal.

And he'd stepped in to personally lead that case.

"See, Miles, I keep those keys in my locker because they remind me of my unique point of view. People think I'm a little nuts. Sarcastic. A drunk."

"You can be all those things," Miles said.

"But there's your core, you know? You always know your own core."

"Are you sarcastic at your core?" Miles asked. "Or a drunk?"

"I'm a detective," I said. "There's a lot of cops out there in the world. Good guys. Mean well. Smart." I stared Miles down. "But only a couple good detectives."

The house phone rang in the other room.

"I kept thinking that my father-in-law was giving Lena a push start with his car at the roadside," I said. "But her keys were found in her purse. When you got an old stick shift with a shit battery and you get a push, you need the keys in the ignition. You gotta be ready to pop the clutch."

"So now you believe in Marvin?" Miles asked. "After all this time?"

"It doesn't matter what I believe in," I said. "See, I keep those keys in my locker as a symbol. They remind me to think differently than others."

"Okay."

"But last week—the keys weren't there anymore. So I knew a cop from our squad had taken them."

"Taken your keys?" he asked.

"And I said this to Remy last night, and you know what she said?"

Miles ran his hands through his salt-and-pepper hair. "No, what'd the rook say that was so brilliant?"

"She told me there's a camera in that room. Way up in the top corner. Real small one. Because cops put their guns in their lockers. We gotta have records.

"And I'm thinking about this," I said. "And then about what Abe said."

I pointed at Miles's mustache. " 'Stash,' he said. I heard the word a few weeks ago from a guy in patrol. I was confused. I said, 'What's "stash," ' "—and he said to me, 'That's what the rookies call the boss. "Stash." ' "

Miles's face turned pale, his fingers instinctively touching his wide gray mustache.

"So 'Stash' was the other person Abe allowed in that room with the timeline. That's you."

"You're talking crazy, P.T.," he said. "You need to think about what you're saying."

"Miles," I said. "You were the only one who knew we were headed to see Cobb and Meadows at that cave. You warned someone. And then you sent two cops into the hands of murderers."

Miles stood up.

"So first it was Abe who's dirty and now it's me?" he said. "We're all dirty, and you're the big hero?"

My stomach turned. I felt like I was gonna vomit.

"I'm no hero," I said.

"You're out of control, P.T. And you know why?"

"Why?"

"You're racked with guilt about your wife," Miles said. "See, I know what other people don't," he said. "What your father-in-law doesn't know."

A fire began to burn inside my chest.

"I know Lena called you," Miles said, "the night she died."

The blaze spread, the flames licking at my heart.

"I know she asked you to come get her," Miles said. "It's easier to blame your father-in-law. Just like you're blaming this on me."

"No," I whispered. But Miles had led the investigation into my wife's death. He knew things.

"I saw the call on her cell records. Three minutes long, so it wasn't a voicemail. And it was made from the roadside to you—at the precinct."

For a moment I was back there, in my office, working last December. Lena had called and asked if I could pick her and Jonas up. Her car was dead at the roadside.

"But you were too busy to get her, weren't you, P.T.?" Miles said. "Worse, you're the one who told her to call her dad, knowing he drank every afternoon. And why? Because of some little robbery that only *you* could solve? Only the very special P. T. Marsh could handle?"

In an instant, the fire was out.

"The Golden Oaks," I mumbled.

My body was frozen. Remembering the case I'd been working on.

Thirty-three dollars and a Cherry Coke had been stolen from the Golden Oaks Mini Mart.

"That was more important than Lena's and Jonas's lives," Miles said. "And the baby's."

I raised my eyes off the floor. Stared at the bottle of Macallan. Lena had been pregnant at the time, and only a couple people knew. I could taste the whisky hitting the back of my throat.

"So everyone's corrupt except you?" Miles asked. "Everyone's made mistakes, but not you?"

My mind wanted to give in. To drink. To hide. How could I face that I'd let my wife and son die?

But some voice inside told me it was okay. Told me I was already forgiven.

Maybe it was Lena's voice. Or maybe it was someone else. Someone who I never met face-to-face. Like Kendrick Webster.

"You're right, Miles," I said. "I *am* full of guilt.

327

But it didn't stop me from focusing long enough to kill Cobb and Meadows."

In the kitchen, the house phone rang again. "I don't have time for this," Miles said.

"See, we got the state police involved since the murder happened in a state park. So you don't have jurisdiction, Miles. You can't control this."

Miles's eyes went wide.

"That phone ringing in the other room," I said. "It's the sound of the end for you. Oxley is dead. The Order of the South, uncovered. The governor, his days numbered."

Miles turned toward the kitchen.

"I've got proof," I said.

"What—you looked at that camera footage in the locker area?"

I nodded, even though I hadn't done this yet.

"I'll tell everyone I grabbed those keys *for you*," Miles said. "That you were drunk and couldn't get into your own house."

So it *was* him. Inside, my heart fell. Hearing it from his own mouth.

"I've got the girl hidden away, Miles. The state police watching her. She heard everything they said. The calls they got."

"What do you want?" Miles said. "You want my job? Is that it?"

"I want to know why," I yelled. "Was it for money?"

Miles laughed. "It wasn't money. It was this

shit—your arrogance checking into every case to make sure the rest of us got it right."

"I'm your best detective."

"You *were* my best detective. You've been drunk six days a week since your wife died."

"No," I said.

"You broke into a stripper's house and beat the shit out of her boyfriend," he said.

"Like this thing with your wife's keys. You constantly rechecking out her murder book. You think I'm not told by Records every time you do that?"

I stared at him, confused. "But you're my friend."

"We're peacekeepers together, P.T. Nothing more. And if we're lucky, we do that for two decades. After that, we gotta think about what comes next."

I shook my head, useless with the shock of it.

"How do you think small towns get funded for highways?" Miles asked. "This place gets an off-ramp. That place gets a crime lab."

"So you did this to run some friggin' crime lab?"

Miles cocked his head at me. "Jesus, P.T., you still don't get how half the crimes get solved around here? It's not you or your rookie partner and how damn good y'all are. It's relationships."

I smarted at this.

"You think it's these lessons you give Remy on

what to do and not do?" he said. "You're so damn righteous."

Miles exhaled loudly. "So when I needed someone to take a knee for the rest of us," he said. "When people of importance in Georgia came to me. It didn't even take me a second to think of your name."

I was confused. Was it really as simple as this? I'd been sold out this easily?

"Well, you don't get to play God." I stood up. "And you're finished."

Miles started laughing. "From the locker thing?"

"I got information on the Order," I said. "I got the girl. The state will bring in your buddy Loyo and trace the call you made to sell me out. And when I hand everything over, they're gonna put your ass in prison."

"Fuck you," he said to me.

"You ready to have your wife and daughters visit you in jail?" I asked. "Or maybe they won't even come—because they'll be too ashamed. Then you'll have no one, just like me."

"No," he said.

"It's time to call the press and retire, Miles."

"No." He raised his voice. "You report to *me*. To me. Not the other way around."

"You better tell your buddy Governor Monroe. It's you or him that goes," I said. "And I'll bet he saves himself."

I headed for the door. "There are fifty feet between your office and a cell," I yelled. "If you show up at the station house, I'm gonna cuff your ass and walk you there."

"Go to hell, Marsh."

"Hell?" I said. "I've been there a year. I'm its best citizen."

I wanted to hurt him. To see him rot in jail. But the look on his face was easy to read. He knew he was finished.

"Forty-eight hours," I warned. "Have a nice retirement."

I slammed his door and got in the Charger. Started speeding back toward the bridge faster than I should've. A minute later I threw on the brakes and pulled to the side of the road.

Miles Dooger and two thugs weren't enough. They weren't nearly enough to correct the evil that had been visited on this community and these families for a hundred and fifty years.

I grabbed the evidence bag and raided it for a business card. A card that Miles had given me at the cigar room before the press conference a week ago. It had Governor Monroe's private number on it.

Grabbing the burner phone, I called up Neary from the state police.

"It's Marsh," I said when he answered. "I need your help."

"Of course," Neary said. "I told you, P.T.

If there's something going on, don't do this yourself."

"Don't worry," I said. "Right now, you're the only guy I can trust."

"What do you need?"

"A reverse trace on a number," I said.

I supplied him the governor's private cell number, and he told me he'd text me the address.

"What about backup?" he asked. "I can send two cars."

"Have them park a distance away. Keep an eye out for me."

A minute later he texted me an address. A farmhouse thirty minutes outside of Marietta.

I got in and drove in silence, thinking about the two dozen dinners I'd had at Miles Dooger's home. Of Miles at the hospital when Lena had the baby. Of Jonas playing in the backyard with Miles's kids. It was flat impossible to believe he'd ordered my murder.

My GPS dinged, and I took the Tall Oaks exit. Drove until the road became fine gravel.

I hit the high beams and spied a line of white fence that ran beside a curving drive. It was a horse-breeding farm and a big one at that. The stables were larger than the main house, and the main house was huge.

The phone told me to make my last turn, and I slowed as I passed a pair of blue state trooper cars. Neary's guys gave me a nod, but didn't follow, remaining just outside of private property.

The drive dead-ended at a locked gate. There was a small security booth, but no one was inside. I punched the number from the back of the business card into my phone.

"Hello?" a man's voice answered, half asleep.

"This is Detective P. T. Marsh," I said.

"What time is it?" a woman's voice said in the background. Sleepy. Young.

I looked at the phone to make sure I'd hit the right number. The man hadn't hung up yet.

"I know about the Order of the South," I said.

There was just silence.

"I've got a ledger," I said. "Monroe is one of the founding names."

"Is it a wrong number?" the woman asked.

"I know about the snowstorm in '68," I said. "Two kids were killed that year. Now we're gonna talk about this, Governor, or I'm gonna drive to Atlanta. Talk to someone at CNN about how your family got its political start."

"I'll come out," he said. "Just wait a sec."

I heard a noise, and the mechanical wooden gate slid open.

I drove down the drive and parked in between the main house and a giant manicured green field—about ten feet from the porch.

As I got out of the car, the two troopers put on their high beams, pointing toward the farm.

A door rattled open and out came Monroe. He was dressed in pajama pants and a black windbreaker. His normally perfect salt-and-pepper hair was mussed up.

I walked toward the wooden steps that led down from the house. "You own this place?" I said.

"It belongs to a friend," he said. "Produced a Triple Crown winner. I come here to think."

I thought of the woman who I'd heard in the background. A twenty-something voice. Not the governor's wife, in her fifties, who I'd seen on TV a dozen times.

"Is that what you call it these days?" I looked to the house. "Thinking?"

Monroe stared at me from the top step of the porch. "I don't know you, Marsh."

"I'm the guy who's got your family name all over a ledger in my car," I said.

I stood about eight feet from him and pulled up the flannel shirt I wore over jeans. I turned in a circle—showing him I wasn't wearing a wire.

"I'm also the guy who knows that you and your type have been killing kids for a hundred and fifty years—"

"You can't tie me to something I never did."

"I don't need to." I shrugged. "That's the media's job. For all I care, they can crowdsource this shit. Ask the public."

Monroe ran his hand along the wood of the railing. "What do you want?" he asked.

"The Order. When's the first time you knew about it?"

"It's a ghost story, Detective."

I turned and walked the ten feet back to my car. Got in the Charger. "Good luck in the next news cycle."

"Marsh," he said. "Stop, all right."

But he hesitated still, and I fired up the ignition.

"I just left Miles Dooger's house," I said. "So let me tell you what I told him. We saved the girl. We intercepted the money paid to kill her. She ID'd the guys and heard Dooger send them her way—under *your* order. So we're gonna wrap this up in a bow so neat that you're not gonna remember what the governor's mansion even smells like. See those guys?" I pointed at the two patrol cars. "I say the word, and they arrest you."

The governor stared through the mist at the two cars and then back at me. A life spent calculating the odds of ever loyalty and betrayal.

"Okay," he said. "Let's talk."

I got out of the Charger and walked toward him.

"There was a guy named Mickey Havordine," he said. "He was my dad's first campaign manager."

"Okay," I said.

"Mickey was like an uncle. Took care of me when my dad was traveling. One night he was drunk and told me this story about how they got shut out of their first debate. That was the first night I heard the words 'the Order.' "

"This was the night of the snowstorm?" I asked. The article I'd found with Candy in the microfiche.

"Exactly." The governor nodded. "And the guys my dad was running against were no slouches, Marsh. One was a councilman from Atlanta. The other, the sitting governor."

"But they both died," I said. "That's how your dad got his start."

"Yeah," Monroe said. "See, Dad wasn't invited to the debate. He was the number three candidate and was shut out. So Mickey rented this soda fountain in Decano Falls. His goal was to get a crowd there and film it. Drop off a reel at the news stations. Make them look *bigger* than the debate."

"But the storm happened?"

"Not any storm," Monroe said. "By eight p.m., the snow was knee-high, and the only people in the soda shop were Mickey and my dad, getting drunk. The high three days earlier had been sixty-six degrees. But at that point it was thirteen out and getting colder. The storm had driven everyone into their homes, where they were watching the debate on TV."

"So Mickey blew it?" I said.

"Half their budget in one night," Monroe said. "But my dad told him not to worry."

This was 1968, I thought. *Fifty years ago.*

"And then a minute later—there's no debate," the governor said. "The roof collapsed under the weight of the blizzard. Everyone inside died."

Thirteen degrees and a blizzard in Georgia. It was stranger than a four-horse win at a track.

"Dad and Mickey were an hour away," Monroe said. "Dad told Mickey to sober up and write him a speech. But Mickey was frozen. 'What did you do?' he asked Dad."

"And what did your dad say?"

"Nothing," Monroe said. "It was an accident, Marsh. It was Mother Nature. And they drove over there, and my dad made his best speech ever. About how two public servants were lost. And parents and reporters. And how he wouldn't stop until he found out how and why."

"What does 'Rise' mean?" I said.

Monroe shrugged. "My dad had a 'Rise' tattoo. My grandad. When I asked Dad about it as a kid, he told me it was a campaign slogan."

I grabbed my phone, showing him pictures of Donnie Meadows and Elias Cobb. "Do you know these men?"

Monroe looked at the shots, studying their features. "Nope."

"There are big reversals of fortune that happen, Governor. A lotto win in Harmony nine days ago. A big horse race in '93 for the guy whose son got

337

sent away. I've looked into them. And you know what I find?"

"You find that they're random. Coincidence. Acts of God."

That was exactly what I'd found. And suddenly I was pissed. Fuming. That Monroe knew about all this, out ahead of me.

"So you met with Miles Dooger and you knew," I said. "You knew what year it was. You saw Kendrick kidnapped and—"

"I wondered."

"And when Dooger told you it was a lynching—"

"Then I was guessing," he said. "But I don't talk to these people, Marsh. Whoever they are, it's in the shadows."

"You and me." I put a finger to Monroe's chest. "We get paid to make sure life is good in Georgia. That this shit doesn't happen."

"And I try, Marsh," he said. "But sometimes you gotta live with the legacy of your history—whether you like it or not. That was Mickey's point in telling me the story."

"You're going down," I said.

"Marsh." He followed me down the porch. "I never took a dollar from these people. I lost elections. I won elections. And if they're doing some voodoo magic to help me, I don't know about it."

He grabbed at my shoulder, and I spun

around, knocking him down onto the grass by the steps.

"What do you want from me?" he hollered.

"Someone paid these men to kill kids. To them, it wasn't magic. It was a contract murder, and you're tied to it."

"We'll figure this out, you and me."

"No."

"I'll make some calls."

"You better make 'em now," I said. "I want five names by the time the sun comes up."

"What?" he yelled. Incredulous.

I walked over to my car and grabbed the ledger.

The governor's eyes went wide. "Where did you get that?"

"Not so in the shadows now, is it? Jesus, you know plenty."

"The younger generation doesn't know about this, Marsh."

I thought of Wade Hester, who was sick when he found out what his dad had done.

"Then I'll take the old men," I said. "They've been at it their whole lives. But I need one an hour if you want to be in office in the morning."

"How?" He squinted. "You expect me to wake these people up in the middle of the night? Tell them to turn themselves in?"

"Or I can take you down," I said. "Piece by piece. I'll start with your marriage. That young girl inside. I'll drag her ass out of bed. Then I'll take your job. Put you in prison."

"Detective." He swallowed.

"Or I'll make you a deal," I said. "One an hour, and when I'm done, I hand you this." I held up the ledger. "You text me an address, and they surrender to the state police. Admit who they paid and when . . . and nothing comes up from me about the Order. About a conspiracy. Nothing about the governor's office. It's just some racist old boys. They can say it was how they were raised. It clears the news cycle in a few weeks; you can hand this ledger back to your friends— and you keep your job."

Monroe stared. "You're leaving me wide open," Monroe said. "These are my supporters."

"At least you're not in jail. You can stay in the governor's mansion. Come here on weekends and *think*. I bet the Websters would call that a nice life."

The governor didn't speak for a minute, and I waited. His face was as white as the railing that bordered the porch.

"Tell me where to head first," I said.

"Gwinnett County," he said, his voice barely a whisper. "You'll get texted an address in the next few minutes."

I got in the car and waved for the state guys to follow me.

48

I spent the next four hours driving some of Georgia's finest old neighborhoods with my two buddies from the state police.

We drove over to Berkeley Lake in Gwinnett County and were buzzed onto the grounds of an enormous waterfront property. Then to Johns Creek southeast of Alpharetta where we entered a massive home with twelve-foot custom copper doors.

The old were given up to protect the young. And the closer it got to morning, the more signed statements and lawyers were already on hand by the time I arrived.

But no attorney asked for a deal.

They simply handed over five white men between sixty-two and eighty, along with written documentation about how they'd paid to have four black kids killed. I didn't supply them the names, and they matched perfectly with the kids from '93 that I had from the ledger. And with Kendrick and Delilah nowadays.

The looks on the men's faces were blank, and their cheeks were sallow with the expectation of what was to come.

In an estate in Milton I saw a lawyer's name I recognized. Lauten Hartley was the man who had come and visited Bernard Kane in prison. Right before Kane had hung himself.

"I know you," I said to him. "You talked to Bernard Kane in my jail."

The lawyer stood up. "You don't know a thing about me," he said and walked out.

The last of the men was Talmadge Hester in Shonus, where I first got a whiff of the Order. The old guy was slumped over in a chair at his two-hundred-year-old desk when I arrived at seven a.m. There was no grand party this time. No uniforms or stories about debutantes from days past.

"I haven't seen Wade," he said to me. "Will you talk to him about this? Can you try to explain that I did this for him?"

"No," I said, cuffing the old man and putting him in the back of the squad car.

Lawrence Neary from the state police was on hand for this one, and he shook his head at me. "Jesus, Marsh. Did you close four murders in one night?"

I didn't answer. I just turned toward my car. I was worn slap out, and I needed to be done with this case.

These were real crimes, but no one explained how their doing them resulted in something magical on the other end of the spectrum. How violence became luck. And how luck built fortunes.

There was ritual here. I'd seen candles and writings in the cave. The farmer had found a headless lamb burned out in Harmony. But I guess that was part of the trade I'd made with the governor. That I didn't get to know all those details. Instead, I got arrests.

I finished the last of the bookings by eight a.m. and headed to the parking lot outside the precinct.

Deb Newberry from Fox was parked two cars down from me. She had on a red blouse and a short black skirt. There was no cameraman with her this time, but I was sure he was on his way.

"Early bird gets the worm, huh, Deb?" I said, opening the door to the Charger.

The reporter applied pink lipstick by crouching near her SUV's side-view mirror.

"I know that sound in your voice, Marsh," she said without glancing over. "You're wondering how I got here so fast. Who I know."

I made a noise with my nose as if I didn't care. But she'd read me right.

She stood up and straightened her skirt. "I was starting to pile up some juicy stuff on you, Detective. But looks like someone climbed out of the basement. Went from zero to hero. That's my story, at least."

She headed off to the precinct, and I got in my car. By eight-thirty, I pulled into my driveway, and there was a black BMW 7 Series waiting outside. A driver rolled down a tinted window and asked if I had something for him.

I grabbed the ledger from my car and handed it over. I couldn't turn it in as evidence anyway, or everyone would see the name of the governor, who I'd made the deal with. But I was hoping that somewhere deep in the bowels of the university library, Candy's old coworker had made copies of some part of it.

I lay my back down onto the wood of my porch, and Purvis came out and licked my face.

Ten days ago when I got to Virgil Rowe's place, I'd had one idea of justice. One in which I considered removing Rowe from the world. I was at the bottom of the canyon and ready to take a man's life, just because I could.

It had been a year since my wife and son were gone, and it had finally sunk in. They weren't coming back, and there was no one left to take it out on.

49

I spent the rest of the day cleaning up my place. Scrubbing every dish, and even throwing some of them out. I took framed pictures of Lena and Jonas out of boxes and put them back up on the walls where I could see them every day.

At night Sarah came over, and we had dinner. I'd filled the fridge with real food and cooked fresh pasta. The smell of garlic and basil replaced the stench of mold.

Sarah wore a yellow sundress with tiny straps that showed off her shoulders.

I broke out a bottle of Pinot for her, but stuck to ice water myself.

She told me more about Atlanta. What had gone wrong there with her boss. A scandal that she got pulled into and couldn't free herself from. It was a sad story. One in which Sarah had trusted someone and been burned.

I reached out to touch her hand. An hour later we still hadn't let go.

Sarah got up to grab the pie she'd brought and serve it.

We turned on the TV, and at some point we fell asleep. Even better, when I woke up in the morning, she was still on the couch with me. And Purvis on the rug below us.

• • •

On Friday, I came into the office and filled out paperwork for some time off.

I needed to split town for a while, and the place was abuzz with energy.

Miles Dooger had made an announcement on the local news that he was retiring. The whole thing was framed around the big case being solved, and the media was applauding him.

But Miles wasn't coming into the office to offer a formal goodbye. He'd asked to have his things boxed up and messengered to his home, and I couldn't help thinking about my threat to put him in a cell.

I nodded as a patrolman told me the news about the chief.

Miles was my mentor. My first friend on the force. I thought of how impossible it must've been for him to investigate my wife's death. And worse than that, all the while stumbling around, knowing that he was, on his best day, an average detective investigating a complicated crime.

While I was gone, Remy had taken over my office and used the far wall to tape up everything we had on the case. She'd also gone back and untied Cobb's girlfriend from that heater pipe in her apartment.

The story began with the five men who were arrested throughout the previous night, and the four names of the kids from 1993 and now.

But Remy also had new evidence.

"I got a warrant for an apartment that Donnie Meadows was renting in town," she said. "Abe did the same for the guesthouse Cobb had been living in."

While Meadows had kept a neat place with no evidence, Cobb had been messier. He'd left behind a notepad with amounts that Oxley and the Order had paid him and Meadows. As well as details about Kendrick. What time Kendrick got off of school and where he lived. And some of the how and why of it. That the Order preferred a teenage boy, preferably a virgin, and someone whose family had stood for the advancement of black Americans. Another level to the tragedy.

I stared at the wall of evidence while Remy sat at my desk, typing in her iPad.

"So Cobb and Meadows followed Kendrick home from school like we thought?" I asked.

"That was when Dathel Mackey from First Baptist first saw Cobb," Remy said.

The Bearded Man, hanging around the church the same night Kendrick went missing.

"Cobb hung back to keep an eye on the parents, while Meadows followed Kendrick to the sleep-over," Remy said. "The plan was to catch Kendrick with that cable as he rode out in the morning. But no sooner than Meadows had set the cable up, the sleepover ended and out came Kendrick."

I shook my head, looking at other notes she'd written on Post-its and stuck to evidence.

Meadows and Cobb had taken Kendrick to the same cave where we'd found Delilah. The place was originally private land and held some spiritual value for the Order. It was once connected to the hunting compound where I'd shot Francis Oxley.

"The land was donated to the state in 1932," Remy said. "That's when it became a state park."

I looked at a deed for the land, and Remy's notes written on it. The parcel was given to the state by a niece of one of the Order's founding families. But they'd still snuck into the cave and used it. Closed off areas that the public never even knew about.

After the cave, the two men brought in Virgil Rowe to take Kendrick to Harmony Farms and set the field afire as part of their ritual.

"So that's where it would've ended," Remy said. "Except for Brodie Sands, the crop duster, who heard the voice of his wife in the wind."

"Sands putting out the fire with his crop duster caused the Order to get nervous."

"Exactly," Remy said. "So Cobb and Meadows did what any thug would do. Before Kendrick's body was even found, they got to Rowe and silenced him. Killed the arsonist who had failed to set a proper blaze."

"Huh," I said, seeing it all together in one place for the first time.

"We found that photo of you." Remy pointed. "The anonymous one turned in to the police. Of you walking out of Corinne's house."

"Where?" I said.

"Cobb's phone."

And there it was finally. The killers outside of Virgil Rowe and Corinne's place right when I was there. Proof that I *hadn't* choked Virgil Rowe to death.

"They must've pulled outside right after you sent Corinne packing," Remy said. "Pretty shitty timing for you, if you're asking my opinion."

I looked at a photo of the money that had been recovered. "How much did Cobb and Meadows get to kill Kendrick and Delilah?"

"Thirty grand," Remy said. "Ten of which went to Rowe."

"The money I found in the matchbox?"

"Exactly." Remy nodded.

I glanced at a picture of William Menasco, the old man at the lake. "So what have we decided about these people in the Order, Rem?" I asked. "If you help them facilitate murder, even unwittingly, they do you a solid?"

Remy stared at the same photo. "The truth is," she said, "we don't know. Abe asked one of the old-timers about the horse race in '93, but he just shrugged. Said they knew lots of people in the business. Jockeys. Track officials. Trainers. But he couldn't remember ever fixing a race."

I thought about the state lottery win in Harmony.

"And what of 'the luck'?" I asked, turning to see if Remy had an explanation. "The lotto? The farmer coming into money?"

"I guess that depends on what you believe in. Superstition? Coincidence? Or it could be legit."

She stood up. Looked at me with—what? Concern? Pity?

"Are you waiting for me to say it out loud, P.T.?" Remy said. "That it's something crazy out in the Southern ether? Some Civil War–era black magic, handed down from father to son?"

I thought about the wealthy families who had benefited from the murders of the kids over the years. Trading what? A country club membership for someone's life?

"And the five men?" I asked.

"They're all pleading out with the DA. Fifteen- to twenty-year sentences, with no parole." Remy gave me a look. "They all had the same story, P.T. They're sorry. It was how they were raised."

"Did they name the guys they hired in '93?" I asked. "The ones who did their dirty work and killed Junius and the girl?"

Remy nodded. "We picked up one guy an hour ago. Another one's already in prison on a

350

different charge. The crime's twenty-five years old, P.T., so he's no spring chicken."

My partner sat down in my chair again and put her feet up on the desk. She wore white slacks and a pair of shiny black pumps.

"So let's get to it, boss," she said. "You and me—we kinda need a wheelbarrow to carry our balls around here right now. Except you know something I don't. You wanna tell me how you got all these old guys to confess?"

I looked around the station. Remy was right. It *was* buzzing, and we would be hot for a while. But I kept thinking about what Miles Dooger had said to me. About how crimes got solved.

Relationships, not evidence.

Was that what I'd done with the governor? Used a pressure point, rather than a data point?

And was that what the governor had done with the five families to give up these men?

I looked over at Miles Dooger's office, piled with white moving boxes.

"Some things are better left unsaid, partner."

Remy followed my eyes.

"You gonna apply for the chief?" she asked.

"Nah, I don't want that job."

My partner turned back to her evidence. "Well, the corporations related to these men's families," she said. "They're scrambling. PR issues ahead of them. We've had a couple calls offering to help out the Harmony and Mason Falls areas. Looking for good local causes to donate to."

"The kids with typhoid," I said. "It's a good cause."

"P.T., those kids are all on antibiotics and fine," Remy said. "The one in a coma woke up this morning as if nothing was wrong."

January 1. The start of the next twenty-five years. The end of the cycle.

The families had the ledger back. But I'd read enough of it, and they were scared. Or maybe enough of them were like Wade Hester. The new generation, guilty and ready to make amends.

I looked at my partner. At some point I'd considered the possibility that she'd turned on me. "Rem," I said. "We're good, right? You and me?"

Remy pursed her lips. "You cleaned up your act, boss," she said. "But if you don't mind, I'll keep an eye on you."

"You better."

I got up and walked to the office that Abe and Merle shared. Abe was there by himself, bent over his writing pad.

"I owe you an apology," I said, putting out my hand.

Abe shook it and pushed his chair back. "Heard you're taking off for a while."

"I never took my wife's ashes anywhere," I said, thinking about how I'd buried Jonas in a casket, but Lena was still in an urn in my living room. Cremated as her family had requested.

"She loved the Keys, so I thought I'd drive down there. Scatter them in the water at mile zero."

"Nice," Abe said. "The governor called here this morning for you."

"I heard we're getting lots of calls," I said. "He leave a message?"

"Yeah," Abe said. He found his message pad and read it aloud. "Congratulations, P.T. and team. So proud of your arrests the other night. All credit to you guys."

I listened to Monroe's choice of words, silently acknowledging the deal I'd made.

At some level we all trade one choice out for another.

The risk of going against twenty-five powerful families versus making a deal to get five of them? I'd seen the system succeed and I'd seen it fail. I'd take the five solid arrests seven days out of seven.

I thanked Abe and walked out of the station.

50

By noon I got down to the hospital and checked in on my father-in-law. Marvin was due to be released in a week. I told him I'd be back a few nights before that, to take him home.

On my way out of Mason Falls, I stopped at the Websters'. I found the reverend in the church by himself, praying. He was dressed down this time, in a simple white T-shirt and jeans.

We moved out to a garden, and I told him the whole story. Even the parts that I wasn't sure what to make of. The voices heard on the wind, the roadside baptisms, and the signs I'd seen on trees.

I told him about Lena and Jonas. About the accident. How it shaped what I believed and didn't believe in these days. About Cory Burkette and his innocence. How the reverend hadn't failed in saving the soul of an ex-Nazi.

When I finished, Webster's face was wet with tears.

"I don't imagine that's the story that you're putting in your file, is it?" he asked.

"Some of it," I said.

"I'm glad you were the one to stand up for Kendrick," he said. "He would've liked you. For the same reason he liked Cory."

"What's that?" I asked.

"He rooted for the underdog. Kendrick used to do BMX, you know. He'd watch these extreme sports competitions on TV. He always picked the guy in the most pain."

I put my hand on the reverend's shoulder, and we both sat in silence on the garden bench, two fathers who'd lost sons. Two men who'd fed better versions of ourselves to the insatiable soil, the vengeful earth.

"What if the ground goes dead?" I said to him finally. "What if they're right and Harmony fails?"

"Harmony will be fine," Webster said. "The Lawless One uses all sorts of displays of power through signs and wonders that serve the lie."

It sounded like a Bible verse, but I didn't ask. Webster's point was simple. That all those rich folks believing in luck or evil—it gave them strength.

"And the rest of us," I said. "Believing in the goodness of Harmony overcoming—we have that same power?"

Webster stood up and smiled, nodding. "Have a good trip, Detective."

I got in the car then and drove, just me and Purvis.

We made our way through Georgia and into Florida. Past Gainesville and Orlando. We spent the night on Lake Okeechobee and kept going the next morning.

We all live under the shadow of a three-century history that has pitted color against color. And we all need to change.

To me—there are no people more capable of that change than people from here.

We're not ignorant of what outsiders think. They see a mix of beautiful mansions from the 1800s—and weeds thigh-high in the next house over.

But for me, this area of the country is heaven. There's no place I'd rather travel than in the South. And no place I'd rather live in than Georgia.

Even with our history, when I'm at Publix buying groceries, I see interracial couples. Lots of us. More than in other places. So as much as we struggle here with race . . . in some ways, our struggle is closer to the surface. And I hold out hope that this means it's easier to fix.

U.S. Route 1 became a single road leading into Key West. The rains disappeared, and the heat rose. When I was out of land and reached the bottom of the Keys, I parked my car in front of the lime-green hotel where Lena and I had gone on our first weekender.

Purvis and I walked to the shore, and I emptied Lena's ashes in the still water.

I said a prayer, watching as the tiny flakes floated on the surface and then slowly submerged. First into the water. And then down into the ground. To the floor of the earth, which remembered and forgot all secrets.

I sat on the dock with Purvis, who looked at me, his brown eyes wet and shining. He licked my face.

She believed in you, Purvis said.

I smiled, pulling him onto my lap.

Not every memory was a good one, but the year was starting new.

I'd made mistakes. But forgiveness was coming, and I could sleep nights now, without liquor in me, even in the heat of the Keys.

Acknowledgments

Books are magical organic things not written by one person, but influenced by many. To that end, I'd like to acknowledge a couple folks, knowing I'll fail to think of someone obvious.

First of all, I'd like to acknowledge my dad, Hank McMahon, who died three days before this book was bought. The timing was bittersweet, but he was my best friend and role model, and I know he's paging through this in Heaven.

The next nod goes to my superhero agent, Marly Rusoff, who took a chance on my first book. And when it didn't sell, (like a tough-love mom) she simply said, "If you're a writer, go write another book"—which is this.

The third thank-you is for author Jerrilyn Farmer. She has been my workshop critic, cheerleader, and friend for years. Without her pushing, this doesn't happen.

To Maggie, Noah, and Zoey, you are my faith, heart, and ferocity. I love you without limit and am grateful for your patience. To my mom, I thank you for a life of support, unconditional love, and the fearless optimism that is your brand alone.

I would like to acknowledge the writers who have made me a better writer and this a better book: Chad Porter, Beverly Graf, Glen Erik Hamilton, Alexandra Jamison, Kathy Norris, and Eachan Holloway.

To my brother, Andy, who gave great feedback on the first book, and to my sisters, Kerry and Bette, who always assumed it would happen. And thanks to Allison Stover, guide on all things Georgia.

To the folks who hosted me in the great state of Georgia—some of the best people anywhere. To the Putnam team, from art and marketing to proofing and publicity.

Final shout-out goes to Mark Tavani at Putnam. Mark is passionate, precise, and answers all questions with intelligent thought. He helped me rewrite, and as any good teacher will tell you, writing is rewriting.

P. T. Marsh will be back. Stay tuned.

Center Point Large Print
600 Brooks Road / PO Box 1
Thorndike, ME 04986-0001 USA

(207) 568-3717

US & Canada:
1 800 929-9108
www.centerpointlargeprint.com